Wedding Matilda

Also by Heather Hiestand

The Marquess of Cake

One Taste of Scandal

His Wicked Smile

The Kidnapped Bride
(novella)

Christmas Delights

Wedding Matilda

The Redcakes

Heather Hiestand

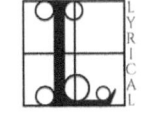

LYRICAL PRESS
Kensington Publishing Corp.
www.kensingtonbooks.com

LYRICAL PRESS BOOKS are published by

Kensington Publishing Corp.
119 West 40th Street
New York, NY 10018

All Kensington titles, imprints, and distributed lines are available at special quantity discounts for bulk purchases for sales promotion, premiums, fund-raising, educational, or institutional use.

Special book excerpts or customized printings can also be created to fit specific needs. For details, write or phone the office of the Kensington Sales Manager: Kensington Publishing Corp., 119 West 40th Street, New York, NY 10018. Attn. Sales Department. Phone: 1-800-221-2647.

First Electronic Edition: August 2015
eISBN-13: 978-1-61650-794-7
eISBN-10: 1-61650-794-2

First Print Edition: August 2015
ISBN-13: 978-1-61650-795-4
ISBN-10: 1-61650-795-0

Printed in the United States of America

For Andy

ACKNOWLEDGMENTS

Thank you to Judy Di Canio, Eilis Flynn, Mary Jo Hiestand, David Hiestand, Delle Jacobs, Abbey MacInnis, and Madeline Pruett for your critique assistance and support. Also, I'd like to thank my editor, Peter Senftleben, production editor, Rebecca Cremonese, and the rest of the Kensington team; and my agent, Laurie McLean and the Fuse Literary team, for their support of the Redcakes series.

Chapter One

April 7, 1890

The fragile April breeze fluttering through Covent Garden seemed like a distant memory to Ewan Hales as he sat in the dank and moldy law office of Shadrach Norwich. Some of the flower sellers had still been wearing their Easter bonnets from the day before, perhaps thanks to late-night carousing, making for a festive, disheveled air in the market.

He had detoured there for a few minutes on his walk between Redcake's Tea Shop and Chancery Lane. As the senior member of staff in town, courtesy of the manager's trip to Scotland, he could do as he liked, a rare thing in his career of secretarial labor. He had toiled for distinguished men, currently Lord Judah Shield, and before that, Sir Bartley Redcake. He liked saying he worked for aristocrats, even if neither man fit the picture suggested by their titles in any precise manner. As a result, he modeled himself after other, more traditional members of the nobility in dress and behavior.

"Ah, Mr. Hales," said a portly gentleman in a dandruff-bedecked black suit as he entered the room from some inner chamber. He gave Ewan a searching glance.

"Yes, sir." Ewan stood and shook hands with the solicitor. "I confess I do not know why I was summoned here. What was the purpose of your letter?"

"The matter was too delicate to put into writing." The man glanced over him again.

Ewan knew his appearance to be impeccable, other than his untamable hair, so that couldn't be the reason for the man's curiosity. "I cannot take much time away from my duties, Mr. Norwich. Could you please be brief?"

The other man sat down, seeming to expand to fit his chair, with the air of one who planned a conversation of considerable length. "What do you know about your family?"

Ewan slicked back his hair as he considered this, his tension heightening from the intent of such a question. Was a legacy due to him? Every orphan, even one of twenty-seven years of age, imagined lost relatives out in the world hoping to find him.

He pressed his hands into his thighs and leaned forward. "My mother died young. When I was about four years old. Her name was Hannah Walker Hales. I think she was from Swansea originally. Welsh, you know. I remember her voice."

Norwich nodded, his underchin wobbling. "And your father?"

"Walter Hales. I was sent to boarding school when I was seven because he went out to Africa. I never saw him again." He had cried until he'd made himself sick that first day at school, and then promised himself he'd never cry again.

Norwich reached for a brown bottle at the edge of his desk, then moved his hand away. "Did you have any contact with him?"

Ewan scratched his chin. "Letters for a while, until I was eleven or so. He went native, I believe, died a few years after that, in 1877. There was enough money to get me through school, then I went to work when I was sixteen."

"Nothing else?"

He tapped his fingers against his thighs. "It's been many years. The solicitor who was in charge of me is long dead."

"You know your mother was Welsh; what about your father's origins?" The man settled back further, his coat pressing against the arms of his chair.

Ewan stared at his fingers. Long and extremely flexible, they were perfect for typing. His father's hands, in fact. He remembered that much. "I don't think he had any family, but he had a London accent. A rather posh one, in fact." He'd been careful to mimic his father's voice at school, not wanting to have his speech coarsened by the other boys, but the years had robbed him of many of the specific memories he'd once had of his parent.

Norwich shook his head and muttered something under his breath. "No family, you say. Why do people run off without explaining their antecedents to their offspring? I have never understood the tendency."

"I was only seven," Ewan stated. He had the vague notion that something had broken in his father when his mother had died, as if his father had been a man who laughed before her death, then had never laughed again. Had she been the only part of his father's life that wasn't grim?

"Very true. There might have been statements made that you missed, letters that were discarded in your father's flight from the country."

He frowned. "Flight?"

Norwich cleared his throat with a phlegmy sound. "He was escaping debtors' prison."

Ewan hadn't known. His hands clutched his thighs, bunching the material of his trousers. He forced himself to relax. "Then where did the money come from to educate me?"

Norwich snorted. "That paltry sum? From your father's uncle— your great-uncle, that is—Lawrence Douglas. He should have had you educated properly, but he must have thought it would never come to this."

Ewan felt his pulse quicken. *Come to this?* Why hadn't this great-uncle helped his father instead of letting him flee? "I do not understand, though I admit the name is familiar to me."

"As indeed it should be. Lawrence Douglas is the eleventh Earl of Fitzwalter. An old, very distinguished family."

"The title goes back to sixteen forty or so, I believe," Ewan agreed. He paid attention to these things because Redcake's Tea Shop and Emporium was owned by the Marchioness of Hatbrook and had a clientele in fashionable society. Once again, he wondered why the earl would not have helped his own nephew, if indeed this story was true. "You are saying I belong to the family?"

Norwich snorted. "I am saying you are now the earl's heir. Someday, Mr. Hales, you will be the twelfth earl."

Ewan coughed in order to hide a peal of laughter. Him, a mere secretary, who had been proud not half an hour before to work for the brother of a marquess? And before that, a mere knight? Why, Sir Bartley hadn't yet been knighted when he came to work at Redcake's in 1884. No, he couldn't be the heir to an earl. *Ludicrous.* He'd seen quite a lot of unusual behavior among their noble patrons over the years, but losing their children? Never.

He pressed his hands against his thighs again. "That is a statement almost too incredible to believe. Are you certain?"

Norwich opened a leather-bound book on his desk and turned it around, revealing a family tree. "Lord Fitzwalter had a brother named Walter. He was the fourth son born and the third to live to adulthood. When he was forty his son, also Walter, was born, himself a second son."

"That would be my father?"

"Exactly. I don't imagine the Walters were ever expected to sire sons. Incidentally, your name isn't really Hales. That was your grandmother's name. Your father's full name was Walter Hales Douglas."

"I see."

"Your father quarreled with his father and no surprise, because the man was a few slices short of a loaf, or so my father always told me." Norwich's soft face creased with embarrassment.

Ewan was too anxious for the information to care about the solicitor's rude remarks about family he'd never met. "Go on."

"He went his own way, married outside of aristocratic circles. You were born in 1863, in wedlock. I have the papers."

"I never had any doubt. How did the family line become so thin?"

"Eccentrics with weak chests, most of your ancestors," Norwich said, sniffing. "My family has served yours for a hundred years. We've watched them come and go. At least you've had some tougher stock bred into you."

He had the unruly dark Welsh hair and eyebrows to prove it. "I must have a title," he said as his thoughts spun. Was there money attached? Could he leave his position, live more like Redcake's patrons than its employees?

"I'm afraid not. You are the heir presumptive, not the heir apparent. The late heir was Lord Ritten."

Ewan blinked. "Lord Ritten died over the winter, correct? In his mistress's arms, somewhere in the south of France?" He remembered the scandal. There had even been a ballad shouted out by newsboys to sell papers.

Norwich sighed. "Scandalous. Considering what you do know about Lord Ritten's demise, you can imagine what I managed to cover up."

Ewan searched his memory. "Not a young man."

"No, he was the third son, the second to live, Lord Fitzwalter's brother. I won't claim there aren't other relatives branched off from the current earl's grandfather, but you are the next in line."

Ewan searched inside himself and found anger. He, who had lived a productive life, was less valuable to his relatives than the notorious late Lord Ritten? "I should have been told. It's not as if the family would have been surprised the title would come to me, given the age of the man preceding me."

"The Walters were deeply unpopular," Norwich said, staring longingly at the unlabeled brown bottle at the edge of his desk. He folded his hands on his desk, possibly to avoid showing a tremble in his extremities.

Ewan suspected the bottle held a patent medicine, which was likely full of alcohol or opiates. "You are in luck, sir. I get along with everyone. It will be a sea change for you and the family."

Norwich smirked. "I'm sure your father thought the same thing of his relations with the natives, until they boiled and ate him."

"He died of a fever!"

The solicitor shook his head. "So you think, Mr. Hales, so you think. The Walters were notorious for tone deafness in their relationships with others." He peered at Ewan, as if expecting him to shout out in a disturbed manner.

Ewan had not been indulged in his life, however, and did not give Norwich the satisfaction of a display. "I was not raised as a 'Walter.' "

Norwich's expression might have been categorized as a smirk if his fleshy face could fold in such a manner. "Actually, you were christened as a Walter. Your full name"—he paused to pull a sheet of paper from a scattered pile on his desk—"is Walter Ewan Hales Douglas. Here you are."

He handed Ewan a page, which appeared to be copied from a church registry, as it contained the names of various children baptized. Finding his own, he recognized the birthdate listed. "At least I'm not a year older than I think I am, or something equally monstrous."

"Naming you Walter is pretty monstrous, considering," Norwich said, giving in to his lust for his brown bottle and taking a sip.

With that, Ewan suspected the interview was complete. He pushed his chair back.

"I'll need you to return to my offices tomorrow," Norwich said over his bottle.

Ewan stood. "Why?"

"Your great-uncle needs to meet with you, of course. Be here at two in the afternoon."

"I cannot continue to leave my place of business."

"Surely you do not think to retain your position under these extraordinary circumstances?"

"I must give notice. I am the man in charge at the moment. My manager has taken his wife and their five-month-old son to Edinburgh to introduce the baby to his sister, who lives there."

"Why do you care?" Norwich said, taking a more generous sip from his bottle. "They are no longer your concern. You are an earl's heir."

"My manager is the second son of a marquess."

Norwich set his glass down. "I wish Lord Fitzwalter had paid for additional research." He sighed. "You work for a lordling?"

Ewan nodded.

Norwich sighed again, his underchin emphasizing the lowering of his lip. "Don't leave your position. You might as well enter Society with a spotless reputation, difficult as that will be for any member of the Douglas family."

"I am not difficult," Ewan replied.

Norwich snorted without humor. "We will see you tomorrow, Mr. Hales."

"Is there anything I can take with me, a history of the family or some such?"

Norwich shuddered. "Why would anyone want to spend his time writing that?"

Ewan suspected whatever was in the bottle was taking effect. He could only imagine what the solicitor behaved like by the end of the day. When he left the dank room and returned to the street, the hint of spring had vanished under lumbering clouds. He'd never make it back to his desk before the rain.

He cheered himself with the notion of a hot cup of tea and a scone at his desk. That was the beauty of working at a tea shop, even if he did spend most of his day compiling reports. The office always smelled delicious, and Redcake's was famous for quality, unadulterated pastries.

On his return walk, his thoughts went to his current project, compiling a manual to be used by the new Redcake's Tea Shop and Emporium. The marchioness had decided to open a second location in Kensington, and a lot of the details had fallen on Ewan. He didn't mind, of course. He had expected to be appointed the manager there when Lord Judah returned. Now, his life had turned upside down and he had the feeling that Lord Fitzwalter was going to upend his career plans.

Ewan smiled as he passed the street that turned toward Covent Garden. A flower seller, her bonnet askew and bags under her eyes, stood on the corner, selling violets from a box around her neck. He, usually so careful about money to build his nest egg, purchased a posy and tucked it into his buttonhole. With that simple gesture, he turned himself into a dandy. The twelfth Earl of Fitzwalter, indeed.

Matilda Redcake passed through the open iron gates at the corner of Regent and Oxford Streets. The neatly cobbled courtyard exerted the force of gravity on her as she reflected on how much she had once detested this place, the clear and visible sign that her family was engaged in commerce. The Redcakes were nouveau riche to the extreme, so much so that she and her younger sister had been raised in very different fashion compared to their three older siblings. Now, as the heir apparent and current manager of the Redcake's factories in Bristol, she still winced as she looked at the façade of their flagship tea shop and emporium, because she was here to discuss a problem. She had been requested to meet with the manager here to discuss failures with the factory cakes.

An establishment that prided itself on the best quality goods in London and sold itself to fashionable society in that manner could not afford to have inferior goods.

Just ahead of her was the famous Redcake's display window, always full of an assortment of tasty goods. She squared her shoulders and stepped toward it, feeling like a soldier under review, and felt a pang of regret when she discovered not a single factory product in the display. Also, the Easter decorations had gone, a sign of a well-managed shop. Nonetheless, the window displayed all the beauty of spring, with fresh flowers tucked around plates of queen cakes decorated with pastel sugars. Towers of tea tins had labels that matched the sugar colors. Handmade cake squares wore sugared violets on top and looked very similar to her bonnet, which had a spray of the flowers around the flat brim.

All in all, the window was attired far more colorfully than she. When meeting with men, she attempted to appear as businesslike as possible, in a gray coat and skirt more suitable for a walking tour than a visit to the fashionable streets of London. A small moonstone pin was her only decoration besides her bonnet. Once, she had been the Redcake family's fashion plate, wearing gowns from Paris. Now, she assumed a very different appearance.

Oddly enough, the restraint and formality of her tailored suit complemented her in a way gowns did not. Her carrot-colored hair worked very well with a narrow palate of colors. Even the violet-trimmed bonnet was too much, in truth, a hint of leftover vanity.

She opened the front door of the shop, ready to be firm with Lord Judah, a relation by marriage due to her sister's wedlock with the Marquess of Hatbrook. In business, it did not pay to be too ingratiating, too friendly, too feminine. While she could not replace her father, or even imitate her brother, Sir Gawain, she could forge her own competent identity, and hide the youth of her twenty-four-year-old self in severe tailoring and hairstyle.

It worked, sometimes.

She ignored the bustling tearoom to the left, the glass cases of the bakery to the right. Her destination was directly ahead of her under a canopy of healthy ferns: the door that led to the back rooms of the enterprise. The industry contained within the building would surprise the ladies who drank tea in front of the large window in the tearoom, showing themselves as attractively as any tea cake in the display window.

Her heels clicked on the polished wood floor as she approached the door and rapped smartly. A moment later, it was opened by a beautiful woman wearing a coat over her simple black uniform.

"Miss Redcake!" she exclaimed. "You look so much like your father. I've never met you, but I'm Irene, the cake decorator."

"I thought Betsy Popham was the Fancy's manager." Matilda's sister, Alys, had founded the cake decoration department before her marriage. The male bakers in the next room had nicknamed her rooms "the Fancy."

"She is, but I do most of the decorating."

Betsy and her father had come down from Bristol with the Redcakes when Matilda's father, Sir Bartley, had opened his London flagship, some six years before. He'd intended to establish the family and marry off his daughters. Alys had married well, and Rose was engaged. Matilda's life had taken a very different direction, thanks to her former suitor, Theodore Bliven.

"I see," Matilda said.

Irene smiled, an expression that made her face even lovelier. "I love the creative work. It is so exciting that you are in charge of the factories. A woman at the helm, just like in my little department!"

Matilda nodded and smiled, though she had not obtained her position by ability, rather by default, thanks to her brother's refusal to continue to run his father's businesses when his own was so prosperous. "If I can think of any good advice I will be happy to share."

"Thank you so very much. What may I do for you today?"

"I have an appointment with Lord Judah."

Irene frowned. "He is in Edinburgh with his family."

Matilda closed her eyes for a moment. "Mr. Hales telephoned my secretary with this date and time."

"I'm so sorry. Perhaps you should speak to him? I do not think the trip was planned."

Irene smiled vaguely and gestured her into the back rooms. Immediately, the genteel atmosphere of the front rooms vanished. The warm wood floor met sparkling white tile. No greenery hung from baskets and pipes were exposed. They walked past racks of products, ready for restocking the bakery. On the other side were storage rooms full of utensils and crockery. Eventually, they wound their way to the back of the building, and Irene pointed to the steps leading up multiple stories to the manager's chambers.

Matilda debated having Mr. Hales summoned to her in a show of her position compared to his. Either way, though, she'd have to walk upstairs in the end. He was a mere secretary, but the truth was he'd been involved in the enterprise back when she was little more than an empty-headed debutante. She should treat him like an asset rather than an irritant, but his attitude had always bothered her. He was obsequious to the men of her family and overly pleasant to the women. Simultaneously, his vanity bothered her. Too aware of his good looks, she'd thought many a time. He kept his hair slicked back with an overabundance of Macassar oil, as if he was afraid of its natural exuberance.

Her pulse jumped traitorously as she wondered what else Mr. Ewan Hales felt the need to keep under lock and key. Although, four years ago, she'd have been happy to have a dose of his self-control, given the mistakes she had made. He'd done better keeping himself in check. It saved a person from serious consequences.

Irene smiled at her uncertainly. "Would you like me to summon Mr. Hales?"

"No, I'll just go up and see what he has to say about Lord Judah's schedule. I did come all the way from Bristol for this meeting."

"I'm terribly sorry, Miss Redcake. I hope Mr. Hales can assist you."

Matilda nodded as she reviewed the details of Lord Judah's letter to her, complaining about the cakes the factories under her control were supplying. He hadn't bothered including details or a sample, so he had the upper hand. Sometimes he still thought like a military man, only sharing the most minimal details, as if everything was a security matter.

As far as she knew, no espionage had entered the world of London cake shops, so they were both safe from spies. She went up the three flights of stairs, glancing at the framed, hand-tinted photographs of cakes with envy. No need for anything this decorative at the factories.

At the top of the building she reached the manager's aerie. The secretarial area was as full of ledgers and paper as the accounting office on the floor below. She knew Mr. Hales was the spider at the center of a web of information about Redcake's.

The man himself had his back to her, one finger on a row of figures in an open ledger and the other on a typewriter key. She had no idea how to operate such a machine, but it did make reports easier to read, so she had insisted that her own secretary, her cousin Greggory Redcake, learn to operate one.

"Mr. Hales?" she inquired.

The finger went up in the air in a request for silence. Her eyebrows lifted. When had the man become so imperious? He probably thought she was a cakie, the Redcake's name for waitresses. Still, she'd have expected him to be more charming. Her sister Alys said he was notorious for relationships among Redcake's female employees, having worked his way through accounting, the Fancy, and the bakery staff.

His finger moved down the row of neatly printed numbers in the ledger. The keys clicked a few times. A pause. He turned a page in the ledger and repeated the sequence.

"Mr. Hales," she tried again.

His fingers stopped moving, pinched around the page he was turning. His back stiffened as he slowly resumed his page turn. His other hand left the keys and he swiveled his chair around.

"Yes?"

He remained cold. No little bow, no small obsequious smile, as she had seen from him in the past. His hair had been mussed, she now realized.

Didn't he recognize her? "I'm Matilda Redcake."

Her announcement brought no change in his demeanor. "I know who you are, Miss Redcake."

Taken aback, she cleared her throat delicately. "I had a meeting with Lord Judah. About the factory cakes?"

His eyes narrowed. "The first delivery of the Easter shipment, to be specific."

"Very well. Lord Judah was not specific in his letter."

"I regret that he went to Scotland somewhat unexpectedly."

"No one canceled his appointment with me."

He nodded gravely. "I do apologize. Holidays are hectic here."

"I came all the way from Bristol, Mr. Hales. Surely it is your duty to manage Lord Judah's schedule."

His head tilted as he considered her. "He has a girl in during the mornings to handle certain details while I work on reports. While I am aware of his schedule, she handles the mundane tasks."

"I am not a mundane task; I am the manager of the factories." She wanted to stamp her foot, but her professionalism prevented her from doing so. Why was he affecting her emotions? He was merely a rude employee. She would tell her sister that her employee had behaved badly.

"Yes." He drawled the word.

"My understanding is that you are in line to manage the new Redcake's shop when it opens in Kensington. I hope you realize, Mr. Hales, that you will have to work closely with me in your capacity as manager there. That is, if the family decides to keep you on after today's rude display."

"Rude display? I have been nothing of the kind, Miss Redcake." His gaze perused her from her hat to her shoes.

She noticed her bonnet's decoration matched the cluster of small flowers tucked into his lapel. If they were on the street together, people would think they were a courting couple. The thought froze her, for he wasn't even being polite, much less flirtatious.

"Are you ill?" she asked.

He frowned. "Why do you ask? In fact, none of you Redcakes has ever shown the faintest interest in me before. That must be the first personal remark you have ever directed at me."

"We think of you as a machine, like that typewriter there, or one of Cousin Lewis's automatic mixers." She spoke without thinking but saw from his wince that she'd made a cut.

"Really." His tone was dry.

Impulse and curiosity won over caution. "Which is odd, because you have such a rakish reputation, and we were all once unattached girls, my sisters and I. But you never showed that side to us."

His lips tilted. "You were above me."

She heard the past tense in his sentence and felt it like a wound. True. She was no longer above him, but a *fallen woman*.

Chapter Two

"I cannot account for the tone of this conversation," Matilda said. "I must be the one becoming ill."

"Train fumes will do that to the susceptible," Ewan said calmly.

"I travel all the time," she protested.

"Does your son travel with you?"

How kind of him to remind her exactly why she was a fallen woman. Her one sexual experience, with a man she thought would marry her, had resulted in her son Jacob's birth. Thankfully, she had the sort of family who would train her for a position rather than casting her off, because no one would marry her now. Except the father of her child, who had eventually returned to press his suit, but by then he was ill and unbalanced and she could not see becoming Mrs. Theodore Bliven even to clear her name. No, she'd had too much pride, too much money, and too much education in the ways of the world.

"I am just here for the day, so no. I don't like to disrupt his routine. He is only two years old."

"I am glad to hear you are a sensible mother." He had turned fully now. She saw the fingers of his left hand were stained with ink and about to touch his trousers.

"Don't do that!" She rushed forward without thinking and took his arm by the wrist. With her free hand she whipped a handkerchief from her coat pocket and wrapped it around his inky fingers.

He stared at her, his eyes widening, but the tilt of his lips had turned into a full grin. "Miss Redcake?"

She looked at his face, then at the wrist she held. Her cheeks warmed. "My goodness, I am so sorry."

He squinted at her until she released his hand, so he could wipe away the ink as best he could. "Motherly instinct?"

She laced her fingers together behind her back in order to remind herself not to touch him. "I am afraid so. Jacob is fascinated by pens, and we have had some spectacular accidents. Please forgive me."

He shook his head. "Not at all. It was an endearing impulse."

His smile entranced her: a little crooked, a lot rakish. She felt like some trembling waitress, hoping to be courted by the great Ewan Hales, rather than his business superior. How charismatic he was when he showed his true self. Neither of them spoke until he gave a little shake of his head.

"I should wash up. Should I return with a cup of tea for you, or something more substantial? I can tell you what I know about the cakes."

"I haven't eaten today," she admitted. Did that explain her reaction to him?

"I'll have a tray brought up," he said, rising.

She had never noticed how tall he was. The top of her head only reached his neck. The perfect height difference between a man and a woman. "Should I go into his office?"

"If you like. I find it too warm for the fire today, but I can have it lit."

"No." He'd warmed her quite enough.

He gestured with his stained hand. "That ledger there, on the top of my desk? You can look at the reports."

"Very well." She forced a smile as she took the ledger and tucked it against her chest.

If he noticed her self-protective gesture, he was too polite to say anything, but she wondered why she felt a sudden need for armor against him. Ewan Hales would never make an inappropriate gesture toward a Redcake.

"Ewan!" A dark-haired Pocket Venus appeared in the doorway, holding an exquisitely decorated miniature wedding cake. "I wanted your opinion on this design for Lord Murchie."

"Ask Mrs. Short. She knows what our most discerning customers like." The side of his mouth tilted up as he turned to Matilda. "Mrs. Short is the tearoom manager."

"Haven't you developed your own eye? If you are going to manage the new operation . . . ?" Matilda let her question die off as something hot and hungry lit in the Venus's eye.

"Is it really going to happen?" the young woman demanded. "Oh, I must write Alys." She thrust the cake at Ewan and trotted off.

Matilda stared at her, bemused. "Good heavens, was that Betsy Popham?"

"Yes, the Fancy manager. Her father manages the bakery."

"I met Ralph Popham once." Right around the time she'd met Theodore Bliven, in fact. Both of them had been suitors for her sister Alys, who was five years older than Matilda. Now she was Marchioness of Hatbrook and Matilda was the spinster. How she would have laughed four years ago if someone had told her how it would all turn out.

"Yes, he and your father are rather close, I believe." He glanced down. "I should wash."

"Shall I take the cake to Mrs. Short?"

"Ah, I suppose so, if you like."

She smiled. "It will give me a chance to select my lunch."

"Very well, then. I will meet you here in twenty minutes." He waved his arm toward the door, indicating she could pass out first.

She did so and walked downstairs. No wonder Alys had been so drawn to working here, despite their father's displeasure. Never a dull moment. She'd never realized how bored she had been until she started training with her father after Gawain abdicated his role as the chief heir to Redcake's, which left only her. Rose had been confined to home in Sussex due to her severe asthma. Now, the silly girl was marrying a Liverpool dye manufacturer, which would probably kill her off within a year. Rose was so desperate for a home of her own. Tragic, really. Matilda had a difficult time faking gaiety any time the upcoming nuptials were mentioned.

She found the bakery service area and Mrs. Short, a rotund, sharp-faced woman who was as obsequious to her as Ewan Hales had been in the past. She clucked over the wedding cake sample and declared that Betsy should stick to managing and let Irene do the decorating, then bustled off with the plate outstretched before her like it was some kind of cake-shaped abomination.

Another cakie helped Matilda with a selection of treats to take upstairs with her.

"No cake selections?"

"We are already out of cake because the factory cakes are unsuitable and the downstairs bakery did not make enough today."

That explained the air of delirium Matilda had sensed. They were disappointing customers, a rare and upsetting occurrence. "What is wrong with the factory cakes?"

"They taste powdery," the cakie said. "Not up to our usual standards. It's one thing to sell a shilling cake of that quality, but our tearoom customers expect absolute purity in our ingredients."

"You mean we're selling off-quality cakes in the bakery?"

She pursed her lips. "I have no idea, Miss Redcake. I only know about the tearoom."

Matilda wished Lord Judah hadn't needed to go to Edinburgh. She supposed Mr. Hales didn't have the authority to keep the operation in check. She wondered if she did as she chose a bannock, a trio of preserved fruit tarts, and a bowl of raspberry cranachan, beautifully layered with cheese so fresh-looking it might have been made from a cow milked yesterday morning. The tearoom selections continued to show a Scottish influence, but all of those treats, courtesy of the Royal Family's obsession with Scotland, were made here and had nothing to do with her factory goods from Bristol.

She paired her choices with a pot of single estate Darjeeling, one of her brother's special finds. Her meal was fit for the aristocrats they often served. Why, the Redcake bakery was so in fashion that noble ladies sometimes picked up their own cake orders these days.

Mr. Hales had returned to his post by the time she reached the top floor, puffing a bit with the effort of taking a tray for two up all those stairs. She'd have thought lifting Jacob would have trained her for the weight, but she couldn't cuddle the tray against her like she could her child.

Mr. Hales opened the door into the inner sanctum for her, and she set down the tray, somewhat ungracefully, on a table in between three chairs next to the fireplace.

"As you can see, there is an absence of cake," she announced when she straightened.

"I would imagine so. It has been hard for the bakery downstairs to keep up."

"A cakie told me the cakes from Bristol have been powdery? I haven't heard this complaint from our other retail outlets."

"We only received the first rotten cake last Thursday," he said, gesturing her to be seated. "We keep a very close eye on any complaint we receive, given the nature of our patrons."

"The fashionable world is so small that one truly angry customer could damage our reputation irreparably," she agreed, wincing at his use of the word *rotten*.

"We cannot take that risk. The entire shipment was discarded, and Lord Judah hoped to work with you to fix the problem before the next shipment on Thursday."

Matilda picked up her glass bowl of the beautiful raspberry cranachan, then took a round spoonful of the creamy oats layered with cheese, cream, and preserved fruit. Her eyes closed involuntarily at the taste of so much rich goodness. Yes, she should have had a bowl of the navy bean soup first, but as usual, she'd wanted to go right to the best part and skip the preliminaries.

When she opened her eyes, she found Mr. Hales regarding her closely, the faintest hint of a smile hovering at the edges of his mouth. His lips were red, and his smile telegraphed itself at the corners even when his lips didn't move. Altogether he had the most attractive mouth she'd ever seen on a man, and now that his hair appeared more in its natural state for the first time, she could see how utterly appealing, how utterly heartbreaking he would be to a susceptible woman.

The problem was, she could be that kind of susceptible woman. Thank heavens he was only a secretary. At least for now. When he became manager of Redcake's Kensington, he would not be so far below her. But he would not live any closer to Bristol. All for the best, she told herself hastily. A man who dangled after waitresses was not for Miss Matilda Redcake, even the fallen Miss Matilda Redcake.

"Whatever went wrong with the cakes started with last week's production then," she said, ignoring the tingles that had started in her body when she had perused his mouth.

"Definitely. No problems before that."

"Can you explain the powdery reference?"

"Bad flour," said Mr. Hales succinctly, choosing a preserved pear tart and biting down.

Large white teeth, and utterly rude. He had not even asked permission to dine. Ate her food as if he were her equal. "What is wrong with you today, Mr. Hales?" she said without thinking.

Juice from the tart stained his lower lip as he lifted his head. His eyebrows rose as he chewed, then set the rest of the tart down on a napkin he had pulled from somewhere. "You weren't going to eat all of this yourself?"

"I'm not in the habit of serving secretaries," she snapped.

One side of his mouth tilted up. "And yet you brought a large pot of tea and two cups."

She glanced down at the tray and remembered he was correct. "I suppose I did expect you would drink."

"But not that you would pour?"

Resigned, she set her bowl back on the tray, expecting it to still be half full, but she had scraped it quite clean already. "Sugar or cream, Mr. Hales?"

He ran his free hand through his hair, tousling it further. "I am amused by how much more formal you are than the rest of your family. Of course, I do not know Miss Rose, but I know Lady Hatbrook and Sir Gawain quite well."

"Our educations were entirely different. Rose and I went to finishing school. Alys and Gawain were working in the factory by the age of nine, as was our late brother Arthur."

"So you younger girls were raised to be ladies and the others weren't?"

"Exactly."

He squinted, as if considering a major decision. "I will take cream."

She poured a generous dollop into a cup, noting how fresh it was, then poured the tea. "I find the first flush of Darjeeling doesn't need anything to improve it." She handed him the cup, then took her own dark brew.

"I did not know that was what you had chosen. You are, of course, correct."

"Have you become a connoisseur, working here?" she asked.

"I'd like to think so, despite my lack of finishing," he said, that hint of a smile on his lips.

"I suppose you are allowed to sample whatever you like?"

"Lord Judah and I often lunch together," he said. "I make the selections. And Sir Gawain gives us samples of every new tea he brings in from India. I probably know his product line better than ours."

"Will you stock the tearoom in Kensington with the same selections, or do you have your own ideas?"

His brow furrowed suddenly, a quite fierce expression overtaking his face. Matilda was taken aback. Had she said something wrong?

Her understanding was that the position was his when the new tea-room and emporium opened in late summer.

"I think we should discuss the cakes," he said after a moment.

"Very well," she replied, wondering how she had overstepped her bounds with him. It wasn't as if she was at risk of losing her position over a few spoiled cakes, irritating though it was. "Tell me what is wrong so I can fix it."

He stood and went back to the outer office, then returned with two of the white and gold Redcake's cake boxes, utensils, and plates. She put her bakery tray on the floor so he could set down his cargo.

"One of these cakes has been cut into; the other has not, but they are both from last week's shipment." He opened the first box, showing three-fourths of a cake.

She wiped her fingers on her napkin as he sliced a piece from the cake and handed it to her on a plate. "Smells fine."

"I've never thought cake could be smelled over frosting."

She put her finger to it, rubbed the cake. "Seems a bit crumbly, but then, it's been open to the air for a while."

He nodded. "Taste it."

Somewhat reluctant after just having eaten, she took a sip of tea to clear her palate of tart and took a small bite of cake, avoiding the frosting. She frowned. "Unusual."

"Powdery."

She took another bite and rolled it around in her mouth. "Talcum?"

"Some adulterant like that."

"Our suppliers haven't changed," Matilda said, putting the plate down. "Don't we use the same suppliers you use here?"

"Lady Hatbrook made some changes recently, trying out suppliers from Liverpool your sister's fiancé told her about."

"I see. What about the other cake?"

He opened the second box and wiped his knife clean, then allowed her to slice into it. She noted a few crumbles as she sliced, more than normal. He shook his head when she automatically offered him a sliver of the cake. It had the same taste when she took a bite.

She inventoried the ingredients of the shilling cake in her head. Everything tasted as it should except for the powdery aftertaste. "Do you remember Trumble's Cakes from when we were children? That's what this tastes like to me. Just standard, a cheap cake anyone could buy anywhere. We didn't eat it at home, but I remember having it at a friend's home for tea."

"We didn't have Trumble's Cakes at school. I think they did all the baking in the school kitchens."

She set her plate down. "What we have is a fine Redcake's brand cake tasting like any other inexpensive cake. Not good. Of course I don't understand why we're selling shilling cake slices in our tearoom. You'd think we would sell better quality."

"They redecorate them with seasonal fruit and add a dollop of frosting."

"Even so. I never realized." She wanted to feel pride that her cakes were so good, but under the circumstances that was impossible.

"What will you do now?"

"Go back to the factory. We have an additive problem, or an adulterant."

"You'll need to move fast to fix the problem before the next shipment."

"I'm hoping it was one bad batch of flour," Matilda said. "I wish the entire shipment hadn't been bad. Thank you for speaking in Lord Judah's stead. I can't waste time."

He inclined his head. "I am happy to serve Redcake's, as always."

She sensed a hint of irony in his tone, not something she had ever associated with him before. "Are you unhappy here?"

His chin pulled back. "What?"

"You are not yourself, Mr. Hales. I may not know you well, but I have known you for years."

"There is nothing you need trouble yourself with."

"If you are ill, you should return home."

"I'm not ill."

She had to agree he appeared to be in fine fettle. If anything, she'd say he had a martial light in his eye, but she had no interest in doing battle with him on any subject. She had to return to Bristol. "May I use the telephone?"

He directed her to it, and she rang her Bristol office, asking her secretary, Greggory, to have the cake factory manager meet with her at nine A.M. the next morning. She would start with him.

By the time she was done with the telephone, Mr. Hales had put the cakes into a larger box and tied it with twine so she could carry it.

She took it, then braced herself and stared up into his eyes. "You clearly do have some kind of trouble. Nothing you say to me would be repeated to my father or Lord Judah. If I can help, just say the word."

"You are not known for your compassion, Miss Redcake."

She shook her head, as if she could cleanse her brain of his words. "You do not know me."

He pressed his lips together for a moment. "I am realizing that. Thank you, Miss Redcake. I hope you solve the problem with the cakes quickly. If you cannot, please notify me so that we can increase our production in the bakery here. I can bring on some extra men."

"When does Lord Judah return?"

"I hope it will be a short trip."

Upon reflection, she did think he appeared tired. Overwork, perhaps? But she couldn't advise him to rest, not with the entire operational responsibility resting on those admittedly broad shoulders. He was gaining useful experience. She made a mental note to ask her father if the new shop and tearoom would have a bakery on the premises. It would be wise for just such emergencies as this.

"I do hope he returns soon. At least his departure created a learning experience for you."

He raised an eyebrow. She held her ground despite his obvious derision. "You will have days like this when you are manager. I have learned that the hard way."

His expression smoothed to a near perfect blankness. Instead of reading his expression, she noted the high cheekbones, the square chin, the skin that molded tightly along his perfect jawline. She could see a hint of beard under his lower lip. It would scratch her if she touched him there this late in the day.

"Miss Redcake?"

His tone was gentle. She had been staring.

She forced a smile. "I am woolgathering. I am not a fan of trains."

"I will go downstairs with you and make sure you get those boxes safely into a hansom for your return journey."

"Thank you."

She followed him downstairs, admiring his lean, tapered body from behind. How could she turn off her admiration for handsome men? It would be best if her body learned what her mind already knew: She was doomed to spinsterhood as a consequence of her foolishness with Theodore Bliven.

* * *

The next day, Ewan returned to the law office of Shadrach Norwich for his first meeting with his great-uncle, the Earl of Fitzwalter. He felt unprepared. Did he call the man uncle or Lord Fitzwalter? He was a man unused to family. How did one behave? With more familiarity than you would otherwise? Would the man consider him an equal?

He still hadn't resigned himself to the idea of being an heir to an earldom. This morning, in the mirror as he shaved, he saw a strange sort of expression in his eyes, like hope. For once, he wouldn't have to do everything alone. Something was going to be handed to him on a plate, as if it was no more than a tea cake.

A title, no less. Matilda Redcake must have thought he was mad, the way he had behaved to her. Those adorable freckles, so large and brown across her nose and forehead, had all but darkened in confusion at his unusually democratic treatment of her. No longer did he have to bow and scrape to the Redcakes. Sir Bartley only held a title due to his knighting. Meanwhile, Ewan could call himself the Honorable Ewan Hales in correspondence now.

He did wonder, as he gazed at the sagging front door of the law offices, why an earl would hire someone from such a miserable-looking law office. Had Norwich come down in the world? Was it mere loyalty to a long-term relationship that kept Lord Fitzwalter with the man? Perhaps the earl didn't understand that Norwich made rude comments about the family. Ewan's head had positively swum with *Walter* comments after he'd left. It had been a wonder that he'd made it through the Matilda Redcake conversation with such aplomb. He'd explained the flour problem well enough and sent her back to Bristol to deal with it.

If he still cared about his position, he'd advise Lord Judah to bend Lady Hatbrook's ear about why her sister didn't exercise proper quality control at the factory. Those cakes never should have left Bristol. On the other hand, would that be dangerous to his career? You didn't tell tales on the sisters of the owner of your company. You buttressed up their mistakes and moved on.

He wondered if Lord Judah would consider buying his cakes from another factory if the Redcake's offerings continued to be unacceptable. But who made such high-quality products other than the Redcakes?

No one he knew of. No competition had tried as hard. But now Matilda was at the helm. Would Redcake's lose its edge?

"I do not care. I do not care," he repeated to himself. If he kept saying it, he might believe it.

Once inside the main door, he found the anteroom as deserted as it had been on his visit the day before, but Mr. Norwich entered from his inner sanctum almost immediately, as if Ewan's presence was more important this time.

"Mr. Hales," he said with a nod.

Ewan noted the man's eyes were dilated. Had he been at his brown bottle earlier today? When he became earl, the man would be fired if he was still in the family's employ.

Ewan nodded back. "Has my great-uncle arrived?"

"Oh, yes. We had certain matters to discuss." The solicitor rubbed his hands together, transferring ink from one index finger to the other. He must have been taking notes. One ink-stained hand went to the door, holding it open. It would leave spots when Norwich pulled his hand away. "If you will, Mr. Hales."

Ewan entered, a sharp eye on the figure seated on one of the two brown leather chairs in front of the desk. The man tapped one liver-spotted hand on the armrest of his chair. From his hand alone, Ewan thought the man must be in his sixties. He had thick, steel-gray hair, though there was a bald spot on the back of his head. When he turned, Ewan had the impression of an unsmiling soul, spotted again around the corners of the eyes, and scored deeply with wrinkles. Late sixties, then. The thin lips were pursed together. Ewan searched for some sign of resemblance and found none, other than the man's shoulders, which were not stooped with age and seemed to be the same width as Ewan's own.

The earl perused him in return, then nodded. "Walter's boy," he rasped.

"I had not thought I had any distinguishing characteristics," Ewan said.

"You have the same hangdog expression in your eyes, as if you are desperate to be liked and cannot understand why you are not."

Ewan felt his face go blank. He had been prepared to smile, it was true, despite the irritating presence of Norwich. Surely such a re-union or, indeed, first meeting between earl and heir should be private? But no, this earl was prepared to insult, not appease or welcome. Good Gad, he was worse than any Redcake or Shield.

"I am forced to accept your interpretation of my looks. I cannot say with any accuracy what expression was habitually on my father's face. It has been too long since I saw him."

"Talks in speeches, too," the earl remarked to Norwich. "Tiresome."

Ewan turned to the solicitor's desk and saw no evidence of the brown bottle. It had been hidden away for the duration. Norwich caught his eye for a moment, then went behind his desk. He seated himself, his knees creaking.

Ewan suspected Norwich was a decade, or even a decade and a half, younger than the earl, but not as well-maintained.

"Norwich here tells me you had no idea of your ancestry," the earl remarked, staring not at him but straight ahead.

"Correct," Ewan said, with brevity.

"I paid for your education."

"So he led me to believe."

"Your father?"

"No, Mr. Norwich. I knew nothing of my finances, only that there was nothing for me upon leaving school, so the headmaster helped me secure a position directly upon completion of my studies."

"And you've been with Redcake's ever since?"

"No, I worked elsewhere early on, then the Redcake's business was broken up. I stayed in my position and now work for the Marchioness of Hatbrook, who was born a Redcake."

"What skills have you?"

"Gathering information, writing letters, typewriting, general duties." Ewan shrugged.

"And your masters? Would they give you good characters?"

"Yes. Sir Bartley wrote me an excellent one when he gave the business to his daughter. Just so I would have it."

The earl nodded. "You'll need to use your talents on behalf of our family now. Estates and such. Know anything about the Fitzwalter properties?"

He had wondered what was coming. Not a life of leisure, obviously. "Nothing, I'm afraid."

"Any experience in land management? Rents?"

He kept his tone level. "I assume my skills can be universally applied."

"I will take that as a no." The earl sighed and took out a cigar case. "Nonetheless, without developing your knowledge, you can have no hope of success as earl. So we must make amends, and quickly. I never thought to find you my heir, but here we are. I only had a daughter, you know. Lady Honoria, who is now Mrs. Keep of New York."

"I remember. Redcake's supplied her wedding cake. Has she had children?"

"A daughter. Never met her. In America."

Ewan realized his time as heir might be brief. "How old is Lady Honoria?"

"Twenty-seven. She married rather late."

Still plenty of time to have a grandson for the earl, however. "I see."

The earl peered at him over spectacles perched on the edge of his nose. "There is no hope of another child. She had difficulties. But any son of hers could not inherit in any event."

"I see. I am sorry." He did not entirely understand inheritance law.

"But you must understand why I never thought you would be the heir. At the time you were being educated, I might even have had another child, but my wife died and I have never remarried."

"You still might," said Norwich, more hopefully than Ewan would have liked.

"I would rather slit my own throat," the earl said. "I finally have peace in my own home."

Norwich clutched at the edge of his desk. Ewan thought he was hoping to find his brown bottle there.

"Then we are bound together," Ewan said.

"At least you are respectable."

"Yes, sir."

The earl coughed. "Good. We'll find you someplace to live, suitable to your station. I haven't the funds to set you up in London, but you need to learn estate management."

Norwich frowned but wasn't able to speak before the earl continued. "Hampshire, I think. We have a large dairy operation there. Good source of income; our best, in fact. Think the steward is stealing, however."

"Lovely," Ewan muttered. "Anything less rural, sir? Not that Hampshire is very rural."

"It is good land," the earl replied complacently.

"Anything more industrial?" Ewan inquired. "My skills are modern."

"Yes, I have tried to diversify. We have wheat farms in Lancashire and use the grain within our holdings rather than selling the raw product."

"That's something," Ewan said hopefully. But Hampshire was preferable to Lancashire.

"It's a good source of income. The problem with the landed classes, is, of course, land. Too much land, not enough money. Which is why my daughter married an American. She can have all the finer things now."

"I'm assuming the land is entailed."

"Precisely." The earl sighed. "I am glad you understand that much, but it will take a great deal of time to acquaint you with the specifics. Norwich here, with his family's long history of service, has a good understanding, and I suggest you write him with any questions. How soon can you leave London?"

Chapter Three

"I cannot give notice to my manager as he is away," Ewan said. "Are you certain I should leave? I am acting manager of Redcake's now, and I am going to have my own tea shop and emporium when Lady Hatbrook opens the Kensington branch this summer. Things are delayed a bit as she is, err—"

"Due to hopefully birth Lord Hatbrook's heir any moment, yes?"

"Exactly, but I expect to be managing my own enterprise by summer's end. That's a good salary, sir, enough for a house and servants. Should I really walk away from it given your financial concerns?"

"Of course you should," the earl snapped. "Have you been woolgathering? I will not live forever, sir, and you need to learn your responsibilities. While my father's direct line has come down to me, my daughter, my granddaughter, and you, my grandfather's line has left us a passel of dependents, not to mention the tenants, and land stewardship itself. I expect you to write Lord Judah immediately and give notice. He will need to return to his post."

"I cannot command the brother of a marquess," Ewan said.

"You can do what I tell you to do," Fitzwalter snapped.

Ewan wanted to stand up and leave, but this man was family. Regardless of how it was presented, he needed to take responsibility for his birthright. "I shall send a telegram. I do not think he has access to a telephone."

"Very good. Today is Tuesday. I hope Lord Judah can be back at his office by Monday, which means you should determine whether you want to go to Hampshire or Lancashire in the next few days."

For the first time since his school days, Ewan had a sore stomach. Bile burned his throat. He had not realized how much independence he really had at Redcake's until this moment, when he found himself falling under this elderly person's thumb.

"I will be in touch, my lord."

The earl nodded. "Speak to Norwich. He has a telephone. You can conduct your business that way, if you wish. Personally, I can't understand a word any man says through the things." He pushed back his chair and rose.

Norwich looked at the ceiling. Ewan suspected from the loud pitch of the earl's voice that he had some hearing deficit. Now that he was standing, Ewan did see the earl's body stoop. He looked older. Was he ill besides?

Ewan stood as well, holding out his hand, but the earl ignored it.

"Norwich," the earl said, then walked out.

Norwich rose, too, then gestured to Ewan to close the office door. "You understand now," he said, as they both sat down again.

"Understand what?"

Norwich sighed again. "There is no hope of you escaping it. You will be the next earl."

Ewan waited for the brown bottle to appear, but Norwich had enough self-control to keep it hidden for now. Still, he felt he needed to put the man out of his misery soon. "What do you suggest? Hampshire or Lancashire?"

Norwich snorted. "Neither. The Douglas men always die between the ages of seventy and seventy-two, unless they are killed in battle or taken off by enemies in some fashion. Given the present earl's age, you have three to five years to learn your responsibilities. You don't want to be buried on a dairy or a wheat farm."

"Then you will advise the earl to keep me in London?"

"He can't afford that unless you live with him."

Ewan held back his shudder. "What if I go to one of these farms for a year and make it profitable? Will he let me then live on those profits, in London, and learn the rest of my duties?"

"You can't bargain with earls, Mr. Hales. You must begin as you plan to go on. If you set foot outside London, I doubt you'll be seeing it again until his lordship's funeral."

Ewan ran his hand through his hair. "Are there any London properties? Anything I can properly manage here?"

Norwich clutched at the edge of his desk again. "Nothing that I cannot handle. It's too bad you weren't a law clerk rather than a secretary."

Ewan suspected he could do better than Norwich and his brown bottle, but until he had a look at the files he wouldn't know for sure. "Could you suggest to the earl that I stay here for the rest of the spring and work with you, to give me a more global sense of where I can best be used? I can pay my own way out of my savings for that long."

"A clever suggestion," Norwich conceded. "I shall let you know in a day or two."

The Redcake's holdings in Bristol were situated in a complex of their own, with multiple redbrick buildings built along a central green. Matilda mostly worked in the building that held administrative offices, though she made an effort to go into the factories and meet workers. She wanted to understand every level of the business. Her father had impressed upon her the idea that surprises were always injurious in business, and she believed knowledge would keep surprises at bay.

Therefore, she knew to be wary when approaching Stephen Hay, the manager of the cake factory. He had accepted her the least of any of the managers. Even her brother had warned her about the man, saying he was excellent at his work but would probably lose his position at some point due to his attitude.

When she walked into his office, Mr. Hay stayed behind his desk, chewing on an unlit cigar, instead of showing her the respect due her either as his employer or as a woman.

"What now?" he barked, an intimidating, bulldog-like presence.

"I'm sure you received the note from Greggory regarding this meeting." She dropped a cake box on his desk.

"Something wrong at the box factory? I never thought we should have started making boxes ourselves," Hay sneered.

"The box is fine. It's the cake. Taste it."

He patted his bulging waistcoat. "Trying to fatten me up, Miss Redcake? Like a big man, do you?"

"It's adulterated." Ignoring his remark, she found a fork in a box on a shelf and scooped up a piece of the cake. "Here."

He leaned over his desk, leering, and took her hand in his hairy paw, then sniffed. She had the feeling that he sniffed her hand instead of the cake. Disgusting pig.

"The cake," she said, in her most disinterested voice, the one she'd practiced years ago to fend off inappropriate swains. She'd never had much of a chance to use it because of her misbehavior with Theodore Bliven.

He opened his mouth, his oversized red tongue darting out to lick off a crumb. Her stomach contents seemed to do a full queasy upturn, and she was grateful that she had eaten only a rock bun and some tea for breakfast. After a moment, he opened his mouth and took the full bite of cake from the fork, then sat back, releasing her wrist with a satisfied smirk.

She kept her expression as neutral as possible while he chewed.

"Had to make sure you weren't trying to poison me," he said, after he swallowed.

"Yes, because I hope to kill off my employees."

"You'd probably poison yourself in the process."

"If I'm dead, I would not be of much use to the businesses."

"Think you're of much use now?" he inquired in a mock-casual voice.

She couldn't help fisting her hands, but she had them behind her back before he could see the involuntary gesture. Her brother had been correct. The first slip in Hay's performance and he would lose his position, unlike other men to whom she might give a second chance. Stephen Hay was odious.

"I hold your livelihood in my hands, Mr. Hay. You have a family to support, correct?"

He sneered again.

"I hope you keep them in mind when considering your behavior toward me." She stayed standing to increase her authority. "What is your opinion of the cake?"

"Something has been added to the batter to give it that powdery taste."

"Redcake's in London has pulled all of our cakes, from the tea-room at least. We have to fix the problem before Thursday."

"Come back in two hours," he said, after staring at the ceiling for a moment. "I will check with the foreman to make sure our recipe hasn't changed for the shilling cakes. If it hasn't, I will check our powdered ingredient supplies."

"Make sure you are checking what was available last week."

"We order a month's supply at a time," he said. "It should be the same."

She shook her head. *Bad news.* "Would last week's powders have been the first of the new supply?"

"I'll check our records. We don't waste anything."

"Why wouldn't anyone have smelled the powder when the bags were opened?" she asked.

"Maybe someone had a stuffed nose. You know how flour hangs in the air. It's hard to breathe. Well, maybe you don't. Unlike Gawain, you never worked in the factory."

There it was, a dig at her more privileged upbringing. She couldn't change any of that now. "I'll go with you, so I can learn."

"No, you won't, Miss Redcake. You want the truth, right? I won't get it in front of the governor's daughter."

"You are mistaken, Mr. Hay. I am the governor. But I will leave and return, because we do not have time to argue the matter. We must have good cakes for Thursday's shipment." She turned and left the room, knowing her shoulders would ache that evening from standing so stiffly.

Holding her son would make her feel better. His chubby arms around her neck usually fixed all her woes. For one evening, at least.

Ewan returned to his office and automatically reached for his clipboard so he could gather the reports. This week, all the information was for his use rather than for Lord Judah's, but he would still take the time to keep careful records. With all of the turnover they'd had in management before Lord Judah came onboard, the historical record had become even more vital.

He turned around to walk down to accounting and found Betsy Popham waiting for him just inside the doorway. She held a tray with a steaming teapot and a plate of orange cakes.

"I thought you might need a midmorning treat," she purred, setting the tray down on the credenza on the wall opposite his desk.

Betsy was one of the few women with the bosom to fill out her otherwise shapeless cakie uniform. On her, the black dress looked almost tailored. Maybe she had done something to it, though the neck and hemline looked like everyone else's. Had she taken it in at the waist or something? Ewan didn't know much about women's clothing. But he did know Betsy's hourglass figure didn't need enhancements of any kind. She had the full breasts and rump of a pagan goddess. They had been lovers once. She'd enticed him away from the copy clerk he had been courting, mostly respectably, in accounting, and into her bed. She'd been a virgin at the time, he thought.

Then she, in turn, had been enticed away by Simon Hellman, the delivery manager. She'd come back to him after two months, tearful, saying she hadn't been Hellman's lover. Ewan had lost his faith in her, though, and hadn't taken her back. Periodically, she made an effort to return to his good graces, though their romance had been over for a couple of years now.

"Do you think I'm going to walk over there to pour a cup of tea?" he snarled.

"You never like me setting it on your desk."

"That's because you like to brush up against me when you do it."

"I do not!" Her large, thick-lashed eyes blinked slowly.

"Maybe I was just imagining that part," he muttered.

She came over to his desk and perched on the edge, then leaned toward him. He took a deep breath. She smelled of fondant and almond paste. Once upon a time, she'd smelled like spilled tea and currant buns, but that was when she was a cakie, before Lady Hatbrook had taught her wedding cake artistry. Rumor had it she wasn't actually a very good decorator, but the department turned a nice profit, and that was due to her.

"Why won't you ever forgive me?" she asked.

"You left me without a word."

"I've been good as gold ever since. You are the only man I've ever been with." She toyed with his lapel.

He sat back. "Still hoping I will propose? It will never happen." Especially not now, when he'd have to marry someone suitable to be an earl's wife.

"Haven't I proven myself?"

"I would not know. I have not paid that much attention. But you know; you left me once. You might leave me again."

She pursed her full, sensual lips. "Fine; you will never entirely trust me on a personal level. I suppose I will continue to focus on my career, as I have done."

"Or find a husband." That would rid him of her.

"I am very good at my work. Will you take me with you when you go to Redcake's Kensington?" she asked.

"Is that what this is about? Not romance at all?" He stopped the search for his clipboard and sat down. When had he become disorganized? He always knew exactly where everything was.

"I gave up on you at least a year ago. I'm not surprised you haven't noticed."

He put his fingers to his forehead, rubbing away the pain there, then ran his fingers over his scalp. If he cared, he'd be irritated by her manipulation, but at least she recognized him as a man with a future. Ironically, it was very different from what she imagined.

"Your hair has been looking very mussed these last two days. Uncharacteristic of you. Has the idea of the new shop put you under a lot of stress? Or is it Lord Judah's vacation?"

"There is a problem with the cakes," he said, rubbing his forehead again.

"That is Bristol's problem." She shifted her torso, undulating slightly.

He attempted to ignore her sensual movements. "You can't be serious, Betsy. Our customers will stop coming here. They wouldn't care that it's Bristol's fault. I don't want to lose half of our tearoom business the week Lord Judah is gone."

"In Lord Judah's place, I'd have gone to Bristol myself, brought them the cake, instead of making a telephone call. Something this important requires immediate action."

"I'm sorry, were we having a job interview?"

Betsy lifted her chin. "I'd like to be your assistant manager. Everybody knows the Fancy makes the most profit at Redcake's, and that wasn't true in Alys's day. I make more profit than my father does in the bakery."

"That's partially due to our reputation in fashionable society, thanks to Lady Hatbrook owning the place."

"If we didn't put out a good product . . ." She had started strong, then trailed off. She put her hand on his arm. "Look, Ewan, I just want to help you."

"How old are you now?"

"I'm twenty." A look of defiance flared in her eyes.

"You don't have enough experience. Men with university educations will be applying for that position."

"You worked your way up and so did I. You know you can trust me. That's more important than learning Greek or Latin."

"It would help to have someone with aristocratic connections there, like Lady Hatbrook." *Like me.* But he knew now that he'd never be the Redcake's Kensington manager. This conversation was pointless chatter and nothing more.

Not only that, he couldn't trust her. Was that not the real crux of the matter? He'd never have considered her, whatever her profit-making skills, because he could not understand her and had never been able to do so. She'd left him; she'd returned. Then he had rejected her right back.

He nodded to himself, completely ignoring whatever it was she was trying to say. "Whatever happens, I don't imagine we'll be seeing each other very much anymore. I sincerely wish you the best, Betsy. I hope you find happiness."

Her face seemed much older as she reacted to his words. "So it's a no, then?"

"It's a no to anything you might ever ask of me, ever again," he stated.

"I didn't sleep with him," she whispered. "You don't understand."

"I understand I was your lover, expecting to become your husband someday, and you betrayed me. For two months I did not exist to you. You cut me dead. No Ewan Hales in your life."

"I had reasons."

"If you did, you never shared them with me. It was long ago." He lifted his hand to stop her from speaking. "I have a great deal of work to do because personal business kept me away from my duties."

"Ewan."

He spotted his clipboard under the morning's mail and pulled it out, then stood. "If you will excuse me, Miss Popham. I need to make my rounds."

She watched as he straightened his coat and tightened his tie. "Your hair is curling over your forehead. You never let it do that."

He smoothed it back. "Thank you. Now, if you want to continue to make a profit for Lady Hatbrook, I suggest you stop wasting time and return to your duties."

"Aren't you going to drink your tea?"

He shook his head. "Not now. Good day." He left the room and went down a flight of stairs to accounting, refusing to look back. She wasn't even attractive to him anymore, but he wished when his brain had a quiet moment it didn't flash to Matilda Redcake. He remembered the days when all his spare thoughts were of Betsy and those lush curves, so newly, perfectly ripened, as if just for him. Now, young as she still was, she looked tired, strained. Odd, when Matilda Redcake, twenty-four and burdened with far more cares than Betsy Popham, appeared so fresh, almost innocent, with those freckles and that carrot hair.

Late in the afternoon, when Matilda longed for a tea tray, she instead sat on the dusty storeroom floor in the Redcake's administrative building and looked through ledgers, tracing the source of ingredients for the shilling cake. By careful perusal, she had been able to break down what exactly had been in those cakes, but it took a great deal of math and knowledge of recipes to figure out the precise details.

"Matilda?" The door opened and a tall figure stood in the doorway.

She recognized her cousin. "Yes, Greggory? I'm down here, doing some quite complex calculations."

"A messenger just came from the shilling cake factory."

She sneezed. This room desperately needed a good cleaning. She found her already dirty handkerchief. "News from Mr. Hay?"

"Yes. It was the flour, he said. They tested a bag of flour left from the last shipment and it had the powder in it. No new additives or adulterants around. Wants to know what they should do about this week's cakes."

"They baked yesterday, right? Tomorrow, they frost." She swore.

"Matilda!" Greggory said.

"Outside the businesses you may be my older cousin, Greggory, but here I am your supervisor. No criticizing me on Redcake's property, please."

"Not very ladylike," he muttered.

She bared her teeth at him. "If you don't think this situation is worth swearing about, I can't imagine what would be. Do you realize much money has been wasted? Cor."

"I thought you went to finishing school."

"Yes, I did. Years ago. Send a boy back over there. Find out if yesterday's baking used the same flour. If they did, they need to give the product to the workhouse and start over. With good flour. Find out if we have any good flour."

"Yes, Miss Redcake."

Matilda glanced up at the saucy tone. Her cousin merely winked at her and wandered off. Even at twenty-six, he seemed superstretched, underfed, and not yet grown into his adult body. He had black hair, stick straight like hers, but the color came from his mother's family. She had some Italian blood and it showed in Greggory's skin tone and hair.

At times, Matilda would have happily traded her hair with him, or with her sister Rose. Now, she just kept it pulled back and under hats as much as possible. That kept her hands out of it. Unlike Ewan Hales, if she slicked her hands through her hair, it would simply come undone from its pins and stick out straight in a witchlike nightmare, like broom straw, rather than tumbling into attractive curls over her forehead, like his did. How appealing he was with mussed hair. She wondered why, for the first time, he'd looked so mussed yesterday. But she didn't have time to puzzle it out.

She went back through her notes and discovered the offending cake flour had come from Douglas Flour. Pushing herself off the floor, she went to a filing cabinet and found the supplier records. Douglas Flour was owned by the Earl of Fitzwalter. He resided in London. She knew that from Alys's prattling about making the wedding cake for his daughter not too long ago. Of course, the earl wouldn't have anything to do with his own flour.

When she dug through the records, though, she found all paths led back to London. The flour had been shipped from Southwark, where the factory was, and her contact information was all there. No sign of a telephone number, either. Could Mr. Hales find someone to investigate on his end?

After she tidied herself, she had Greggory ring Ewan Hales. She explained the situation to him.

"Do you think you can get us any shilling cakes on Thursday?"

"I'm still waiting." A boy appeared in the doorway of her office's anteroom, where Greggory worked. Her cousin gestured him in and opened the note, then handed it to Matilda.

"Sorry, Mr. Hales. It looks like I can get you half of your regular order. We have a backup supplier locally, and we do have some flour in stock. It's clean, though more expensive than Douglas Flour."

"Douglas Flour?" His voice had gone tense.

She frowned. "Yes, out of Southwark." She explained what she knew about it. "Can you get someone to investigate the situation on your end?"

"I think you had better come down to London tomorrow," he said.

"Why? I need to go hat in hand to our backup supplier and beg twice as much flour from them as we usually take. I'm hoping to get you the rest of the week's order a day late. I'm glad we have someone here locally instead of having to bother Alys just before her baby comes, and learn about these new Liverpool suppliers." She turned to the boy. "Look sharp! Go back to Mr. Hay and tell him to take the good flour he has and start making new cakes immediately."

The boy nodded and ran out the door. His trousers were too short for his spindly, bowed legs. She frowned. Not a healthy specimen, but she liked to hire out of the workhouses whenever possible, especially the youths. It might be their only chance of staying away from a life of crime.

"We need to have a conversation." Mr. Hales sounded world-weary on the phone, a decade older than his true age, just a year older than Greggory.

"In person?"

"Yes, please. It's important."

"Is it about Douglas Flour?"

"Yes. In part."

She sneezed again. The dust from the file-room floor must have covered her skirts. She needed to change. "Fine. I will come down to-morrow morning, assuming I can make a deal with our other flour supplier. You can give me lunch and then we shall deal with Douglas Flour together. Any word from Lord Judah?"

"No, I am not about to bother him. Yet. If you can get me a half shipment of good cakes on Thursday, and the rest on Friday, I hope we can put this behind us without too much loss of customers."

Who was going to pay for the expense of the lost cakes and the more expensive flour? She'd like to know that. Her father would turn red with rage when he saw her reports. She didn't look forward to writing those notes to him.

"Very good, Mr. Hales. Thank you for your forbearance, and I will see you tomorrow." She set the earpiece back on the telephone and turned to Greggory. "Have we researched flour suppliers recently? Do you know who is reputable?"

Greggory scrunched his nose and said nothing. She waited. "We do that every autumn, so we have the information as of about eight months ago."

"Start there. Get fresh prices from everyone. And I need a full report on Douglas Flour before I have to leave in the morning. How long have we worked with them, what our relationship has been, did we have any issues with price changes recently? Anything you think I ought to know before I call on them."

"Yes, Miss Redcake."

She grabbed his right ear and tweaked it gently in response. "Don't get saucy with me, underling."

He stood, grabbing her hand, and twirled her around. "I'm still taller and stronger than you, Matilda. Watch yourself."

She laughed and let go of his hand, then went into her office, beating at her skirts to release the dust. At least Greggory didn't seem the ambitious type, after her position. He was a lover instead of a businessman, wrapped up in his nuptial plans. His wedding was in early June. Her parents had decided to buy him a cottage as a wedding gift. Very generous, but he'd been a good employee, and they expected him to spend his entire career working for the family.

The news continued to be bad. All the flour from the Douglas factory was suspect. Alarm spread through the operation as baking was restarted while the flour was investigated. Their backup supplier was thrilled to have the extra business but didn't have the resources to fill their entire order. Matilda needed to have Douglas fix the flour or find a new supplier a week ago. On the train to London, she drafted a memorandum of quality for Mr. Hales to type up. Hopefully, the Douglas manager would sign it. Even better, follow it.

At least she carried proof of a cake with good flour in a white and gold Redcake's box. She'd taken one of the first cakes off the line and finished its preparation herself, supervised by an old woman who'd been employed in the business since Matilda's grandfather's day, back before there had been any such thing as a Redcake's cake.

She'd always wondered if her father had arrived at the idea of becoming a cake manufacturer because of the family name. Or cake making might simply be in the family blood. Rumor had it that the family had gained its surname baking cakes for some medieval Irish king long ago, but she wasn't certain if her father had made the story up or not. She made a mental note to ask him; the story might be useful in promotions.

She entered Redcake's via the door by the loading dock in the back. Arriving earlier than her previous visit, she saw men returning from morning bread deliveries. At least bread flour and cake flour were separate and came from different suppliers.

Men with ink-stained fingers and ledgers under their arms passed her on the stairs as she went up to the offices. They nodded, smiled, and greeted her by name, such a change from a few years back, when her father never allowed her to set foot in the business and she had even less desire for that than he did. Now, she wished she knew every detail of each person's business, because every grain of knowledge helped her to do her own job. There were never enough hours in the day, and there were times she missed her son dreadfully, wishing she could have a quiet morning in the nursery with him, a few childish games of patty-cake or tickles on the hearthrug, but her efforts kept the entire family afloat.

She'd become more important to the family than Alys had ever been, with her once obsessive love of wedding cakes. Now Alys had the life Matilda had expected to have herself. The rough factory girl had become a marchioness and the finished young lady was the mother of a bastard son and had a position in the family business.

Her pensiveness matched Ewan's by the time she arrived behind him. Instead of being at his desk, his fingers running down columns of numbers, he stood at the window, staring at Oxford Street.

"Trying to gather your strength?" she asked.

He turned and blinked, as if he wasn't quite sure she was there. "What do you mean?"

"There is so much energy down below. I thought you were trying to find some. You look exhausted."

He put his hand to his hair, then pulled it away. "I didn't sleep well."

"Management harder than you thought?"

"Oh, it isn't Redcake's."

Her eyebrows rose at that. What else could there be in the middle of a crisis, and his manager not in town? How could he be concerned with anything else? "What, then?"

"I have tea set up in the inner office," he said, shuffling forward with nothing of his usual purposeful step. "Let's sit down."

She followed him, bemused, and set her box down on his leg, then dropped her valise to the floor and unbuttoned her coat. He watched her silently but did not behave as a gentleman and offer to help her remove it. Leaving her hat on, she sat down and poured tea for both of them.

"I brought a new cake, baked yesterday. We can both test it, but it is made with Bristol Flour, not Douglas Flour. The entire Douglas shipment for the month has been adulterated, as best I can tell. The fact that we've had almost no complaints tells you the state of the flour market in general."

"Our aristocratic clients won't accept that."

"No, but then, most patrons at our level aren't eating out of common shops, so they aren't used to common goods."

"You are correct about that, Miss Redcake."

She opened the box and took a knife from the tray, slicing into her cake. "What have you learned about Douglas Flour?"

"It's owned by the Earl of Fitzwalter."

"I already know that," she said, impatient. She slid the knife under a cake piece and moved it to a plate, then handed it to him.

"The thing is, I'm related to Lord Fitzwalter," he said, not taking the cake, his hand going to his hair again.

The knife dropped from her fingers onto the cake, marring her decorative efforts. "What?"

Chapter Four

"Normally, Miss Redcake, I am the first person to be obsessed with my position. Redcake's has been my life since 1884, when your father hired me. I was not particularly qualified for the position, but neither was he qualified to run a retail establishment. We learned together." He clasped his hands around his teacup. It had rained all morning, and the ensuing dampness would have caused him to light the fire, or at least the stove, in the room, if he hadn't been woolgathering. He needed the cup's warmth, but even that didn't quite quell the fine tremor in his limbs.

"I know all this," Miss Redcake said, dropping another slice of indifferently frosted cake onto a plate.

Ewan didn't think he could force a morsel of anything down his dry throat, but he needed to taste the product, so he set down his cup and took the plate. "Why was Douglas Flour our primary supplier and not Bristol Flour?"

"Mr. Hales, kindly finish your earlier thought, about your familial relationship to Lord Fitzwalter," Matilda said.

He noted her light brown eyes had a mesmerizing hint of silver in them when they caught the light. When he'd first seen her a few years ago, he hadn't thought her beautiful, though she had always carried herself well. Her more recent severe style suited her looks. Her hairstyle allowed him to see the planes of her face. She would be far more beautiful in middle age than any apple-faced, plump beauty. But he would not be in the Redcakes' sphere by then. He would be the Earl of Fitzwalter.

"Yes, of course. I do apologize. My parents died young and I went away to school. I had not understood there to be any relations, but as it turns out, my father was merely estranged from his family."

"Go on." She took a bite of cake and smiled.

He thought she was pleased by the taste of the cake rather than his words. Following suit, he tried the cake. "It's fine."

She nodded. "I'm not sure the grain is quite as delicate, but such an improvement over the adulterated flour."

He nodded. "Lawrence Douglas, the earl, was my father's uncle, my great-uncle. I had no idea until very recently."

"I see."

"I'm not certain you could, at least not yet. The earl has one daughter and her children, assuming she had a male heir, could not inherit."

Matilda's eyes went wide and she set down her plate. "Never tell me you are now the heir to Lord Fitzwalter!"

"That is exactly what I have to tell you." He set his plate on top of the box.

"How long have you known this, Mr. Hales?"

"It was news to me just this week. I do wish Lord Judah was in town." He picked up his teacup, cradling it.

She shook her head. "So you can tender your resignation?"

"Can you blame me? I have to take up my duties to the family, now that Lord Ritten is deceased."

"Undeniably a difficult situation. And you in line for the promotion." She winced.

"I am sorry for that. I was looking forward to the challenge. Like you, however, I need to do what my family asks, and in this case, they want me in the countryside, running one of the earl's estates."

"Good heavens. Have you ever been out of London?"

"No." He picked up his cake plate again, noting in detached fashion that his fingers shook.

"Terribly indelicate of me, of course, but how long do you think it will be before you have autonomy again?"

He knew she was wondering how long it would be before the present earl shuffled off this mortal coil, as if anyone could really know that. "It hardly matters to the Redcakes. I will be gone from your lives soon enough."

Matilda swallowed the last morsel of her cake and set down her plate. "Mr. Hales, I do not believe anyone in my family wants you gone from our lives."

"No?"

"Least of all me."

He wasn't sure he'd heard her correctly at first; she'd spoken in such a low tone. "No?"

She put a hand to her temple, as if answering the question gave her a headache. "You've been a great help to me. Your reports are very precise. I know you are the person who prepares them, even if they come from Lord Judah. And you've assisted me with this shilling cake disaster. I appreciate anyone who takes me seriously, as it is hard for men to treat a woman so."

"I see." He forced a smile. "I've worked hard to be an efficient and effective employee."

"And a rakish man."

The unexpected comment made him sit straight back in his chair. "What?"

"You've cut a swath through the ladies of the tea shop." Her lips curved. "I have wondered what your secret is, especially given that I've only ever attracted one man to me, yet you seem to be catnip to many ladies."

He could find no words, at first. Especially because she'd said she wanted to be taken seriously. And yet men discussed such things among themselves all the time. "I had no idea I had such a reputation. I courted a young lady downstairs, then Betsy Popham."

"Then that ended." She raised her eyebrows.

"She left me. My pride was hurt, and I suppose I had flirtations with a few of the cakies."

"Were you affianced?"

"No, but I was expecting it." He winced as he remembered that time. Betsy had never understood how she'd hurt him.

"I am sorry." She leaned forward and patted his hand.

Her interest kept him speaking. "A number of employees go to the Egyptian Hall for the magic show once a month or so, and to some of the music halls. I suppose I might have paid too much attention to one young lady or another."

She smiled and patted his hand again.

He took a deep breath. "Really, I should not have gone traipsing through the halls with the common employees, given my position, but I am the youngest of the senior staff and therefore do not have much opportunity to fit in anywhere here."

"I understand completely. We have that in common, not fitting in." She lifted her chin, obviously considering. "I expect you are well educated."

"Not exactly. I went to boarding school but didn't have the opportunity for further education."

She released his hand and sat back. "You mixed with a different class of boys there, and that changed you. It matched who you really were, rather than who you were given to believe you were. It must have been confusing."

"We both were educated above what we thought our positions to be at the time. We expected one thing and received another."

She nodded, staring directly into his eyes. He liked her directness, but her clear chestnut-brown gaze had begun to stir a different interest in his lower parts. Perhaps his troubles interfered with his work, but he found his thoughts drifting away from Redcake's and cake flour.

"You say you have only ever attracted one suitor?" he ventured.

She nodded.

"Given the situation, it is not such a surprise," he said.

She flinched.

"I am sorry, Miss Redcake, but you have to be realistic. It is not that you are unattractive." Certainly not, given his reaction.

Her frown deepened.

"Quite the opposite," he assured her. "But you fit in as little as me. If you had the family background most of the cakies do, an illegitimate child would be no great thing."

She looked nauseated for a moment, then straightened her shoulders. No sheen of tears was present in her eyes. She had backbone, and he liked her all the more for it. He could see her at the helm of an army with that fierce expression: Boudicca leading a battle charge.

"We tried so hard to leave our background behind," she said. "My father wanted to be a country gentleman. He raised Rose and me to be ladies. But I was so naïve. I made mistakes, and even though the gentleman did eventually wish to marry me, I couldn't bring myself to do it."

"No?" He had never heard this part of the story. He set his things down and leaned forward.

"He'd proven himself to be a cad. Also, he was ill, and by then I had Jacob, my son, and the business to learn. I didn't want to nurse a man who'd treated me so poorly. I was also afraid he'd make me live in India with him." She shuddered.

"Very trying." *Hampshire or Lancashire*. At least his options were better than India. He appreciated her strength. Most women would have married the man regardless. Most families would have forced her to do so. Sir Bartley could have deleted the scandal from his family history but put his daughter and business first.

"Yes. So, I am a disgrace, a scandal, but an old one. Jacob is two and a half now. The last three years have gone by so quickly." She smiled suddenly. He saw dimples in her cheek for the first time. How had he missed those?

"Then you have little time for regrets."

Her cheeks twitched with an almost-smile. "It is good the time passes fast when one is an old maid."

His cock didn't see her as an old maid. "Twenty-four isn't old."

"Not to someone who is older," she teased.

He looked her over again. For the first time, he felt a friendship was brewing with a member of the Redcake family. He didn't really have friends. It had seemed like he did at school, but when he left, his circle moved on to university while he went to work. His friends rarely responded to his letters. He gave up on those chums who had been so important in boyhood and settled in here at Redcake's, where he was treated well but didn't fit in. Now, he'd have a few years isolated on a farm with no social equals, and then, all of a sudden, he'd be meant to take up the reins of an earldom, live in London, and fill his nursery with the children of some aristocratic bride. Someone who would look down on him, probably, for his lack of polish. Then he'd have to enter politics, manage everything. And he'd thought becoming manager of a tea shop was an impressive undertaking.

"Mr. Hales, you are clutching at your tie as if you're being strangled. Are you well?"

He blinked, releasing his hand from his throat. "I think I may have panicked."

"Why?" She tilted her head to one side.

"So much change." He tried to find some understanding in her gaze. "I am not prepared."

She took his hand again. *Matilda Redcake was a toucher.* "I'm sure you will be fine in time. The earl will guide you, as my father has guided me."

"He feels like an adversary."

She squeezed his fingers. "My father does to me as well at times, but I learn. It gets better. You are intelligent, Mr. Hales, and you look the part."

"I do?"

She considered him. "Yes. You have that tall, tailored, competent look about you, and a very charming smile. With the right clothes, you will make the debutantes swoon."

"I am going into exile to manage a family estate. Not wife hunting."

"Oh, you should wife hunt," she assured him. "Better to secure the family now."

"You think so?"

She blushed. "What else will you have to do with your time on a family estate except start a family?"

Her earthiness reminded him of Betsy, but she had a charm entirely her own. "That is what you recommend?" He took command of her hand, stroking her fingers. His senses were on full alert.

"I–I didn't mean—" she stammered. She sat back, but he didn't release her hand.

"You didn't mean to flirt with me?" He'd only just started to remember how.

"I don't know. I mean, I'm not moving to some rural estate to birth future earls. Even if I wanted to, I'm not a candidate for you. I'm tainted."

"At least you are honest. I like honest women. I don't meet enough of them. What is your agenda?"

She attempted to pull her hand away gently, but he held firm. "I just want to fix the flour. We need to go to Douglas Flour and talk to them."

He tugged at her hand. Her lips parted as she was forced to pull away or stand and move toward him. She chose to stand, to come closer. He pulled her down, feeling her breath on his hair as she tumbled into his lap. This woman didn't smell like a bakery but like industry. He smelled coal dust in her hair, ink on her fingers, paste and something like carrots on her coat.

Her scent comprised factories and trains and motherhood. But he smelled her, too, an earthy, passionate note underneath. She couldn't be a wife—at least not his wife—but he wanted her, and it had been so long since he'd wasted time wanting any woman when he couldn't afford a wife.

She smiled quickly, exposing those dimples again, then stilled. "Really, Mr. Hales." She leaned forward, biting her plump bottom lip.

"Really, Miss Redcake. Really, you are absolutely stunning." He traced one of her dimples with his finger, then angled his mouth toward hers.

She inhaled, met him lip to lip. Her warm breath hit him first, tea and frosting and spice. Softness pressed against him, sweet womanly lips. She didn't seem to know how to kiss, and he hardly remembered how, but it didn't seem to matter. She moaned softly and tucked her hands between them, pressing against his coat. Her mouth firmed against his and he licked her bottom lip, sucked it between his teeth, then released it so he could swirl his tongue into her mouth. She met him timidly, sweetly, gasping when he pulled back to take a quick breath before securing her cheeks with his fingers, ready to angle his mouth against hers again.

"Oh, no." She slipped away and pressed a trembling hand to her mouth. "This shouldn't have happened. I need to see to the flour."

"What? Why not?" His intellect had deserted him.

"I can't trust you. You're a rake." She stood in the small space between the chairs, her skirt askew.

"I'm not. I've just explained myself."

She was breathing hard, her color high. "You're a future earl. We can't do this. We need to go to the factory. We need to do our work."

"Your work," he said, feeling stupid and cranky. "My work is to run this tea shop, the bakery. You're my vendor."

She put her hands on her hips. Her hair had loosened from its tight hold. Feathery tendrils laced her temples and forehead. "I thought we were in this together."

A knock came on the door. Ewan stood as the door opened and pulled his coat down. Ralph Popham, the bakery manager, stood at the door.

"The telephone rang downstairs, Mr. Hales. You must not have heard the instrument up here. Gave me a turn. That apparatus never rings."

"What is it?"

"Message for Miss Redcake. She's to call her secretary at once.

Something important, but he wouldn't tell me what." His large eyes stared unblinkingly at Matilda.

She blushed and pushed back the hair on her forehead. When Ewan took a close look at her, he decided she appeared softer, more the young woman she was rather than the ageless businesswoman.

"Thank you, Mr. Popham. We will ring him directly."

He nodded and went out.

"I apologize. He should not have entered without knocking."

"It wasn't locked," she said in a tart tone. "Is there a mirror anywhere?"

"Not up here, no."

She sighed. "I had better call Greggory, then."

He directed her to the wall by his desk, where the telephone hung just within reach of his chair. She stood, her back turned, as she spoke to the operator. He sat in his chair, wishing he could pull her into his lap for a cuddle. A silly notion, but now that he'd had her on his knee, he knew she was slight yet rounded in all the right places. If his body were opened, he expected steam would rise from his veins.

He listened, watching a line of concern appear between her brows, when she was connected to Bristol.

"How long ago did they leave?" she asked. "It was such a lovely morning. I agree that three hours seems a very long time to be away. Has anyone gone to look for them?"

She listened some more. "They weren't at the park?"

He heard a catch in her voice as she asked who had combed the area. Soon, she wiped her eye, as if a tear had formed there, though he couldn't see for certain.

"I'll come right home," she said. "Surely there is some misunderstanding and he'll be found before I reach my house." She hung up and put her back to the wall, facing Ewan.

"Who is missing?"

"My son and his nanny. My housekeeper expected them back when it began to rain an hour ago, but no one can find them."

"Maybe they are having buns in a shop somewhere?"

She clasped her hands together. "She doesn't have any pocket money for him. He's too young. Besides, I don't like him to eat food from shops. Of all people, I know what terrible things can be found in shop food."

"Yes, I suppose you would."

Her hand shook when she lifted it to her hair.

"You look fine," he assured her.

"I feel terrible."

"You are a mother worrying about your child. I expect your nanny stopped to visit a friend or something. You may need to sack her, but I'm sure your son is fine. Jacob, right?"

"Yes. Jacob Michael Bliven."

"Is he as beautiful as his mother?" He'd spoken without thinking, but his words made her smile.

"He has dark hair like his father's, but a face very like my father's. I'm not sure what he will look like when he is older. My mother told me my father was a very handsome youth."

"You take after him. The hair, I mean."

"There are two distinct Redcake looks. The Redcake red hair, like Alys and me, and the cool blond Noble look from my mother. I'd have preferred the Noble looks."

"I don't prefer it," he said. "Blondes wash out. Your face has character."

She sighed. "I have an anxiety-ridden character, Mr. Hales. I am afraid I am going to have to abandon my responsibilities to the flour today. I will answer to my father for the increased expense of using Bristol Flour for now."

"He won't blame you. Jacob is his grandson."

She stepped away from the wall, stumbling on the rug. He stood up swiftly and caught her, not having realized the wall had been holding her up. She felt fragile in his arms, like the vitality had leeched out of her with the disturbing news.

"I'm going to see you home," he said.

"You can't possibly."

"Yes, I can. I'm in charge for now. Let me." He pushed her gently into the chair while he sent a messenger boy downstairs.

Popham returned, flustered.

"I apologize, Mr. Popham, but I'm going to go up to Bristol with Miss Redcake. I will return tonight, but you are in charge of the operation for the rest of the day."

"Yes, Mr. Hales. We'll do our best."

Ewan closed his eyes and recalled all the important details he could, relaying them to the senior manager, then found his coat and Matilda's.

Sooner than he had imagined, they were at Paddington station, ready to leave for Bristol. It would be a few hours before they reached Matilda's home. Surely the child would long since be home, had his tea, and been tucked into his nursery for the evening.

He attempted to distract Matilda during their long, rattling train ride. Wind and rain lashed their carriage, causing them to bump shoulders frequently. Ewan walked Matilda through the genealogy of his recovered family, told her about Norwich, shared highlights of his life so far. Throughout, she spoke little, her mouth pinched and tense. Innate politeness kept her responding to him, though, and he hoped he had entertained her as much as possible.

Good news was not forthcoming when they arrived. Their hansom cab pulled up in front of Matilda's palatial home, which was lit so brightly that it shone through the rain. The door was opened by a pale, drawn, and shaking housekeeper. A maid hovered in the hall, wringing her hands. Black-haired Greggory waited in the receiving room, along with a young male servant.

"Cook has hot broth ready, and rolls, Miss Redcake," the housekeeper said. "Will you eat?"

"I want my son," Matilda said very coldly. Her tone reminded him of the imperious one she'd used a few years ago, fresh from finishing school. But this time, Ewan knew her tone came from holding on to a ragged edge of control, rather than a sense of noblesse oblige.

"We all do, the poor blessed child. Where that Izabela could have got to I cannot imagine." The housekeeper rocked from side to side.

"That's wot comes of 'iring bloody foreigners," a maid muttered.

"Hush, Daisy," the housekeeper snapped. "Izabela may be a Pole, but her mother is a good woman."

"And her father was a thieving Gipsy," the maid muttered.

From the murderous look in Matilda's eye, one he remembered from working with Sir Bartley, Ewan was afraid the girl was about to be sacked. This was the wrong time for it. If Jacob was really gone, they needed people for the search. And they needed people to stay close, in case they somehow had something to do with the baby being missing.

He put his hand on her arm, hoping to calm her. "Can you send the maid to check Jacob's room, and Izabela's? Make sure nothing is missing?"

Matilda took a deep, shaky breath. "Excellent notion." She lifted her chin and gave the order. The girl picked up her skirts and ran down the hall toward the rear servant's stairs.

The housekeeper wrung her hands. "We've looked everywhere."

Greggory nodded. "I can start pulling men from the factories to search."

"We can't do that. We have to get the good cake order out." She sniffed. "I have to think like a woman of business, even when all I want to do is think like a mother."

"It might not help very much," Ewan said. "They don't know the child."

"Izabela is a most striking girl, too pretty to be a servant, really," the housekeeper said. "She won't hide easily."

Ewan winced as he realized the woman's thoughts had already gone to mischief. "Any followers?"

The housekeeper nodded. "A butcher. A rag merchant, but she wouldn't give him the time of day. One of her father's people, a horse dealer."

"Is she really half Gipsy?" Matilda asked.

The housekeeper nodded. "But the man died when she was about seven. Swept her poor mother off her feet, then was a terrible husband. A blessing he died."

"Do the Gipsies have anything to do with his family?" Ewan asked.

"I never saw them around the church, or on the little street of cottages where we lived when my husband was alive, God rest his soul."

"You were neighbors," Matilda recalled.

The housekeeper nodded. "Tera and her family lived next door to us."

"Would Izabela have taken Jacob there for some reason?" Ewan asked.

The housekeeper rubbed her eye. "They have been gone for six hours or more. How can there be any reason? It will be dark soon."

"If her mother took ill," Matilda suggested. "Send Dash with a note to Izabela's mother."

The housekeeper nodded. "Yes, Miss Redcake."

"We also need to check with the butcher, the rag merchant, and the horse dealer," Ewan said. "Can you give me their addresses, Mrs. . . . ?"

The housekeeper said, "Miller. Mrs. Miller. I know how to find the butcher and merchant, but you'll have to go fast before they close up shop. The horse dealer will be harder to find."

"Tell me what you know about them."

"The butcher is on Castle Street. The rag merchant is near the fish market. You'll have to ask Tera about the horse dealer."

"What should I do?" Matilda asked.

Ewan sensed she would start wringing her hands at any moment, too. "Go to the neighbors. Make sure they are on alert. Telephone your parents."

"I can do that," Greggory said. "And I'll alert the factory managers. We want a lot of eyes watching."

Ewan nodded. "I'll be on my way." He squeezed Matilda's arm. It felt like granite from the tense way she held it. To think, a few hours ago she'd been warm and pliable in his arms.

Chapter Five

Ewan spent hours visiting shops in Bristol. He had a photograph of Jacob that Matilda had given him, which he showed at every stop. The butcher and the rag merchant professed to know nothing. Neither had seen Izabela, and they both swore the nanny had rejected their suits. Did that mean she had become betrothed to the Gipsy horse dealer?

Ewan reached Tera's home hours after Dash, the boot boy, had been there. The woman, her head wrapped in a black kerchief, initially pretended not to speak English and acted quite shifty, but eventually Ewan persuaded her to speak with a combination of charm and threat. She hadn't seen Izabela since Sunday. She knew the horse dealer's name, Andrzej Majewski, and that he met buyers at the White Horse tavern, then took them to his camp outside of town. But she swore that her daughter had never been to the camp and probably did not know where it was. She also insisted Izabela was not engaged to Majewski.

"She's a good girl, works very hard," the woman said.

"What do you think happened to your daughter and Jacob Bliven?" Ewan asked.

The woman looked shifty again. "I have no idea. We must be patient, no?"

With that useless and dispiriting experience, Ewan returned to Matilda's home and sat in the drawing room until Greggory turned up with equally useless adventures to report. He took Ewan home to his father's house for the night. Not as fine as Matilda's home, which was set back from the street amid lush plantings, the junior branch of the Redcakes had a large ramshackle house on a busy square, packed to the roofline with various relatives and servants, as well as an assortment of mongrel dogs.

He didn't sleep well, with his dreams punctuated by images of Matilda's anxious face. It had not seemed wise to leave her alone, flagging visibly as the hours passed, but he could not sleep in her house without family present, and none of her family would arrive in Bristol until the noon hour.

Greggory and Ewan met over the breakfast table the next morning and ate quickly. Greggory had a list of the houses Matilda had visited last night near her home and checked them off, then handed Ewan an assignment of doors to knock on.

"When do you need to return to London?" Greggory asked.

Ewan shook his head. "Yesterday. Never. Lord Judah would stay in this situation."

"You had better write him." Greggory yawned. "I'll fetch a cab to our door. Come out as soon as you are done so we can get started."

Ewan spoke to an assortment of tenants in the houses, the voices slowing and slurring as he moved down the economic scale to the smaller properties. Some of them recognized his description of the Polish Gipsy nanny with her cherubic, brown-haired charge, but none had set an eye on them the day before.

"It was raining a bit yesterday like, just coming down like you see in the spring . . . well, I'm not likely to look out of doors on a day like that, still sort of had the lamps lit and the fire going, fair smoky really," reported one bored young mother.

That seemed to be the consensus. Too wet of a spring day to pay much mind. He suspected something foul had been afoot from the first. What had the nanny's scheme been? Surely Matilda wouldn't want her two-year-old son being taken to the park in the pouring rain?

Dripping wet and soaked to the skin, he trudged back to Matilda's house and was let inside. Droplets from his clothing puddled on the rug in the front hall as the housekeeper clucked at him and took his outerwear.

"I'll have Daisy fetch you a spot of tea," Mrs. Miller promised. "The family has gathered in the parlor."

"Who has arrived?"

"Miss Redcake's parents are here. Came up from Polegate. A long day for them."

"I'm sure they wouldn't want to be anywhere else under the circumstances."

When Ewan arrived in the drawing room, however, he wasn't so certain about that. Sir Bartley was in one of his red-faced moods, which could lead to an explosion of anger if it wasn't diffused.

"I have too many daughters," he roared. "Why can't any of you live quietly? Alys about to give Hatbrook an heir, Jacob missing, Rose plotting her wedding, and a less likely bride I've never seen."

"Surely likelier than me," Matilda shot back.

The lady of the house was chalky pale under her freckles, and dark half-moons had sprouted under her eyes. Her hair was pulled back so tightly that her skin looked drawn and stretched. Pale lips moved with minimum effort as she spoke as if she were too tired to bother.

Ewan, used to Sir Bartley's rants, interjected, "I've just come from knocking on doors, Miss Redcake. Were you aware that it rained heavily yesterday? No one was looking out of doors because of the rain. Did you like Jacob to go to the park in the rain?"

Matilda frowned. "No, of course not, but it wasn't raining when I left for London."

"You have to give clear instructions to your staff," Sir Bartley said.

Matilda blinked slowly as she turned back to him. "This situation has nothing to do with my instructions."

"First the problem with the cakes and now a problem with your son. You must hire more wisely, daughter."

"We don't know that Izabela is at fault," Matilda said.

"Hales reported that the mother is shifty. Like mother, like daughter, I say."

Ewan winced at Sir Bartley's palpable rudeness. His wife Ellen, Lady Redcake, put her hand on his arm.

"We have more to worry about than cake," she said. "Alys will have her baby this week. Rose's wedding is next week. And now poor little Jacob is missing."

"Someone has to worry about the cake," Sir Bartley snarled. Then he turned and saw Ewan. "Well, boy, what do you have to say for yourself?"

"We know where the bad flour came from but did not have the time to follow up. Meanwhile, Miss Redcake came up with a plan to ensure Redcake's has the cakes it needs and changed suppliers for now. She's doing everything she can, especially under the circumstances, sir."

Sir Bartley snorted. "I remember when it was me you toadied up to. Think Matilda's got the stuff to manage an enterprise of this size? I wonder."

Common wisdom had it that Matilda had done very well managing her father as well as the businesses. She had spent a great deal of time at Redcake Manor in Sussex at first, but it had paid off. Now, she stayed in Bristol, managing on her own, while Sir Bartley focused on his estate and the life of a country gentleman. He'd even taken up hunting and whist, according to Lady Hatbrook, who watched her father's transformation with bemusement. It did not seem that he'd ever lose the bluff manner of a manufacturer, though. Not for him a dose of Town polish.

Ewan hoped that Matilda didn't lose her position with her family over the cake mess, even though at this very moment, it might be a blessing due to Jacob. How could she concentrate with pressure from her father to do her job? She looked as though she hadn't slept a wink the night before.

"Is it going to cost more?" Sir Bartley barked.

"Yes, sir, but we will still make a small profit, even so," Matilda said.

His red-circled eyes narrowed. "How small?"

"I need more instructions," Ewan interjected. "Please, Sir Bartley, we need to focus on the missing child. I need to learn where the White Horse tavern is, and the Gipsy encampment outside town. The nanny might have taken Jacob there."

Lady Redcake put the back of her hand to her forehead. "He's been kidnapped by Gipsies?"

"Izabela came highly recommended by Mrs. Miller," Matilda said. "I don't think that is likely. She's only half Gipsy."

"Her follower is a Gipsy horse dealer," Ewan said.

Matilda swallowed hard, looking like she might be ill. Ewan wondered if she'd eaten today, as she grasped the back of a chair and used it to support herself. "I didn't know she had a follower until this happened."

"She had three," Ewan said. "But as best I can tell, the first two can be ruled out for now."

Sir Bartley swore. "He's a pretty child. They'll sell him!"

Matilda wrapped her free arm around her stomach. "There's Theodore Bliven. Could he have hatched a plot to kidnap his son because I refused to marry him?"

"We'll need to consult with Gawain," Sir Bartley said, startled into paying attention to the primary crisis. "He'd know best if the man needed money."

"Or he might simply want to raise Jacob as his own. He's never even seen his son," Matilda said.

"A man like him," Lady Redcake said faintly. "Who behaves as he has. I cannot imagine."

"Mother, we must consider the possibilities. And frankly, thinking Mr. Bliven has him is more soothing to me than the idea that the Gipsies have taken him. He might have hired someone." Her gaze swept the room and met Ewan's.

He nodded. "Is Sir Gawain coming here?"

"He's on his way," Sir Bartley said. "He'll help me sort out the business while Matilda focuses on motherly matters. Hales, you need to return to London and Redcake's. You are supposed to be the man on the spot."

"Recall Lord Judah," Ewan said. "If you have the right, given that Lady Hatbrook owns the tea shop. I cannot in good conscience leave Miss Redcake under these circumstances."

Matilda and her parents stared at him. While the silence ensued, Mrs. Miller and Greggory walked into the room. When Ewan met his eyes, the young man shook his head regretfully.

"That's it, then; we've done all the neighbors and every house on the way to the park," Ewan said. "It's time to concentrate on finding Majewski."

"Should we call in the police?" Greggory asked.

"No," Matilda said firmly. "I'm sure Mr. Bliven has him, and we don't want gossip reaching the papers. He seemed unbalanced when we saw him last. It has been over a year, so he must have returned from his most recent trip to India."

"And the Gipsies?" Ewan asked.

"Mr. Bliven may not be alive," Lady Redcake said. Her expression turned anxious. "Darling, if he was on his deathbed, you could marry him without any risk."

Matilda visibly gathered herself, but her expression was still pinched. "Mother!"

"He might have taken Jacob to get your attention one last time," Lady Redcake said, her hands fluttering.

"Good heavens, Mother, you say that like it's romantic. Jacob is two years old and he's just spent a night away from home, in who knows what conditions. He might not even be—"

Alive. Ewan finished the thought Matilda couldn't. He wished he could take the exhausted beauty in his arms, but he could not comfort her in front of her family, even if she'd allow it at all under such fraught circumstances. All he could do for her was take action.

"He's fine," Sir Bartley said. "They'll want a ransom, whoever took him. Mark my words, it's a money matter, whether it's Bliven or the Gipsies. Let us keep the police out of it lest we panic the criminals."

"Or worse," Greggory said.

Ewan put his hand on the other man's shoulder. "Why don't you and I find this White Horse tavern," he suggested.

Outside the parlor door, voices rose, and the stomping of boots could be heard in the corridor. The door was flung open and Ewan recognized Sir Gawain Redcake, trailed by his exotically beautiful wife, Ann, who was half-Indian royalty. Ewan noticed cynically that the pair had not brought their son, Noel, who was about a year younger than the missing Jacob.

"Came up from Battersea in my horseless carriage," Gawain said to his father. "Made good time."

Ann gave Matilda a hug, but she scarcely bent her elbows to return the gesture. Ewan couldn't tell if she disliked her sister-in-law or was too emotionally exhausted to care.

"I can hunt down the tavern," Greggory said in Ewan's ear. "I would suggest you follow up on this Bliven situation. Plus, Uncle Bartley will not be satisfied until you return to Redcake's and he knows someone is in charge there because neither Alys nor Lord Judah can be present."

"I don't care about your uncle; I care about Miss Redcake," he said.

"Either way, it makes sense that Bliven would be behind this," Greggory said.

Ewan nodded. "Sir Gawain, might I have a word?"

Matilda's brother, a tall former soldier with the scars and slight limp to show for his adventures on the north-west frontier of India, pointed to the door. Ewan followed him out into the corridor.

"I remember the gossip," Ewan said. "I heard more than a few of Sir Bartley's rants at the time. You knew Bliven best, correct?"

Gawain rubbed his chin. He had circles around his eyes from the goggles he'd worn on the drive to Bristol. "No, he was a school friend of Alys's husband. I have only worked with him on a professional level."

"Is he in England?"

Gawain nodded. "He's been back about a month. In London, but I can't imagine he's behind this." He grimaced. "I have my reasons for thinking that, but he did me a good turn, and he's been a useful business associate, so I tend to be more forgiving than the rest of my family."

Ewan's eyebrows rose. "He seduced your sister, got her with child."

"Matilda thought she could persuade Bliven to marry her if she trysted with him. She believed that was how our sister won her marquess. It's an old story. Matilda has always been utterly headstrong and she paid the price."

"So he was sinned against," Ewan said.

"He should have married her when she turned up pregnant, but he refused, claiming another woman had a previous claim on him. But that marriage didn't materialize, and he lost his spot in the succession to an earldom when a cousin had offspring. He then showed up in England again, offering to marry her."

Ewan realized he had never heard the entire story. Matilda was as headstrong as Betsy Popham. "No one could persuade Matilda to do so?"

"Bliven was not much of a marital catch by then," Gawain said.

Ewan frowned. "Surely anyone would be better than no one, under the circumstances. Your sister must have loved him once."

"Headstrong," Gawain repeated. "Always does what she wants, which isn't always what she ought."

Ewan remembered their kiss and suspected Gawain was correct in his analysis. "Then that leads me to another question. Could there be another lover?"

"Of this Gipsy girl?" Gawain asked.

"No, of your sister. If she's as headstrong as you say, could there be some secret lover who might have taken the child, perhaps to persuade Matilda to marry him, or just to extort funds? No one intimate to her could fail to see she's wealthy."

"I don't know of any lover, but I don't live in Bristol any longer. I think she's too busy."

Ewan lifted an eyebrow. "We're both men of the world. Everyone has time for that kind of thing, if they really want it."

The parlor door opened. Ewan had his back to it.

Gawain grinned. "You're right. Maybe she has a dozen lovers. Maybe there is a brothel catering to women. I don't know."

"What on earth?"

Ewan turned to see Matilda, her freckles stark on a paper-white face, her hands on her hips.

Gawain lifted his hands. "Look, Matilda, cards on the table. Is there anyone else you've let get as close to you as Bliven did?"

"How dare you!" she shrieked, lifting her arms as if to strike.

Ewan went to her and took her hands. They were icy cold.

"We have to know," Gawain said, sounding irritatingly reasonable even to Ewan's ears. "It's a fair question, and Jacob's well-being has to come before your privacy, repugnant as that is."

"There is no one," she hissed, not looking at Ewan, even though he still held her hands. "How could you think that?"

Gawain shook his head. Matilda turned blazing eyes on Ewan. "You?"

Ewan pressed his lips together. "I am just trying to be thorough."

"Leave," she said. "Go back to London, deal with the flour. You're the best person for it anyway because that factory will be yours someday." She wrenched her hands away from his and flew back through the door.

"What?" Gawain said, his tone flat.

"I've discovered I'm the new heir to the Earl of Fitzwalter," Ewan said.

Gawain put his hands on his hips. "Are you Lord Ritten's son?"

"No, I'm the son of another, younger son. Both of my parents have been dead for years."

"How unusual," Gawain said. "She's right, you know. This is a family matter and you aren't family. Go keep Alys's business from falling apart."

Ewan swallowed hard against the lump in his throat. He was never anyone's family, not really. Anger filled him when he remembered his high birth and prospects compared to Gawain's factory worker past, his army days. He shouldn't let Gawain talk to him like this, treat him like this. Yet this was a terrible time for them, and he'd soon be free of the Redcakes forever. "Very well, if you think it is more important than having another pair of eyes searching for your nephew."

Gawain huffed out a breath, clearly offended. "You've upset her. What do you want me to do?"

Ewan pushed his fingers through his hair. "I suppose there is no one I need take my leave of."

Gawain shook his hand, then went back into the parlor, leaving Ewan alone in the hall. He couldn't decide if the Redcakes were a cold lot or simply distracted. A man in his position had never been close enough to find out. His conversation and kiss with Matilda Redcake had been the first time he'd felt like any Redcake's equal. The thought of her in distress had shocked him like a physical pain. He'd wanted to help find the child, not deal with business back in London. But he wasn't a friend of the family, merely an employee, so he might as well leave now.

Ewan went to Redcake's two hours earlier than usual the next day. He straightened his desk and packed away the few personal items that had accumulated over the years. Ewan wondered when he'd be able to leave his position. He had too much pride to simply walk out and never return, and he didn't want to anger the Marquess of Hatbrook and his family.

When he deemed the solicitor's office to be open for business, he abandoned his box of possessions and walked to Chancery Lane, his brain churning with thoughts of the abduction rather than the flour issue. Could it be that the horse dealer had intended to kidnap Izabela the nanny to be his bride, and Jacob had merely been in the way? It didn't matter what he thought because no one cared about his opinion. He hoped Greggory had found the tavern the night before and someone had told him where the Gipsy camp lay.

At Norwich's office, he found the man staring dolefully into his teacup, the brown bottle back at the edge of his desk. "Come in," he said as Ewan rapped on his door.

"Hullo, Norwich."

"Have you given notice? Decided on Lancashire or Hampshire?"

"You sound raspy this morning. I thought you were going to try to keep me here."

"I am always miserable in the spring. The earl said no to London." The man blew his nose in an already stained handkerchief.

"You aren't as miserable as the Redcake family." *Or me.*

"Do I care?"

"It's good gossip, what with a son of the family being kidnapped shortly after someone sold us—I mean, Redcake's— adulterated flour."

Norwich raised a fluffy eyebrow. "Redcake's prides itself on selling the best. It's the one emporium where it's said even a newborn would be safe eating its goods."

"Exactly. And guess who sold Redcake's the adulterated flour?"

"Who?"

Ewan made a fist and pounded it once on the solicitor's desk. "Douglas Flour."

The man's half-mast eyes widened. "How dreadful. I hadn't realized Douglas Flour was known to be the best flour purveyor, but it is one of those smooth-running businesses. Steady profit. No involvement on my part."

"I'd suggest you send me there, rather than to Lancashire or Hampshire. It must be worth a great deal of money, the prestige of supplying Redcake's. With the family distracted by the kidnapping, I might be able to turn things around before Douglas Flour loses its best customer."

Norwich abraded his nostrils with the handkerchief again. "Yes, yes. I see your point."

"How do we make it happen?"

"The earl left for his country seat last night, so he put me in charge. I think under the circumstances, temporarily at least, you make a fine point."

Ewan sat still. A position in London, or at least nearby in Southwark? He could not have done better for himself under the circumstances.

Norwich straightened in his chair. "I will write a letter to Corwin Vare, the present manager of Douglas Flour. He will report to you now."

"I'll need to draw a salary," Ewan said. "I don't have funds of my own."

Norwich turned away and opened a file cabinet with a key on his watch chain, then paged through some files. "We pay Vare three hundred a year. I'll give you four."

Ewan blinked. He wouldn't live like a lord on it, but at least he could live like a factory manager. "Very well. I should take on authority for all the associated businesses as well. Can you draw up a list and notify me, and them, of the details?"

"Of course. I'll have it to you next week." Norwich called to the outer office for a secretary and, when the man came in, dictated a letter to Corwin Vare with all the details.

Ewan was gratified to hear himself called regional director of Douglas Industries. He had come up in the world.

When the secretary was gone, Norwich poured a dram of the brown bottle's contents into his teacup and leaned back. "There, you've got what you wanted, at least until Fitzwalter returns. Now, tell me about this kidnapping."

Matilda paced her breakfast room floor, alone for a moment, too exhausted and nervy to eat any of the contents of the covered dishes her servants had put out. Everyone she'd seen so far that day had red-rimmed eyes and the air of a sleepwalker.

Her mother, who heretofore had been more focused on Rose's wedding than her grandson's disappearance, came into the room and immediately opened her arms to offer a hug. Matilda accepted the embrace but pulled back when tears welled in her eyes.

"I need to go upstairs," she said. She shook her head firmly and turned to flee the room, almost colliding with her father as he entered.

"Kippers?" he asked.

"Yes." The mere scent of them would turn her stomach when he lifted the dish cover, so she trotted out before he reached the sideboard.

She climbed the stairs, blinded by tears, until she found herself in the nursery. Tucked under the eaves, it wasn't the most cheerful of rooms in its natural state. It had a sensible cork linoleum floor and plain, hygienic white walls. The furniture had been old when Matilda was a baby, though she had a new modern chair for Jacob and the latest perambulator.

Where had that gone? It hadn't turned up in the park or on the street anywhere. If Izabela had abandoned it, the expensive, useful item had probably been stolen before any of the family searchers saw it. She wished she could believe the nanny was a victim, too, that she was cuddling Jacob, that Izabela and her son were in this together, that she was protecting the child. But it made no sense that some stranger would kidnap Jacob from a private park, that he would even know to do so without the nanny's help.

She picked up the stuffed bear Gawain had given Jacob for Christmas. It had been taller than her son at the time, but now they were equal in height. She hugged it against her chest, pretending it was her little boy. Would she ever see him again in this life? She pressed her cheek against the bear's head. It smelled like hair and stuffing, but it also smelled like spoiled milk and powder.

She took the bear to Jacob's rocking horse, which had been Gawain's during his boyhood, and bounced the bear on the horse's saddle. She still loved to rock Jacob in the chair by the fireplace, the same chair where she'd been rocked to sleep, but her little boy loved the rocking horse best. Sometimes she was afraid he would break the springs, but they were free of rust and had held heavier children than he presently was. For a moment she stood there, allowing herself to pretend he was bouncing away on the horse, the springs squeaking in a headache-inducing ruckus, in counterpoint to the childish laughter that was an unending source of delight.

He'd shriek, "More, Mummy, more!" when Izabela went to remove him so he could eat his bread and milk. Sometimes she would send the nanny off to her mending and sit on the chair next to the horse while he played. But she hadn't done that nearly enough.

And she had trusted the wrong person. She went to the wall and stared at the family portraits there. Her other lost boy, her brother Arthur, had died from a lung complaint at twenty.

He'd be thirty or even thirty-one now. Funny; she couldn't remember his birthday. She'd been working so hard this past year, and sleeping so little as a result, that certain details of her childhood had slipped from her memory. Why hadn't she named Jacob for Arthur?

His second name was Michael, named for Alys's husband, who had allowed her to hide away at his farm while she waited for the shameful birth. Jacob Noble was her uncle, her mother's brother, who had done precisely nothing for her then. She must have had hopes at the time that her mother's Noble kin would be of use to her, more so than a dead brother. So practical after being so foolish.

"Watch over him, Arthur," she whispered, staring at the picture of the solemn and much too thin youth staring so seriously out from his portrait. His hands were too large for his arms, and his coat in the photograph was slightly too short in the sleeves. Gawky and not full grown.

The thought that some other Redcake, a decade or two in the future, might look at the studio portrait of her own darling boy in the nursery on a day like this, and not know who he was or what he'd meant to her, made her head swim. The room spun around her. She sank to her knees in front of the trivet where Izabela had heated Jacob's milk.

Someone had pulled the fender away from the fire. It was meant to protect Jacob from the flames. Had someone been hoping he would injure himself, or had a cleaning project been interrupted?

She put her hands to her head and let it sink to the floor. The cool linoleum felt good against her cheek. She closed her eyes, but the darkness behind her eyelids swirled with dizzying colored shapes. Not sleeping last night would cost her.

Time passed in a dull haze. She could hear the telephone ringing floors below, and wondered how the sound could carry, but couldn't rouse herself enough to wonder if it was news about Jacob. It was likely to be Redcake's business.

A couple of minutes later she heard footsteps on the stair. Mrs. Miller appeared in the open doorway. Matilda tilted her head slightly to see her housekeeper's red face. Her chest heaved with the effort of hauling her bulk up all those stairs.

"Jacob?" she asked. Her voice sounded rough to her ears.

"Family news," Mrs. Miller said. "I'm sorry, lamb." She put her hand to her mouth.

Matilda pushed herself into a sitting position. "It's quite all right, Mrs. Miller. I don't mind you calling me 'lamb,' not today."

"Such a special boy," Mrs. Miller whispered. "And you all alone up here. You should allow your family to comfort you, but"—her gaze swept the room—"I understand why you would be happiest here. When my little Victoria died, I slept in the nursery for months, just to feel I was closer to her."

Matilda knew Mrs. Miller had lost her entire family a decade before to tainted meat.

"I don't want my family," Matilda said. She knew she sounded petulant, but the only person who had comforted her at all was Ewan Hales, and he'd turned out to have feet of clay. How could he have gone from that demonstration of quiet competence and help in London—not to mention his show of attraction to her—to accusing her, behind her back no less, and to her own brother, of having a lover who had absconded with Jacob?

Chapter Six

Matilda never wanted to see Ewan again. He'd been more practical than she could tolerate in his inquiries, his a mind with no hint of feminine sensitivity. She might have appreciated that under ordinary circumstances, but not when she was frantic with grief.

She held out her hand so that Mrs. Miller could help her up. "Do you know what happened to the fender?"

Mrs. Miller clucked when she saw the fire was open to the room. "That Daisy. She's a bit overwhelmed. I'll find it and have it returned to its proper position," she promised.

Matilda nodded. "Have we heard anything from Greggory about the White Horse tavern?"

"No word yet, but news came from Sussex. The family is in the parlor waiting for you."

Alys. She'd probably had the baby, been delivered of the Marquess of Hatbrook's perfect male heir, while her sister was prostrate with grief and loss. Just how their lives had turned out.

She swallowed hard, refusing to give in to self-pity. She patted her housekeeper on her sleeve. "I'm sorry you lost your daughter."

"It was a long time ago," the housekeeper said absently, straightening a table covered with pencils and paper. "None of my children lived."

"I'm sorry," Matilda repeated, then went downstairs, holding tightly to the railing. She was still dizzy and didn't trust herself. How she hoped she wouldn't soon have something so tragic in common with her housekeeper. The thought of having a child no longer living was beyond her capacity to understand, now that she was a mother herself. Yes, children died, but not *her* child.

Arthur had died, but at twenty. He'd had a life, even though it had been a short one. Gawain had nearly died, but he'd lived, was married with a child of his own now. His wife, Ann, had lost her first child, a stillbirth just after her first husband had died. But her mother and Ann never spoke of their lost ones. Perhaps the sadness was too much to share.

If she lost Jacob, though, how could she never speak of him again? But she'd have nothing to share: no new tales of achievements or funny little stories. Every memory would be encased in amber, a complete story with a beginning, middle, and end. Soon all her stories would be told and no one but her would care to hear them again.

She had to write it all down. Swaying on the steps, she grabbed for the railing again and slid down along the wall, digging into her pocket for a pencil. That first time Jacob had felt sand against his bare toes last summer. The first Christmas present he'd opened last year, just old enough to understand it was a secret only to be opened by him. The way he chortled when he chased his puppy, Sir Barks, who he had named himself.

Where was Sir Barks? Matilda blinked. She hadn't remembered the puppy. Too much else going on with kisses and disappearances and upset servants and family bounding around the place. And the bloody flour issue.

Gawain appeared on the stairs, quite from nowhere. "What are you doing? You need to come."

"I don't. It's just about Alys's baby."

"It's a boy. He's a courtesy earl. Not sure of what. I had no idea Hatbrook had multiple titles. I should have thought of that."

"I expected he'd be a viscount if he was a boy." How jealous Theodore Bliven would be. Back when they were courting, he'd told her he'd be an earl by fifty, when the old unmarried men ahead of him were dead. But then one had married a twenty-year-old girl, and she'd produced an heir within a year.

"Yes, well . . . look, Matilda, you need to pull yourself together." He squinted, which made the scars under his bad eye more pronounced. "There's a note just come for you."

"Where is Sir Barks?" Matilda asked, not really hearing Gawain's words.

"Who?"

"Jacob's puppy."

"He's downstairs," Gawain said, rubbing at the scar under his eye.

He still had headaches sometimes, though he'd regained enough vision to stop wearing his old pirate patch.

"The puppy?"

"Yes. A boy brought it. He had a note tucked into his collar."

She shifted, pressing her back to the wall. "Where did the boy find him?"

"Running around the park where Izabela was meant to take Jacob."

"It's been two days." She rubbed her forehead, willing her brain to function.

"Yes. They must have taken the dog with them."

"In the rain?" *No.* That wasn't right.

"It was deliberate, Matilda, obviously. Izabela took Jacob and the dog out on a rainy day quite deliberately. No one was watching out their windows for kidnappers."

"How is it Friday already? How is it that I have a kidnapped son?" She reached out, grabbed Gawain's sleeve. "He's dead, isn't he?"

Gawain shook his head and plucked her hand from his sleeve, then held it between his large hands. "You're too cold, Matilda; you need a good cup of tea."

"You would say that, being a tea merchant." She vaguely noticed his smile, though she hadn't meant to be funny. She didn't mean much of anything. Jacob had been kidnapped.

Someone spoke down below. She didn't really hear the words, but Gawain yelled down, "Order a tea tray, would you, Mother? I'm bringing her down."

Gawain reached underneath her. Matilda thought she shrieked at the unexpected arms under her knees, around her back, but he hefted her without so much as a creaky joint and slowly walked downstairs, steady despite his damaged hip.

She didn't demur. What was the point? In a few minutes, Gawain had her deposited on the sofa in the parlor. Her father silently wrapped a plaid blanket around her.

"This room is for guests," Matilda said. "I don't spend time in here. Where did this old raggedy blanket come from?"

"It was in a chest in the room we are staying in," her mother said. "I remember it."

"Alys used to use it as a picnic blanket. She'd read under that apple tree in the garden on Sundays," Gawain said. "I remember because Arthur hit her in the face with a ball once when we were play-ing catch around her. She screamed like a banshee."

"Arthur," Matilda said. "Mother, you never speak about him. Why not?"

Her mother stared at her blankly. "I suppose there is so much else to speak about when we see you, dear. It is not like I see any of you often, except Rose, and she is about to move to Liverpool."

"Alys isn't so far away. You aren't abandoned," Matilda said.

"No, dear, of course not." Ellen's arms crossed her body and her hands clutched at her flowing sleeves. "But, dear, Arthur has been gone over a decade now. I do think of him every day, of course, when I say my prayers."

"Do you pray to him, or about him?"

"Matilda." Her father spoke sharply, as if she'd blasphemed, but her mother smiled.

"A little of both," her mother said with a soft smile.

Her father frowned.

Gawain had left the room. Now he came back just behind Daisy, who carried a silver tea service on a large tray. He held the brown-and-white–spotted puppy, distinguishable instantly from any other by the octagonal white patch around his left eye. Matilda wasn't sure quite what breed he was, given that his sire was unknown, but she would always recognize him.

Gawain dumped the puppy onto Matilda's blanketed lap and then held out a scrunched, rolled-up piece of cheap paper. "It was in his collar."

Matilda ran her hand along the puppy's back. "He's damp."

"Raining again," Daisy said. "Shall I pour, Miss Redcake?"

"I'll do it," Ellen said. "Go about your business, Daisy."

The maid curtseyed and trotted out of the room.

"Read the note," Gawain said.

Matilda unrolled the paper, her hands seeming to work separately from the rest of her body. She couldn't make the words resolve at first. There was only a vague impression of thick black marks against the white.

"Focus," Gawain ordered.

She blinked three times, then, slowly, the marks began to form words. "i am rite you want yer baby. You goin to pay for the littl one. 5000 pounds."

The writing was all but illiterate, the spelling horrendous. The money demand offensive.

"There's no proof of anything," her father said.

"They had the dog," Gawain pointed out. "Though I admit a lad finding him in the park, rather than the kidnappers sending him to the door, is a bit odd."

"Could be an opportunist," her father suggested.

"They don't even say where to take the money, or when," her mother said, pouring tea. She sighed as she added milk and sugar, then held the cup and saucer out to Matilda. "It's cool enough. Drink it right away."

"I don't think I can," Matilda said, squeezing her eyes shut. She hugged the puppy tightly, until it beat its tail against her arm and she had to soften her grip. He might have been the last creature Jacob hugged.

"You need to keep your strength up," Gawain said. "And warm yourself." He took the cup and saucer in one hand, reached under the puppy with his other, and traded the damp animal for the warm cup.

Her hand shook as she lifted it to her lips, but she managed to swallow the first sip of the sugary fluid. In all these years her mother had yet to doctor a cup of tea to her satisfaction. When she was younger, Mother never added sugar to a girl's tea because she needed to protect her figure. Now, it seemed Mother had given up on her ever finding a husband. And no surprise.

Her father glanced at his pocket watch. "I can get you the money by Monday afternoon. I'll go down to London to my bank, then bring it back. If we've heard something more by then we'll be ready."

"I think I should storm the Gipsy camp," Gawain said. "That rabble is not likely to give an ex-soldier a fight."

Tea slopped as Matilda forgot her cup. "Don't you dare, Gawain. Jacob could be killed!"

Gawain's gaze turned on her with no hint of sympathy. She knew he must think Jacob already dead. Her stomach lurched at the thought, but no, she mustn't think such things about her child, her baby. Gawain wouldn't think them about his own son if the situation were reversed. He wouldn't admit the truth until he held Noel's tiny body in his own arms. And she wouldn't either.

"It doesn't matter for now, until we find out where it is."

"You will not go near that camp," Matilda told him, using her most emphatic voice. She didn't use it often because she mostly employed Greggory to give orders, knowing the men in her employ would take direction better from him directly. So often the men she met with refused to even look her in the eye, their gazes hovering somewhere around her bosom.

Gawain shrugged. "We'll do what makes sense at the time."

"We don't even know the Gipsies have Jacob, not yet," her father said.

"Or why," her mother chimed in. "That Izabela may be as much a victim as our boy."

"I still think Mr. Bliven is behind this," Matilda mused. Could he have charmed Izabela into helping him? She stared into her murky tea. She wondered what her fortune would reveal if she took her teacup into the Gipsy camp and asked one of the women to read it. Doom, perhaps?

But it was an idea. A woman, a tourist really, could probably enter a camp, claiming to look for a fortune-teller. She'd have to be accompanied. Mrs. Miller might go.

"I assure you, he is not," Gawain said.

"How do you know that?"

"Let's go to London tomorrow," he suggested. "I know where he is. You can talk to him."

"He wanted his son quite desperately, once."

"I know," Gawain growled.

"He sent Jacob a wooden train for his birthday and a matching boat for Christmas. He hasn't forgotten his son."

"Did you give them to him?" her mother asked.

Matilda nodded. "As long as he isn't present in our lives, I don't mind Jacob receiving the gifts. I'll have to explain the situation someday. I hope by then I can explain it."

"I agree that he might be involved," her father said. "His behavior was not that of a sane man in the past."

"Yet you wanted me to marry him."

Her father frowned. "You can understand why, Matilda. Jacob's prospects would be much improved. But I wouldn't want my daughter tied to such a man."

"I can't leave Bristol right now. If—I mean *when*—Jacob is found, he needs his mother." As if the thought gave her strength, she took a sip of the tea.

"I think it is important that you see Theo as soon as possible," Gawain said.

"Can you bring him here?" She drank again.

"No, I cannot," he said in a monotone.

Matilda stared at her brother as she considered.

"I think we should bring in the police," her mother said. "Now that money is involved."

"No," Matilda said. "They might react as Gawain has, and want to storm the Gipsy camp. I can think of no way better to lose Jacob forever." As she said it, she knew she had decided. "Will you stay here while Gawain and I take the train to London to see Mr. Bliven? Then, when we return, you can obtain the money from your bankers, just in case."

"We need more people looking," her father said. "Clearly these Gipsies are elusive, if Greggory cannot find the tavern."

"What about Lady Elizabeth's husband, the one who is the private inquiry agent?" her mother asked. "He might be able to help."

Lady Elizabeth was Lord Judah's sister. But she and her husband lived in Edinburgh. He wouldn't have any local contacts, though he did have strong opinions about kidnappers. "He might help," Matilda conceded.

"I'll contact him," Gawain said.

"I want to search the park," Matilda said. "Has anyone done that since Sir Barks was found?"

"You haven't the strength," Gawain said. "I'll do it."

"I'll pack a few things and check the railway timetable," Matilda said. Resolutely, she drank down her tea, every sugary drop, then popped a biscuit into her mouth. "There, I'm restored."

Her defiant glance fooled no one, but it was the best she could manage. She did feel steadier as she went up the stairs to her bedroom, however.

The next day, Matilda and Gawain, in the Redcakes' best carriage, pulled up in front of a row house near Grosvenor Square. She had dressed in a black coat, feeling already in mourning. If she could make Mr. Bliven understand her pain, surely he would tell her where he was keeping Jacob. She didn't discount the idea that her baby was being kept in a Gipsy camp, just thought that Mr. Bliven was behind it. With his dark eyes and mahogany curls, who was to say he hadn't been hiding some Gipsy blood himself, despite his ties to an earldom?

Sleep had been hard to come by the night before. She kept wishing—imploring God, really—that Jacob would be in his bed by morning and this nightmare would all be over.

When Greggory had returned from another useless day of searching for the White Horse tavern, she'd sent Mrs. Miller to visit with Izabela's mother again, but she hadn't seen the girl. Mrs. Miller reported that the woman had seemed very frightened and properly concerned for her daughter's well-being.

Truthfully, though, Matilda wondered about the character of a girl who had attracted three followers despite spending most of her time indoors, tending to a young child. It seemed absurd to be able to manage to attract three men with so little effort.

As Gawain helped her down the step, she wondered if it was only petty jealousy due to her having no suitors to Izabela's three. No one had shown any proper interest in her . . . well, ever, really. She imagined a tall man next to her in this time of trial, someone like Ewan, her head leaning gratefully on his shoulder. It sounded lovely to have support like that, yet it wouldn't make the situation any better, not really. Not when Jacob was missing.

She pressed her glove to her mouth, stifling a moan as they went to the door of the house. Gawain checked her face, his expression passive.

"Hold it together, Matilda. It's going to get worse before it gets better."

She glanced away, not wanting to ask what he'd meant. After this, he'd probably go home to Battersea and kiss little Noel and be so very grateful he wasn't her. Her bitter thoughts carried her past the parlor maid who opened the door and allowed them into a waiting room, then a male servant who took them up two flights of stairs, past the public rooms and into a private section of the house. She didn't listen to anything Gawain said, but as they went down the hall, she smelled strange animal odors that had no place in a properly run house. Blood and waste and old food.

Gawain stopped in front of the open door instead of following the servant in. He wrapped his hand around Matilda's upper arm. "Buck up, old girl. He isn't what you remember."

She frowned at him and wrenched her arm away. Didn't he realize that the worst thing had already happened to her? She was wrapped in the cotton wool of horror already.

Ignoring his presence in the doorway, she stepped around him and slid into the room. The stench of the sickroom hit hard. Not just the animal smells but camphor and lavender and laudanum. Coal and smoke, too, which seemed to hover under the ceiling thanks to an un-opened window and insufficient flue.

She approached the bed, ignoring all of this. The figure under a white sheet and multiple wool blankets was unrecognizable. Patches of scalp showed under graying, curly hair. Cheekbones and the over-all shape of the skull were visible. The mouth was the dried rictus of a mummy. But the papery eyelids fluttered open and she recognized those eyes. *Theodore Bliven.*

Oh, God. She put her hand to her mouth. This man was far too ill to scheme. To think, he'd wanted to marry her and manage the Red-cake's factories when this was his fate. He'd already been ill then, but nothing like this.

"Can you speak?" she whispered.

His corpse's head moved restlessly on his pillow. She noted the in-congruously cheerful yellow daisies embroidered along the open edge of the pillowcase. "Ears buzzing."

She raised her voice. "Mr. Bliven, it is Matilda Redcake."

His eyelids fluttered. He still had thick eyelashes, though his eye-brows were wispy, threaded with gray. "Matilda?"

"Yes. I came to see you about Jacob."

His arms were bent, his fingers placed along the top of the sheet, which was folded over the blankets. They fluttered. "My son."

"Yes."

"How old?"

"Two and a half."

"It's been more than three years since you loved me." His lips curved upward, and she was afraid they would crack open. "Why visit me now when . . ."

She wondered what he meant to say, but it seemed he had fallen asleep.

Behind her, Gawain exhaled and put his hand on her shoulder. They had become close in a way they never had been since he had helped teach her the business. Over time, she knew her older brother had learned to respect her. His irritation and disgust had turned to a grudging admiration and friendship. She welcomed the comfort he offered, now that she realized the gravity of her situation.

"I'll marry him now," she said, remembering what her mother had said. "Take responsibility for burying him."

"He won't last long enough for that. Malaria, you know."

"We can afford the special license," Matilda said. "Would it give him comfort?"

Bliven's eyes opened a fraction of an inch. "Want to see Jacob."

"He's gone," Matilda said, her voice catching. She could say no more.

"Not dead," Bliven whispered, his dry gray tongue touching the center of his lip as if to try to moisten it.

The servant leaned over the edge of the bed and attempted to spoon water into Bliven's mouth. Most of it went down the side of his lips onto the pillow, but it seemed to restore the dying man.

"Not dead," Gawain rasped. "Missing. Kidnapped."

"Who?" Bliven's eyelids fluttered.

"We don't know. The nanny disappeared, too. We've had a ransom note but no real details yet."

"Not me," Bliven said in a faint whisper. "I don't need money. I have plenty."

"I know," Gawain said. "That was a good shipment you brought me."

"And my corpse, ready for burial," Bliven said, a hint of his old humor showing.

"Do you want a wife?" Gawain asked. "Matilda will marry you now."

"Very kind of you," Bliven murmured, "but find Jacob. That's important. I left money." He frowned.

Matilda glanced at Gawain. He shrugged.

"My will," Bliven continued. "Money to Jacob."

Matilda sighed. Her son had no need for money. Their son. "Our marriage would help his prospects."

"Then do it. I have a cousin who is a vicar," Bliven said, the words slowly spaced. The servant leaned over with another spoonful of water.

"He can't take food anymore." The servant and Gawain shared a significant glance.

Matilda frowned. She knew the end was near. And she needed to get back to Bristol. If they could marry today, or after Jacob was found, she would do it, but otherwise Bliven himself was correct. She needed to focus on the search for her son. If he wasn't responsible, who was?

An hour later, they had consulted with Theodore's cousin, Hiram Bliven, who owned the house and had taken responsibility for him in his illness, and had him send for his younger vicar brother, who was somewhere in Surrey. Gawain went to inquire about a special license. Matilda found herself dropped off at the loading dock in the back alley of Redcake's, with orders to eat something so she could get through the day. She intended to telephone Bristol and check on her family.

When she reached the manager's office, she found Ewan Hales at his desk, though it was Saturday afternoon and he probably had the afternoon off.

She felt her back stiffen. "Mr. Hales."

He swiveled in his chair, his hair flopping over his brow. "Miss Redcake!" He leaped to his feet.

"I wanted to use your telephone."

He peered at her. "Have you eaten? You're white as milk. Better than gray, I suppose."

She did feel her legs wobble, but whether it was from hunger, shock over Theodore Bliven's appearance, or the sight of this man, who had so insulted her, and in her own home, too, she could not say.

"Sit down, Miss Redcake. I'll be back in a moment."

She heard rapid footsteps as he went into the hallway, and he was back in under two minutes.

"There. I asked a messenger boy to run downstairs to fetch you a tray. Everything that's been going on has taken the wind out of you, and no surprise."

"I am amazed you are being kind."

He frowned. "I hope I would always be so, Miss Redcake."

She scoffed.

"I am sorry for what I said to your brother. I was trying to be thorough. It's part of my position, you understand; to anticipate problems and prevent them."

Her hands shook as she tucked one over the other across her chest. "You thought I might have a lover because I let you kiss me?"

"I am sorry," he said again.

"You think I have loose morals," she said, louder.

"I don't know you well, Miss Redcake."

Her brain seemed to tilt when she turned her head from side to side. "It was only the one time, you know. One indiscretion with a man I thought would marry me. Everything happened because of that one time. It's not so rare, you know. People do indulge themselves. Not everyone is so spectacularly unlucky. I'm sure you have engaged in such activities."

From the way his eyebrows rose, she suspected she had gone much too far. "Miss Redcake."

"Why did you kiss me?" she asked, closing her eyes.

He ran his fingers through his hair. "Does it offend you to know that I scarcely remember? It feels like it happened a century ago."

"That's why I asked." She sighed. "I don't remember either."

He cleared his throat. "Any word on your son? I dearly wanted to stay in Bristol."

"I know you did, and I appreciate that, Mr. Hales." She had no energy for anger at him anymore. "No word since the ransom note. I was so sure Jacob's father was behind everything, but he's dying."

"Are you sure?"

"Oh, yes. We were just there. Such a handsome, laughing rogue of a man. He was a school friend of my sister Alys's husband. He was meant to be one of her suitors, but he liked me better. I was such a fool. A friend of ours from finishing school—she's Lady Bricker now—told me how to get him to propose, and I thought Alys had done the same with her husband." Her laugh sounded hollow. "It turned out Mr. Bliven already had a fiancée. My father is usually more thorough in his investigations."

"You thought he was a true suitor."

"Yes. We weren't used to suitors. We didn't know any better."

A knock came at the door, and Mr. Hales leapt up to answer it, then returned carrying a tray. "Let us get some food into you and we shall decide how to proceed."

He poured a generous amount of milk into her cup, then added tea. No sugar. He had remembered her preference.

Chapter Seven

Matilda stared at Mr. Hales's head, bent over the tray. He looked up with a smile and handed her the tea.

"Here, drink this, then your soup should be cool enough to eat. Cream of mushroom today."

Her hand shook slightly as she took the cup. Would this be how she remembered this time in the future? Every hand offering her endless cups of tea and no hope? She downed the beverage as quickly as possible, thinking she might become a coffee drinker when Jacob came home. If he ever did. And if he didn't, she might just throw herself into the River Avon.

"You are thinking too hard," Mr. Hales observed.

She emptied her teacup and handed it to him. "I am going to marry Mr. Bliven, if he can last long enough for Gawain to obtain a special license."

"What good will that do?"

She took a biscuit from the tray and stared at it. "It will be better for Jacob."

"And for you?"

Her mind went blank. How could she explain how desperately she'd wanted Mr. Bliven, then how desperately she'd avoided him? "It won't matter very much to me, not at this time. I'll be a widow soon enough."

He took a biscuit, reminding her to bite into her own. "What about mourning?"

The rich chocolate and marmalade topping soothed her throat enough for her to swallow the dry texture underneath. "I hadn't thought of that." She stared down. Her skirt was a muted red and blue tartan. She'd have to wear black for a couple of years, but that would only make her more severe-looking, not a bad thing. Terrible for her complexion, but then she wouldn't be hunting for a husband. "It will be fine. I don't care."

"You are clearly a woman who would do anything for her child." His gaze was sympathetic.

She didn't want him to think she was a martyr. "No, I wouldn't marry him before. He came back, you see, wanted to marry me then, and I refused. About a year ago, a little longer than that. Before he returned to India."

"Why didn't you?"

She worried her lip, tasted a stray fragment of orange peel. "He seemed mad. I was afraid to put myself under his power, and I was arrogant, thought Jacob and I were better off alone." The biscuit turned into a rock in her stomach, weighing her down. "But it wasn't true. Maybe if there was a male in my household Jacob wouldn't have seemed such an easy target."

Mr. Hales leaned forward. "He wouldn't have done you any good. The nanny would have known he was bedridden, ill."

She squeezed her eyes shut, wanting to believe him. "Are you sure?"

He took her hand, his own so warm that it seemed to add life to her skin. "Yes, Miss Redcake. I am sure. The opportunity would still have been there. What do you think, now that this avenue has been ruled out? Why was your son taken?"

She stared at his hand, the fine hairs covering the thick wrist, the ropy veins. Once she had thought such a hand in hers was her right. Then the only hand she could claim was a small child's. And now, nothing. "I suppose it was just for the money. Gipsies are kidnappers. It is well known."

"It is rumored. I do not know if it is true." His hand squeezed and pulled away.

How she wanted a hand to hold hers again. She sat, doing nothing but breathing, remembering the feel of Jacob's small, fragile hand in her palm. She had taken her son for granted, forgetting what a miracle he was.

"Miss Redcake?"

She glanced down, pulling the shreds of her professional personality over the frightened mother, and realized she had downed her biscuit. "So sorry, woolgathering. I think I can eat that soup now."

He lifted the cloche off the bowl. "It is probably better eaten at my desk."

She nodded and stood slowly, then reseated herself as he placed the bowl of steaming white soup on his desk, on top of a closed ledger. His presence loomed at her back as he pushed her chair toward the desk and handed her a spoon.

"Lord Judah is coming back on Monday and will retake the reins of the enterprise," he said, as he came to the side of the desk and placed his hand on the shelf. "But between my duties here I took the time to go over to Douglas Flour and test some samples."

"And?"

"I specifically asked to test the flour sacks earmarked for us in Bristol. It was all bad. I didn't have time to check any other flour sacks, but the manager said he'd look into it. Obviously, if it is all bad we won't be able to reorder until the problem is fixed. I'll take a look at their books next week to see how they do things. Is our flour batched separately from other factories' and so forth. I wonder if yours was sabotaged on purpose because we were experimenting here in London with the Liverpool supplier."

"I'm sure you know what to do. I'll leave you in charge."

"That's the thing, Miss Redcake. You see, I am in charge. Of the factories. I'm going to stay in London and oversee the earl's businesses here. So I'll be leaving Redcake's."

She'd never see his hand holding hers again either. The thought hurt more than it should, considering the fact that, so recently, he'd been nothing more than a too-handsome, too-rakish secretary, an underling, a subordinate. "I suppose I knew that. It will be strange, though. You are such a fixture here, Mr. Hales."

"Like a piece of furniture." He didn't smile.

She kept her eyes on her soup as she fished out a piece of mushroom. "I hope you don't think I feel that way."

She glanced up as she swallowed. Far from his usual obsequious yet ultimately blank expression, she saw a hint of pain, a faint line between his brows. She felt the need to reassure him. Had she just seen a first crack of vulnerability in the handsome secretary's face? "I know better now. Other than you thinking I'm a woman of loose morals, you've been very supportive and kind to me."

"How could I be anything but, under the circumstances?" He sounded confused.

"You could have ignored the situation, ignored everything that wasn't a part of your paid duties."

"I've worked for your family too long for that."

"I'll think of you as a friend now." Her voice caught. "If that is acceptable to you."

His hand pressed gently on her shoulder. She closed her eyes, soaking in his touch, and when she opened them again, he'd stepped back.

A knock came at the door. She ignored the conversation, focusing on her soup, liking the warmth that filled her stomach.

"Sir Gawain has news," Mr. Hales said, coming to her side again. "There are so few places to get a special license, and it won't be possible until next week."

"I see." She nodded. "I suppose I won't be getting married, then."

"A week's delay?"

"It will be too late for Mr. Bliven. It's just one more thing I cannot do for Jacob."

"There are more important things to do for him now."

"Like finding him?" She had spoken without taking a breath, heard the shrill pitch in her voice.

"Don't become hysterical, Miss Redcake. You said we are friends, correct? Then please give my poor choice of words the best possible interpretation."

She sniffed. "Of course. I can do no less."

"Sir Gawain is downstairs, ready to take you back to the train station."

She nodded and pushed back her chair, and forced herself to face him, hold out her hand. Instead of shaking it like a man, he took her hand between both of his. She shuddered at the warmth, the touch. Good heavens, she was starving for it. "Best of luck to you with your new endeavors. We shall miss you terribly."

"You will?" The left side of his mouth tilted up. She hadn't noticed how lopsided his smile could be.

"Yes. If your position ever brings you to Bristol, I hope you will stop by."

"Miss Redcake, I want to help you."

She didn't want to cry. "You will. Fixing the flour will protect my job, keep my company's—my family's—reputation in good standing. If we start losing customers, we'll lose money, and what if we couldn't pay the ransom?"

He nodded, sobered by that. "I will do everything I can, and stay in touch with you besides."

"Greggory will have to be in the office Monday, even if I cannot. Please let one of us know what you find out."

"Very well. Have a safe journey home." He squeezed her hands again, then released them.

She felt like a corpse walking as she left the office. Home to more disappointment, more emptiness, more fear. Where was Jacob?

On Monday, Ewan went to Redcake's very early, but he found Lord Judah Shield there even earlier still. He'd stepped onto the street just after sunrise, but Lord Judah must have walked over in the dark.

His manager smiled at him from his office doorway and said, "Why don't you fetch us up a pot of tea and some of those nut scones and we'll catch up? I haven't dined yet."

Ewan knew he wouldn't be able to eat. He'd made himself oatmeal over the fire that morning in his room and had barely managed two bites. Besides, he had meetings at Douglas Flour at eleven A.M. He noted that Lord Judah had his diary of events open on his desk and knew most of the catching up could be done from his notes, so he nodded and went back downstairs.

The late round of bakery deliveries was just going out and it was nearly seven thirty before he made it back upstairs with a teapot and fresh-made scones, still too warm for their sugar glaze. He set the tray down on the table between the armchairs in Lord Judah's office for the last time, and poured the tea.

The telephone rang and his ears pricked. He went to answer it, hoping for news of Jacob Bliven. He'd fretted in his room all Sunday, closed off from the telephone at Redcake's, wishing he could go to Bristol instead of preparing for his new life; making sure his clothing was spotless, doing some marketing, touching up where his landlady had left surfaces less than gleaming. By the end, his room might have been freshly moved into, it was so clean, and his clothing was in perfect repair, plus he'd spent money on a nearly new overcoat, all the better for protecting his suits from dust and soot on the trains. He'd ordered a new pair of shoes as well, from the cobbler who lived in his building. His best pair of shoes was too scuffed to take polish perfectly anymore.

The telephone call was from a restaurant with an emergency

order. It should have come in downstairs, but Ralph Popham must not be answering the telephone yet. The poor man worked all hours, not seeming to have any kind of home life despite his daughter still being unmarried and living with him.

If he'd had to peg a woman for having an illegitimate child it would have been Betsy Popham, not Matilda Redcake, at least until he'd learned to know Matilda better. That kiss they had shared was pure fire, more passionate than anything with Betsy, even though they'd been far more intimate. If he hadn't been so busy, he'd have become obsessed with reliving that kiss and scheming how to have another. On Saturday, though, he'd contented himself with touching her. She had not been ready for kisses. He wondered if they would meet in a few years. He, an earl, she, an established spinster running the Redcake's factory. Would she consent to be his mistress then?

"Run downstairs, would you, Ewan?" Lord Judah asked, behind his desk now. "Turn in the order, tell Simon Hellman to send it over, find out where Mr. Popham is?"

Ewan knew if he did that the day would erupt into its usual Monday chaos. "I really need to speak to you, sir."

"You know Mondays are not a good time," Lord Judah said, staring at the towering stacks of information for him to follow up on. "Particularly today."

"Yes, sir, but that is the problem. Your Monday is going to take a much worse turn." Ewan folded his arms over his chest.

Lord Judah narrowed his uniquely striated amber and brown gaze at him, stood up from his desk, and went to his favorite armchair, then deliberately poured himself a cup of tea. Ewan was reminded that this man had been a military officer. When the battle was at its most heated was when a man like him became calm.

He waited until Lord Judah took his first sip, then sat down opposite him.

"What?"

Ewan unfolded his arms and spread his fingers over his thighs. "I am the heir to the Earl of Fitzwalter, courtesy of Lord Ritten's recent death."

"Scandalous something or other, what?" Lord Judah commented, finishing his first cup of tea and pouring another.

"That is not my point."

Lord Judah's eyes, so reminiscent of a tiger's-eye stone, caught a ray of sunlight and gleamed gold for an instant. His lips curved. "I would imagine not. I had no idea you were so closely related to an earl. Sir Bartley never mentioned it."

"He didn't know any more than I did. But the problem is, I have to start work in a family business today. Ironically, it is one of the Redcake's suppliers. I am going to oversee various businesses, including Douglas Flour, which has shipped the factories bad product recently."

"So your fortunes are still intertwined with ours."

"Precisely. I am also deeply concerned about Matilda Redcake, and I'd like to resolve the flour issue from the Douglas end; that is one less issue for her to worry about."

"Don't you mean you are concerned about her missing son?"

Ewan was silent. Lord Judah set down his teacup and nodded to himself. "I see. So you are interested in Matilda."

Ewan let out a breath.

"I cannot tell you how unhappy all of this makes me. I never should have left the office. So often in the army you could take a leave of months and nothing would happen, but in business that does not seem to be the case." Lord Judah ran a finger over his lower lip.

"No, sir."

Lord Judah held out his hand. "It seems we are to be colleagues." Ewan hesitated, then took the proffered hand and shook it.

Lord Judah grinned. "Good luck with Matilda. You are going to need it."

"She needs support, not a lover."

Lord Judah sobered instantly. "I had an update last night from my brother. He's down in Sussex, of course, due to his heir's birth, but he's been in close contact. Terrible business. We've had no indication anyone has taken Jacob out of Bristol, correct?"

"The ransom note was attached to the baby's dog's collar and left in that same park by the Redcake house."

"Right. By Jove, I hope the child still lives."

"It will kill her if he does not."

It was hard to meet Lord Judah's gaze directly, given his gleaming eyes, but in this moment, they shared a long glance of mutual concern.

"If I were you, I'd put off the earl for a few days and go back to Bristol. The child is more important, and the Redcakes need help. I'd have gone myself, but now I need to do your job, too."

Ewan nodded. "When this is all over, try to bring Greggory Red-cake down here. He's a smart man, and if you train him here, he might be able to take on the new shop in Kensington by summer's end. Betsy Popham wants to go as well."

Lord Judah pursed his lips. "Doesn't help me today."

Ewan shook his head. "No, I understand that." He stood. "I leave for my meeting at Douglas Industries in two hours."

"Then to Bristol?"

"Do you really think it is wise?"

"Yes. The family trusts you. They need help."

"Then I will return to Bristol. Jacob has been missing for five days."

"It doesn't look good for him. For all of Matilda's faults, she doesn't deserve this."

Ewan gritted his teeth. Why did everyone have to keep damning the poor woman? "What faults? She made one foolish mistake, the same as many a woman before her, with a man who had concealed his engagement from her. Her own father introduced him to her as an honorable suitor."

Lord Judah stared at the fire. "You have to understand how Society works. She was a tradesman's daughter who was attempting to enter fashionable society. Her actions cost her younger sister any hope of an aristocratic marriage. They tore her family apart."

"It was one mistake," Ewan repeated. "One small mistake. I have no doubt her character has been formed by it ever since. I have never met a woman more self-contained, who so desperately needs to be held. That mistake took her out of Society, denied her any chance of an honorable marriage. Meanwhile, her own brother gave her seducer a position!"

"Matilda's family didn't ostracize her but trained her for a good position, too. She lives in a mansion with servants to care for her and the child. She hasn't done badly at all."

"She's all alone. Who does she turn to when her son is gone? Clearly her servants are less than honorable."

"Her family is there with her."

"Arguing with her, second-guessing her."

"I understand she was convinced the boy's father was behind the entire mess, and she was wrong about that."

"So easy to mistrust the judgment of a fallen woman," Ewan snarled.

"He is quite literally on his deathbed," Lord Judah emphasized. "Gawain saw him two days ago."

"I know that," Ewan said. "I saw Matilda that day myself."

They stared at each other. Lord Judah shook his head. "Never argue with a man in love. I would tell you, man to man, that you cannot have Matilda. She's soiled goods, and a future earl cannot have that. She's not good *ton*, or even *ton* at all. You will have enough problems, thanks to your own background. Thank God you didn't marry Betsy Popham. Matilda is no better, not with Jacob."

And what if he's dead? The thought passed like lightning through Ewan's mind and was just as quickly suppressed. It would not matter. He'd never been a secret, though he'd never been in London. Besides, he hadn't been joking when he'd said the boy's loss would kill Matilda. That boy was her exposed heart. Without him, all you'd ever see of her was a cold, clear-minded woman of business. The rest would die.

"I believe earls can do as they wish, but that is not the present topic. I will take your leave, Lord Judah, and will be in touch regarding the business relationship between Redcake's and Douglas Flour, though I expect most of my dealings will be with Matilda if you retain the Liverpool suppliers."

Lord Judah didn't respond, merely bit into a scone. After he chewed and swallowed, he said, "No glaze?"

Ewan closed his eyes and shook his head. "I chose speed over perfection today. Not my usual style. I apologize." Not bothering to wait for Lord Judah's response, he went to the outer room and picked up his box. He'd take his things directly over to his new office, wherever that might be. After settling in and putting in orders to hire a secretary of his own, he'd take his meeting with his managers, then go to the train station.

Matilda paced the parlor floor at teatime as her mother fluttered her arms. Her sister Rose sat in an armchair, very pale.

"Then it is final. I will cancel my wedding," Rose said.

Happiness had put some weight and color into Rose's face, Matilda had noted as of late, though she had spent too much time in

London, breathing in the air that was so destructive to her compromised lungs. "I am not asking you to delay your happiness in any way; I am merely saying that I cannot be in Liverpool on Wednesday to witness the happy event. You can wed without me."

Rose bent her head. Her beautiful white-blond hair, so often the focus of Matilda's jealousy, suited her like a halo suited an angel. "I cannot have a big event when my nephew is missing. Mr. Courtnay will understand."

"Doesn't he have a lot of his business partners coming to the dinner afterward?"

Rose folded her hands over her skirt. "He had a party not too long ago to belatedly celebrate Cousin Lewis's marriage to his daughter."

"It was a lovely event," her mother reflected. "Such flowers in early March!"

"We'll do the same thing, when Jacob is found," Rose said.

Matilda wiped away the tears that sprang to her eyes at her sister's brave voice. Poor Rose. She'd wanted marriage so badly, so much so that she was risking her health by marrying a widowed Liverpool industrialist just to have a chance at a normal life. Now the kidnapping had ruined her pleasure at a proper send-off.

"I wish we would hear again from the kidnappers," Gawain said. "Resolve this."

Matilda wasn't sure she agreed with that. While they waited for the news, there was still hope. She vacillated from minute to minute between hope and despair. Surely such blackguards would not want to keep a child alive, at risk of being found. So much easier to . . . well, she couldn't reason that out, even in the privacy of her own head.

Rose stood. "I need to telephone Mr. Courtnay. He is waiting to hear from me. And I shall have to go to Liverpool on the evening train."

"Why, dear?" her mother asked.

"I have to cancel everything," Rose said. "There are so many people involved."

Matilda squinted at her sister. She was up to something. For a moment a crazed fantasy swept through her mind. Her sister, changing her mind about wedding a man old enough to be her father, has her nephew kidnapped in order to cancel her wedding. But no, that was absurd. Besides, Rose didn't have a cruel bone in her body.

Daisy entered the parlor with a silver tray. Sir Bartley took the card.

"Ewan Hales is here," he said.

Gawain looked up with a frown. "Surely he wouldn't come here uninvited to discuss the flour problem."

"Daisy, send him into my study. I'll be there in a minute," Matilda said.

"You don't need to deal with him," her father said.

Matilda shook her head. "He might know something useful."

"I'm going back to London tomorrow to get the special license because Theo still lives," Gawain said. "I'll take Hales back on the train with me and have a firm chat with him about showing up here."

"Special license?" Rose asked.

"Our idiot sister thinks now is the time to marry Theodore Bliven."

Rose stood suddenly. "What?" Her parents echoed the word.

"It will help Jacob. Mr. Bliven is dying," Matilda said, holding herself very still.

"That is madness!" her father exclaimed.

Matilda put her hands to her throat, wanting to strangle her father instead. "I don't know that I can even manage it before he dies. Obviously we've had trouble securing the license."

"How much longer does he have?" her mother asked.

"He could be gone any moment," Gawain said. "It didn't look good. I'm all for it, to be honest. Anything to help poor Jacob."

Their mother made a keening noise and slumped into an armchair. Rose bit her lip, looking faintly irritated.

"I am going to pack," she said. "Gawain, will you take me to the train station?"

"Of course."

"I am going to see Mr. Hales," Matilda said. Her feet felt like heavy bricks as she passed over the carpet and into the hallway. She needed sleep, yet couldn't rest.

Lines of fatigue bracketed Mr. Hales's mouth, Matilda could see, as he rose from the chair in front of her desk. She noted his scuffed shoes, the valise next to the chair.

"You look like you are on the run."

He stepped forward and took her hand, pressing it between both of his. She soaked up the warmth of his hands, while noting the tired sag of his suit and the smell of soot and train on his hair and clothing.

"It has been a long day. I went to Redcake's and resigned in person to Lord Judah, then I went to my new office at Douglas Industries and met my subordinates, then I packed and caught the next train here."

"Why did you come?"

One of his hands left hers and, outrageously, caressed her cheek. "I could not stay away."

"I'm returning to London tomorrow to marry Mr. Bliven," she whispered, knowing before she said the words how foolish she sounded. She ought to be scouring the streets for her child, but she'd wandered for hours this morning, despite the rain. What was she supposed to find? Greggory and a team of men were combing every tavern in the city, trying to find Andrzej Majewski, the horse dealer. They had men watching Izabela's mother's house, just in case she was involved somehow. Mrs. Miller had been interviewed repeatedly, even on the telephone by Dougal Alexander, the private inquiry agent. They had soaked up all the advice the Scotsman had on finding a missing child, pasting notices on lampposts, talking to street sellers and the proprietors of local shops, sharing sketches and photographs of Izabela and Jacob.

Nothing had brought forth any useful clues.

"I wish you would not," Mr. Hales said. "I do understand the impulse."

"Why do you care?"

His dark eyes stared into hers. He sighed, and she wondered if his exhaustion was bringing out a new aspect of his personality. Certainly she'd seen sides of him recently that had never been evident before. He'd been tossed into a stormy, uncertain phase of life, just as she had.

His fingers caressed her cheek again. "I simply cannot stay away. I do not know how to be more eloquent than that, Miss Redcake."

"You cannot think to court me now," she whispered.

"I cannot court you at all," he said. "You understand that."

She thought of Alys with her marquess, Gawain with his Indian princess, and told herself, *No, I do not understand that.* And yet she had not hidden away her child, her shame. She was beyond Society. It was completely out of her reach now. But this was Ewan Hales, too, her father's secretary. She wanted to laugh at the sheer absurdity of it.

Betsy Popham's discarded follower was now above the touch of Sir Bartley Redcake's daughter.

"Then you should avoid me," she said, her voice gaining strength as she stepped back from him. "Why cause either of us pain?"

"You need help." His hands dropped. "I can be an extra body on the street. We need to keep knocking on doors until the right person answers. Someone knows something. People don't vanish into fairy rings."

Behind Matilda, the door opened. Quick footsteps sounded on the carpet.

"I found it!" Greggory called.

Chapter Eight

Matilda whipped around. Ewan let his hand drop, knowing her hope was probably far greater than the reality. *It* was not likely to mean her son.

"What did you find?" he asked.

Greggory spread his fingers across his chest. "The White Horse tavern. It's on the northern outskirts of Bristol. The Gipsy camp is supposed to be in Fiddlers Wood."

"Isn't there coal mining near there?" Matilda asked, brushing fine hairs off her forehead. The tiny hairs poked straight out, giving her a hint of a lion's mane.

"Used to be." Greggory bobbed his head. "It's a pretty wild area."

"Good place to hide a Gipsy camp," he said, wishing he knew the Bristol area better. "We can finally find the horse trader."

"I'll get my things." Matilda smiled, and his heart ached to see the naked hope in her eyes.

"We'll need lanterns. It will be dark soon," Greggory said.

Ewan stared at the Redcake cousin. "You can't think to take Matilda out there, to a lawless camp, after dark?"

"You can't think we'll wait until morning."

"Did you go to the tavern yet?" he asked.

"No," Greggory said. "I only just found out where it was. I went to one called the Folly and they told me. I thought I'd better come back for more men."

In the hallway, they found Matilda's brother and father, throwing on heavy coats. Ewan thought he saw the handle of a pistol going into Sir Gawain's coat. Matilda's mother made wringing motions with her hands as Matilda tucked a heavy scarf around her neck and pulled on a cloak. A bonnet covered her red hair. The boot boy had to be sent to hire a hansom so they had room for their party, Greggory having let his go back to the stable after the six-mile journey he'd taken to the Folly.

At least they had almost two hours of daylight left, though they would burn most of that checking the tavern and the camp. A brief argument ensued as to splitting up the party.

"I'm going to the camp," Matilda insisted. "I might see Jacob there, or even Izabela. You won't recognize them."

Mrs. Miller appeared in the doorway, a heavy cloak around her shoulders. "I should go too, Miss Redcake, to see if I can spot Izabela."

"Have you ever seen this Majewski character?" Gawain asked as they went outside.

Mrs. Miller shook her head. "I'm not really sure. All those dark men look alike to me. I'd have sent off anyone who loitered around the house, but if he visited her mother's home, I might have."

"Take her," Ewan said. "Another pair of eyes to spot the nanny."

Gawain nodded. "Father, you and I should go to the tavern. I think Greggory, Ewan, and the ladies should go to the camp."

"Unarmed?" Sir Bartley asked, incredulous.

Gawain grinned. "They aren't going in for a battle. They are merely escorting two ladies who want their fortunes told."

Sir Bartley shook his head. "What if you see Jacob or Izabela? They might need to be taken by force."

"Matilda," Gawain said, "if you see them, mark their location but don't get into a fight. We'll meet back at your house and we'll call in the factory men."

"If I see my son, I'm going to take him," Matilda retorted, her color high.

"We'll be fine in a fight," Greggory said. "I box, you know, and Hales here looks to be in good shape."

"I know those Gipsies are likely to be a puny lot, but don't risk it," Gawain said. "You hear me, Greggory?"

Greggory sneered at him but didn't respond, just handed Mrs. Miller into the carriage.

"We need to leave," Ewan said.

Gawain shook his head. "No fighting, Hales, understood?"

"We have to let Matilda have her head," Ewan said. "Whatever comes."

"You're a braver man than I," Gawain said, clapping his hand on Ewan's shoulder in soldierly solidarity. "But try to be inconspicuous. We don't want the kidnappers on the run. Gipsies are a mobile lot."

"That is rather the point," Ewan muttered as he followed Matilda into the carriage. He watched her fight anxiety as the carriage rumbled north through Bristol, over bumpy cobbled streets, wishing he could hold her hand. Staring out the window, he saw the hansom turn off behind them, heading for the tavern. They continued down muddy farm lanes toward Fiddlers Wood and the Gipsy camp.

The first thing they saw was smoke from campfires. Then they saw a motley collection of covered wagons, proper caravans, and tents. The low canvas tents predominated, and the scent of animal hung as thickly in the air as smoke.

"They are called *vardos*, the wagons, I mean," Greggory said. "I went to a Gipsy horse fair with my father once, and we ate food prepared on a stove inside one. They actually have chimneys and can be very beautiful and gilded inside."

"Ironic that they have the same taste as the highest aristocrats," Ewan said.

Only one of the wagons was of the brightly painted variety, probably belonging to the head man. He saw some donkeys hobbled near tents, but no horses. Had they really found Majewski's home, or was this some other, poorer camp?

When their carriage stopped, a dozen children, some wearing nothing more than a shirt, ran toward them.

"Secure your money; they are fearsome pickpockets," Greggory advised. "This is when I'd want a pocket with teeth."

Matilda sighed and pulled a small purse from her reticule, then tucked it into an inner coat pocket. "I might need money, though. I wonder if I can bribe possible informants."

"Let's ask about Majewski first," Ewan said. "If they've never heard of him, we're sunk."

"Or Izabela. Her last name is Pickett."

"I don't recognize any of the women," Mrs. Miller said, playing with a long thread on the hem of her shawl.

"What about the men?" Ewan saw three men huddled at the side of the fancy *vardo*. The doors were covered in carvings of horses and the rest was painted brightly in stripes of red and green.

"I can't see that far away so clearly," Mrs. Miller confessed.

Two girls, old enough to be minders of the children though not quite their mothers, approached.

"We want the *drabarni*," Greggory said. "That's the fortune-teller."

"We want Majewski," Matilda said in response. "I am not going to play a game, some sort of idiotic subterfuge. Anyone would look for Izabela's suitor under the circumstances. There is no point in being underhanded."

"But Gawain said—"

"He's not here," Matilda snapped.

The girls stopped moving, confused by Matilda's tone. Ewan could see her forced smile at them was hard-won.

"Andrzej Majewski?" she asked. "Is he here?"

One of the girls darted away. The other one stayed, but her expression hardened, and Ewan wondered if he'd mistaken her small size for youth. He nodded at Greggory, who wandered off, keeping the runner in sight.

"We need to get Mrs. Miller close to the men," he whispered to Matilda.

She didn't nod, but she took a few slow steps forward while reaching into her coat. Her hand came out with a couple of shillings. "Andrzej Majewski?" she repeated.

"What you want?" the young/old Gipsy girl asked.

"A horse," Ewan said when Matilda hesitated. "He is a horse dealer, yes?"

The Gipsy relaxed slightly. "He doesn't do business here."

"We came all this way," Mrs. Miller said, smiling sweetly. "Do you have a *drabarni*? I'd love to have a cup of tea and have my leaves read."

"That's kitchen stuff, not for us," the Gipsy sneered. "Our *drabarni* reads runes and cards."

"Not palms?" Matilda asked.

The Gipsy snorted. "Our *drabarni* is the real thing. She's read for Princess Alexandra."

Ewan sincerely doubted the Princess of Wales would have visited a dilapidated camp like this one, much less received a reading from the local wisewoman. He exchanged a cynical glance with Matilda, who tossed the coins at the Gipsy's feet.

"There will be more if you take me to Mr. Majewski."

The Gipsy swept up the coins and dashed away, her bare feet blackened with dirt.

Mrs. Miller looked confused. "What is that girl doing?"

Matilda shrugged. "Majewski is here. The question is, what does he know?" She glanced around, her weight balanced on her toes.

"We should walk the camp, see if you can spot Izabela," Ewan said.

Matilda nodded and he took her arm. Mrs. Miller strolled next to them. He kept an eye on the men, watching for signs of trouble, as they scanned the faces of the women and children. Within five minutes their task became harder as mist started to drift between the trees. Twilight descended. The Gipsies steadily fed the fires as they prepared their evening meals, and the flames sent their faces in and out of shadow.

They strolled the camp, circling the edge of the woods. Ewan spotted Greggory next to a man, talking animatedly.

"Think that's him?" he asked.

The walnut-skinned man looked to be about thirty, with thinning black hair that stood up in tufts. He had a well-defined black mustache and sideburns. In waistcoat and shirtsleeves, he stood with arms folded across his chest and legs spread wide, his head at an arrogant tilt.

"Handsome devil," Mrs. Miller said. "I can see Izabela liking him."

Greggory spotted them and they walked over. "This is Mr. Majewski."

Ewan shook the man's hand and his companions nodded. Thankfully, Matilda kept her emotions in check.

"I was just telling him that Izabela Pickett has gone missing," Greggory said.

The man clicked his tongue against his palate. He had an air of defiance, with no hint of surrender in him. This characteristic reminded Ewan unpleasantly of the Earl of Fitzwalter.

"What do you say to that, sir?" he asked.

The man shrugged and pulled a half-smoked cigar from a waistcoat pocket and stuck it in his mouth. "What's it to me?"

"We thought you were planning to marry the girl," Ewan said.

Majewski sneered. "Too fast, that one, too flighty. If she cannot make up her mind who to wed, I say to the devil with her."

Mrs. Miller blinked next to him. Ewan wondered how much freedom Matilda had inadvertently granted her nanny, that she seemed to have so much time for men.

"When did you see her last?"

The man shrugged again and strolled toward the nearest campfire. He bent over the open flame and puffed on his cigar until it lit. Matilda's lips were tight.

"I want a look in that *vardo*," she said.

"Has Izabela ever been here?" Ewan asked.

The man turned to them with a feral grin. "How would she have the time for that, all but enslaved to that one?" He pointed at Matilda, and tilted his lean hips in her direction. "Such a polite household for that bastard child of yours."

"What do you know about him?" Matilda asked in a voice that might have been chiseled from ice. Ewan pulled her arm closer to his body.

"I know his name," Majewski said. "That's a dangerous thing, you know, sharing a name with the world. People can use it to hurt him."

"Who do you know who wants to hurt my son?" she asked, taking her arm from Ewan's hand and stepping toward the campfire. Ewan stayed close.

The man smirked. "Anyone who is jealous of such a fine healthy boy and his rich mother, I suppose."

"Where did Izabela take him?" Matilda asked. "Is she a victim or a kidnapper? You know I can pay you plenty for the information."

"I know you can call the police. Have them come in here with clubs and send us into the wind. Maybe we'll go now and save you the trouble."

Ewan heard a muttered imprecation in a language he didn't understand, and an older woman stepped forward, majestic in numerous brightly colored shawls, though her dress underneath was a plain mourning gown.

"We haven't called the police," Matilda said. "I want my son back, quietly. I won't cause any trouble to your people. Just give me my son."

"We don't have your son, Miss Redcake," the woman said. Her air of dignity matched Majewski's. Was he her son?

"You know my name?" Matilda rejoined.

"My son has heard Izabela speak of you," she said, confirming her identity. "But the girl has not been here, nor has your son. Andrzej broke with her last month."

Ewan narrowed his eyes at the man, who nodded significantly. He swore as insight hit him. Had the break spurred Izabela into some folly? "Was she expecting a child of her own?"

The old woman muttered something that sounded foul, whatever language it was in.

"It wasn't mine," Majewski muttered, sounding abashed for the first time. He puffed hard on his cigar stub and gazed at the sky.

Matilda put her hand to her forehead. "There is yet another man, then."

Mrs. Miller shook her head. "I cannot believe all this was going on under my oversight. I am so sorry, Miss Redcake."

The housekeeper seemed kindly enough, but she'd had a blank spot in front of her eye where the nanny was concerned. She had found the girl the job, though she was apparently little more than a whore, and ignored her doings.

Matilda swayed, and Greggory grabbed her arm. She slumped, and Ewan, shocked, caught her with one arm behind her back, then slipped another behind her knees as they buckled completely.

Majewski pointed to the *vardo* impassively. "Take her in there."

Ewan followed the old woman into the *vardo*. It was difficult to balance on the steps, which were as much ladder as staircase, but thankfully, he only counted to seven before his feet touched the boards of the wagon itself. He saw the bed on the far wall but decided to set her down on a narrow, cushioned bench built into the side wall, opposite the stove, for fear that beasties would be lurking in the bedding. While Majewski and his mother looked clean enough, the black-bottomed soles of the Gipsy girl made him question camp hygiene. Miss Redcake didn't need lice or bedbug bites on top of her other woes.

The *vardo* was crowded with all six of them inside. Majewski cursed and pushed a small table aside, then gestured to his mother and Mrs. Miller to sit across from Matilda's prone form. First, though, his mother went to a cabinet and pulled out a vial. After she opened it, she pulled out a bit of dry leaf and crumpled it under Miss Redcake's nose.

Ewan watched as her eyelashes, ginger like her hair, fluttered. Her lips moved. He thought she said her son's name. The old woman muttered something and capped the vial, then put it back in her cupboard.

"I'll tell you that one's fortune," she said in English. "She's going to waste away without her son. Isn't she eating? Sleeping?"

"He's been missing since Wednesday," Ewan said. "That's a very long time to be separated from your child, especially under the circumstances."

"Wednesday?" Majewski said. "Are you certain?"

Ewan remembered that day so clearly. He'd been kissing Matilda, feeling like his own world was falling apart, sensing that she might anchor him back to earth, and then it rocked again and she was cast onto the waves as well.

"Why do you ask?" Greggory said sharply.

The horse dealer exchanged a glance with his mother. "I saw Izabela on Thursday."

"Holy Mother," Ewan swore. "Where?"

Matilda moaned, and he knelt beside her. "Listen if you can, Miss Redcake; this is important." He rubbed her hand between his palms.

"On Corn Street, in front of the bank."

"Was she alone?" Ewan asked.

"I was on my way to the Commercial Rooms to meet with a merchant about a matched set of grays," Majewski reflected. "She saw me, stuck her nose in the air, and turned away."

"What was she wearing?" Mrs. Miller asked.

The man shrugged. "Just her everyday blue dress. No apron." He blinked. "No shawl either, now that I think of it."

"It was raining heavily that day," Ewan remembered. Who had she handed Jacob over to? There could be no more doubt that she'd been involved. She hadn't returned to Matilda's home.

"She might have just come from the bank. I don't remember her looking damp. Must have been a break in the weather. She seemed to be alone, but I'm not sure."

"You had no reason to speak to her," his mother said.

"No. I broke with her," Majewski confirmed. "I hadn't seen her from the time we argued until Thursday."

"You didn't try to get her back, promise a scheme that would bring you the money to marry her?"

Majewski waved his arm around the neat room. The places where there were bare walls showed fine wood. Everything looked fresh and clean. Nothing needed repair. "By the standards of my people I am a wealthy man. I want for nothing."

"This is your place, then, not your mother's?"

"I have my own *vardo*," the woman said. "Parked in the trees on the eastern edge of our camp. I do not like all this gaudy paint, and mine blends into the landscape."

"You are the fortune-teller," Greggory said, frowning. "Don't you need to draw attention to yourself?"

The woman smiled. "I have all the trade I need, young man." She stood and walked toward him, the floor creaking underneath her feet, then lifted her chin to stare into his eyes.

Ewan watched Greggory flinch as the woman took his hand, as if she'd shocked him with electricity. Shaking her head, the *drabarni* said, "You have a rough road ahead of you, *gadjo*. Much to endure before you find peace."

Greggory's expression went stony. "Shouldn't I cross your palm with silver first?"

She chuckled. "That prophecy was free."

Matilda struggled into a sitting position. Ewan wondered if she hoped to escape before the *drabarni* inflicted a doom-filled prophecy on her as well. Instead, the old woman took the small table and pushed it toward the bench where Matilda was, then took a small pouch from a drawer. A card-shaped pouch.

"For the love you bear for your child, and the sorrow I feel that a member of my people is involved, I will give you a free reading." She opened the pouch reverently and placed the deck in front of Matilda. "Ask your question."

Matilda sat up and placed her hand on the top card, then squeezed her eyes shut. Ewan was surprised that she acquiesced, but perhaps she thought it the quickest way to get out of the *vardo*. A moment later, she took her hand away.

The *drabarni* nodded and placed three cards from the deck in front of her, then frowned in concentration. "In your past, the hermit. You have done this alone, the birthing and raising of your child, Miss Redcake. You have been willing to do anything for the baby. You were wise to follow the course you did."

Matilda's eyebrows rose, and Ewan wondered if she thought of her recanted decision not to marry Theodore Bliven.

"Here in the present, we have the Nine of Cups." The old woman frowned. "This is a happy card. It symbolizes that you have everything you want."

Matilda shook her head. Tears welled in her eyes. "We both know that isn't true."

She tapped the card with a long fingernail. "There is some deeper truth here. In the past, you trusted the wisdom of friends. Perhaps friends will lead you to the truth again. Now, in the future, the card is the Two of Swords, symbolizing the decision you will make. The figure is blindfolded. You are missing some important piece of information, something in front of you that you are refusing to see. You have to understand things as they are and act quickly, before disaster strikes."

"Information like you and your son are charlatans and Izabela is hiding in your caravan in the woods?" Matilda snapped.

The woman spread her arms, palms up. "You are welcome to look. Indeed, I insist. I do not want you calling the police and disturbing our peaceful camp. I gave this reading to you freely and I ask courtesy in return."

Matilda reached into her coat and pulled out a handful of coins. She dropped them onto the table, a shower of silver shillings. Queen Victoria's dour image glared sternly at the Gipsy woman.

"There, I have paid, and I grant you nothing." Her face glowed with pale fire as she stood, a hint of red circles on her cheeks. "Greggory, Mr. Hales, please take a look at this woman's *vardo*. We cannot risk my child for courtesy."

"I do not want to leave you alone," Ewan said.

"Mrs. Miller is here."

He nodded and gestured to Greggory. They went down the steps and walked through the camp in silence.

"I really thought we'd find them here," Greggory said as they reached the woman's caravan. "I cannot believe there is yet another man in this picture."

"Mrs. Miller needs to lose her position," Ewan said. "She is in charge of guarding the servants' chastity."

"It doesn't sound like there is any hope of controlling this one's," Greggory said with a laugh.

Inside, the plain *vardo* was just as tidy as Majewski's, if less ornate and perhaps a decade older. "No one could be hiding here."

"I didn't see any movement in the trees, as if someone ran away when we approached," Greggory agreed. "Lord, but that old woman spooked me. She didn't even bother to look at my palm or read cards or anything before predicting doom."

"She must think she's a true clairvoyant."

"Do you believe in any of that?"

Ewan regarded the younger man. He had dark circles under his eyes, and he remembered that the missing Jacob was his cousin. "It is best not to believe. This is just the situation where charlatans can get a toehold, claiming they know how to find a missing child. And Jacob's father is dying as well. Now we'll get people who claim they can contact his shade for information."

"Is Matilda really going to marry him?"

"I think she will if she can find the time, but I think she should stay in Bristol. Something tells me Jacob is near. He could even be in a neighbor's house, not that we could ever get inside."

"Who would shelter Izabela?"

"Her lover, perhaps." Ewan shrugged. "Though who would want a flighty, inconstant, immoral girl like that?"

Greggory grinned. "You haven't seen Izabela. Even in shapeless nanny garb she's a stunner. Has the proverbial smile that could launch a thousand ships."

Ewan pursed his lips. "She could hang, you know, if the child is found dead and she is caught."

Greggory shuddered. "Let's go tell Matilda the bad news. Tomorrow we need to start over. If neither Bliven nor Majewski are responsible, who is?"

"We need another ransom note," Ewan stated. How else would they find another path through the situation?

Back at Majewski's *vardo*, the men collected Matilda and Mrs. Miller. They returned to their carriage, feeling the weight of the Gipsy's unhappy gaze on their backs.

"Did you think we'd find him there?" Greggory asked, staring pensively at the lantern that swung in the corner of the carriage.

"I am not thinking anymore," Matilda said. "It is too hard."

"At least we found Majewski. I can stop walking Bristol, searching for taverns and camps."

"Izabela's lover might be another Gipsy," Matilda said. "Who can say?"

Ewan watched Mrs. Miller. Expressions flitted across her face. Studiousness, confusion, recognition. She blinked hard, as if something had landed in her eye, but then her head turned.

"What?" he asked.

"I remember seeing a man in a fine suit pacing in front of the house the day before Jacob vanished," she said. "I thought he was waiting for Miss Redcake to return."

"But he wasn't?"

"No," Mrs. Miller said. "He was gone before Miss Redcake came, but now that I think about it, I didn't see him after Izabela took Jacob to the park."

"He was there late in the day?" Matilda asked.

"Late afternoon."

Matilda frowned. "I thought she took him at about eleven."

"Sometimes she took him twice, or I sent her out to do a bit of shopping. She's a sharper girl than Daisy, and when my rheumatism was acting up, well . . ." Mrs. Miller's hands fluttered above her skirts before settling again. Her head dropped. "I'll be giving you my notice, Miss Redcake."

"Not now you won't." Matilda's voice cut the air. "You are not going anywhere. I will keep my household together until my son returns. Who can say what any of us knows? Something small might bring Jacob home."

"Can you give us a description?" Ewan asked. "Of that man?"

Mrs. Miller stared at her hands. "Dark hair. But he had a hat on, of course, so I didn't see much of it. A neat beard. The clothing was nice, though. I recognize a bit of good tailoring when I see it. My husband was a tailor."

"Could you say what shop the suit came from?"

"Not a shop. Not ready made."

"Someone wealthy, then. Where would Izabela meet a wealthy man? Did you take her to parties, Miss Redcake?"

Matilda snorted. "Who would invite me? You're sure it isn't some man who lives nearby?"

"I've never seen him before or since," Mrs. Miller said.

By then, they were at the tavern. Greggory jumped down from the coach and consulted with Gawain and Sir Bartley, then came back. "No help there. We're all returning to the house now."

Ewan thought they must have all dozed on the dark drive back to the house. Every window of the four-story redbrick house blazed with light when they drove up, as if inviting the world to enter and tell their tales.

Everyone exited the carriage, but Matilda held back as her family and Mrs. Miller went inside. Then she turned to Ewan. "Let's walk."

"Where?"

"It doesn't matter, but I cannot go inside yet." She took a deep breath and let it out slowly.

"You haven't been well."

She slipped her hand around his arm. "You will keep me upright, Mr. Hales. I think I shall suffocate if I have to go in there again, listen to my mother flutter and worry about Rose's wedding, hear Gawain complain about how difficult the situation is with Jacob, wonder if I should be on the road to London to marry Mr. Bliven before it is too late."

"Don't marry him," Ewan said, squeezing her hand against his body.

"Why, Mr. Hales, one might think you care."

Chapter Nine

"I do care," Ewan said. "I care very much."

"Then walk with me. I cannot breathe inside my own house," Matilda said, with the confidential air of a confessor.

Would she swoon again, or cry, or completely break down? Should he take her away from her family right now? Then again, they were the source of much of her immediate frustration. No one was focused on her. How could they be, with a missing child and a new birth and a canceled wedding? He needed to take her mind off her worries for a few stolen moments.

He pulled her away. They walked two blocks, past houses similar in size and consequence to Matilda's own home. They were the kind of structures Ewan could never have hoped to obtain under his previous circumstances, though he supposed that now he would become accustomed to something even nicer. Someday he'd be going from rented rooms to Fitzwalter House in Mayfair, and country estates.

Matilda opened the gate to a private park, the same one where the dog had been found, the last place Jacob had been taken before he disappeared.

"I don't think we should come here," Ewan protested. "It will just make you sad."

"How can I be anything but?" Matilda asked, releasing his arm and sitting on a bench where the nannies waited while their charges played.

"You need a release from all the sorrow," he said. He stepped behind her and began to massage her neck. It was too intimate a gesture, and yet she held herself so stiffly that he couldn't resist. Beneath his gloves he could feel the taut lines of the muscles under her skin. He pulled off his gloves so he could touch her with his own flesh.

She moaned softly when he palpated a particularly sore spot on the left side. It sounded like the noise a woman might make during the act of love, and it made him harden against the cold iron back of the bench. He felt guilty and more alive all at once. Could this be the way to give her troubled thoughts a rest?

"My hotel is just across the square. It's too cold to sit here for long."

"The bench is damp besides," Matilda said, though she didn't move. Then, though, she slowly let her head drop back, to rest against his belly. Her hat brim protected her from actual contact with his coat, but it felt like a surrender.

He felt a surge of power. She trusted him. "Do you want to go to my room with me?" His cock swelled in agreement with the notion of taking her there.

"I could use some privacy. I shouldn't sit out here."

"No, it isn't wise," he agreed, continuing to rub his fingers in small deep circles on the sides of her neck.

She tilted her head from side to side, and he could hear crackling noises as she moved. So stiff, poor girl, so tense. He moved forward, and his swollen cock brushed the iron again. They could both use some stress relief. If she went to his room, would she know what that meant, to him at least?

Her head lifted from his belly as wind rustled the trees. A carriage passed in the street, and he could hear a dog yipping, and another dog answer. Something darted across the ground in front of them. He saw her shoulders move as she shuddered.

"A rat?"

"It might have been a squirrel. I was just thinking of Sir Barks being left here during the day, when anyone might have taken him, never seeing the note."

The truth being that the note might mean nothing or everything. They could only wait and see. He walked around the bench and held out his hand to her. "Come, Matilda."

She stood obediently enough but lifted her chin to him. "Matilda?"

"Am I being too intimate?" He took her gloved hand between his bare ones, then slid his hands up her arm until he grasped her securely. "I think of you as Matilda. My Matilda."

He let her go as she sighed, her entire body relaxing. "That's nice."

I would like to be someone's Matilda. I need an anchor. I'm so lost, Ewan."

"I know. Let me take care of you for a little while."

"I need that. I'm afraid I won't be able to go on if I can't rest. I can't eat. My entire body is betraying me."

He wrapped his arm around her shoulders, pulling her next to him as they went through the gate on the opposite side of the park, then walked down a block to the small hotel that was on the edge of the residential area. Empty and hushed, the streets seemed to be waiting for news. He hoped that news could wait for a while. His body hummed with awareness, with lust for the woman next to him. Could he make her forget her pain for a while?

The reception desk was empty as they walked in, and they were able to reach his small room on the second floor without anyone noticing them.

He shut the door and drew off his coat, then took off his hat and set it carefully on the table next to the door. He'd spent a lot of money on it, and it would be a long time before he lost the habit of parsimony.

Matilda didn't smile at him, or even look at him really, as she took off her own hat, coat, and gloves. Her hair was matted, as if she'd sweated under the hat for hours. Maybe she had. It had been a hard day. Underneath she wore a simple, severe gray skirt and coat, well-tailored to her curves, something she could take on and off herself.

She unbuttoned and removed her coat without looking at him. At a loss for words, he went to the window to close the curtain. Light from a streetlamp outside provided their only illumination, but he could drop money into the gas meter to bring the lights in the room to life.

He pulled the curtains shut and went to the meter box. Her hand came down on his arm.

"Leave it off. I like the dark."

His throat went dry. "Very well, Matilda." Enjoying saying her name, he fumbled with his coat, as if he had never undressed in the dark before, though he was used to the light of a single candle.

He heard her exhale. Could she possibly be as aroused as he was? Was she in the same dreamlike state as he? His hands went to his suspenders, but then he remembered he still wore his shoes. He sat on the edge of the small bed and removed them, then cast off the rest of his clothing. She made small rustling sounds. He wanted to peek, but it took all his focus just to get his own clothing off.

Concentrating on his own nudity, he was surprised to see only her skirt on the bed next to him. Patiently, he waited, hearing the whispers of fine fabric, his very soul aching with desire to touch her. How long had it been since he'd done this? Could he last more than a minute? What did she expect from him? Release, certainly, and he needed to provide it.

Finally, the soft sounds of her movements quieted, and he felt rather than saw her come to stand in front of him. His mind was in turmoil, so buried in lust, the scent of her body revealed as her clothes came off, that he could not think rationally. Her hands touched his shoulders, then left. He heard the sounds of fingers against skin and lifted his own hand, felt strands of her hair falling around her shoulders as she took out the pins.

"I love your hair." He kissed the flaming strands. The sweet scent of roses surrounded him as he buried his nose in the hair on her collarbone. It seemed to take a long time for her to find all the pins. Her hair covered her breasts, hanging to just below the small, full mounds. "I remember you used to seem larger in this area, though you were always slim."

Her hands went to her chest. "Bust improvers. Such a silly vanity."

He tugged her fingers from her soft flesh. "You have beautiful breasts. They need no improving."

She pushed her hair off her neck so that it drifted down her back. He lifted his head so she could free all the strands.

"I don't remember what I wanted three or four years ago. I am not the same person."

He wasn't sure he entirely agreed with that statement, but then, the Matilda Redcake of 1886 would not have undressed in Ewan Hales's hotel room. As he lifted his hands toward her breasts, she remained still, so he touched the soft, satiny flesh with his fingertips, then circled her nipples before brushing them. They hardened. He leaned forward and softly kissed each one. Bolder now, he parted her legs with his own foot and sank to his knees in front of her, next to the bed.

She gasped. "Oh. What?"

Wrapping his arms around her smooth, warm, naked hips, he buried his face in her soft, musky curls.

"Oh," she said again, as if in understanding.

He followed his desire down, using his lips and tongue to part the way to her inner secrets, oblivious to anything but the scent of her heat. Her pelvis canted toward him, welcoming and eager.

She let out a tiny shriek when his teeth closed over her pearl, already exposed for his delectation, but she didn't push him away, just wrapped her hands around the base of his skull and drew him in, letting him lave her and suckle her and circle her until her knees buckled.

"I want this," she panted. "Oh, Ewan, don't stop."

He had the presence of mind to turn her, then. She half-sat, half-fell against the bed, and then he could truly feast, licking up the nectar her arousal offered. He tested her with one finger, finding her shockingly tight, but as he drove her higher, she loosened enough for two. Sliding them both in, he blew warm air against her pearl, then sucked hard until she shattered a few seconds later.

She bowed on the bed, crying out and shuddering with tearful gasps of pleasure. He stood, almost staggering his one step to the bed, tugging her legs to turn her the long way, so he could mount her body. He didn't give her a chance to second-guess his actions, just climbed up, rubbing his torso along hers as he lifted himself above her, and notched his body to hers. His cock jerked, felt damp at the tip with his own fluids. Grabbing her hips to angle her properly, shaking with eagerness, he pushed the head of his cock into her creamy depths. Still panting, she seemed watchful but said nothing.

"Matilda?" The word was etched with lust, almost staccato.

She put her hands to his cheeks and brushed her index fingers in a circle around his temples, then rubbed her cheek against his chin. Sensing her approval, he slid home, easily, luxuriously, sweetly, until he could feel his sac against her skin. When he covered her mouth with his, he found her lips apart and willing to trade tastes. Her hands grabbed his back and slid lower when he pulled away, mouths still together, guiding him back inside her.

She moved her hands rather than her hips to urge him on, but her legs bent to cradle him, and eventually, she slid her inner thighs alongside the outsides of his legs. Squeaking when he took her thighs in his hands to open her wide, the sound turned to a gasp of pleasure as he moved even deeper inside her.

All too soon, he could feel the pressure building in him. His mouth moved from her lips to her neck, his hips bucking uncontrollably. He felt her clasp at his cock with a silken interior grip, and heard her hoarse cry as she came with him, beautifully, inexplicably, for he hadn't been a suave, experienced lover. Yet he had pleased them both.

His torso calmed over hers, feeling heavy even to him. His head relaxed onto the mattress, his mouth still on her neck. She moved her hips, as if testing to see if he was still hard. He was.

"Give me a second," he muttered. He kissed her throat, then canted his hips, feeling the ghostly aftershock of his orgasm as he pulled out of her. Tilting to his back, he slid his arm beneath her slim shoulders and pulled her to his side.

Her head fell against his shoulder and she molded herself against him. "I just wanted the world to stop."

"Did it?"

"It fell right off its axis for a few minutes."

"But?"

"But." She was silent for a moment, while he played with the strands of her hair. "I shouldn't have taken my hair down."

"I'll braid it for you. I think I can remember how to do it." He made a clumsy braid with the lower part of her hair.

"No, that's not how I had it before." She sat up abruptly and began to smooth the strands.

Sensing her mood change, he got up and started the lights, then found his comb. "Here, this will help."

She nodded. He sat on the single cane-bottomed chair in the room and watched her make her toilette, offering his assistance, silently, only when she turned her back to him so he could help her with her stays.

"I'll walk you back," he said, then realized he was still nude.

Matilda took the chair Ewan had just vacated while he dressed, staring at the powerful lines of his body. His lower body was particularly well-developed, with strong legs and a taut backside. For all the dark hair on his head, he didn't have that much body hair, just a light dusting around his pectoral muscles and a trail that led down to the soft nest around his manhood. This allowed all of his musculature to show, and his skin glowed golden in the gaslight.

"You must walk a great deal."

"Hansoms are expensive and I don't like buses," he said, buttoning his shirt.

She watched him, feeling empty and peaceful, a slight soreness between her legs, until he finished dressing. He put on his coat and hat, then held out her coat, reticule, and hat. He held her coat while she shrugged into it, then did the buttons while she stood like a child. She didn't want to think.

Thought returned when they reached the street. The wind blew through her clothing. The resulting shiver brought reality back. Where was Jacob? What if she had missed something while she was engaging in mindless passion with Ewan? How could he have taken a grief-stricken mother away from her home during a crisis of this magnitude? Was he a predator? He had already told her they could never marry, given his future title and her stained past. She knew for certain this lovemaking had not been a proposal. No, she'd learned that the hard way.

Oh God, what if she'd conceived another child? She keened softly, uncontrollably.

"Matilda? What is wrong?" Ewan wrapped his arm around her shoulders and pulled her close.

She found her strength again, pushing him away. "How could you?" she rasped. For the first time in her life, she sounded like her brother when he had been at his most broken and bitter. "How could you make me forget, even for a moment?"

He held up his hands. "What?"

She pointed a shaky finger at him. "I have no right to comfort while my son is missing. Stay away from me, Ewan Hales. Don't tempt me again." She turned away from him and made her way down the street.

When she heard footfalls, she knew he was following her, but she didn't have the energy to turn around and face him, and certainly didn't want to continue their confrontation so near her home. Just what she needed: further confirmation that she was a wanton slut.

She already felt like one; she didn't want to offer her family any proof. What had happened to her self-control? She didn't even have the excuse of bad advice this time. The mistake had been all her own fault.

When she reached her front gate, she turned back. He lifted his hand in farewell. When she put her hand on the gate's latch, he proceeded down the street.

Inside her house, all was quiet. Her family had gone to bed. No drama of any kind, but also no news. She could only hope tomorrow would change things. The fire had been lit in her bedroom and as she warmed, her mind quieted, like a landscape after a storm. She fell asleep easily, at first.

The next morning, she still felt groggy as Daisy helped her dress. She had tossed and turned after midnight, unable to shake the horrible realization that Jacob had been gone almost a week. If neither Jacob's father nor the Gipsy horse trader were responsible, who was? Who was Izabela's lover?

Downstairs, she poured coffee from the pot and stared at the rack of toast. She needed to eat so that she had the strength to search for Jacob. Her father had aged a decade in the past few days, and even her mother's serene face was unusually lined. Ewan had not appeared. Had she chased him off for good? Gawain sat in an armchair, staring at the ransom note as if some clue remained to be found.

She took a bite of toast, the eggs smelling too sulfurous to touch, and the sausages seemed off, though surely Mrs. Miller would never allow it, and went to lean over Gawain's shoulder.

" 'i am rite you want yer baby. You goin to pay for the littl one. 5000 pounds,' " she read.

"I think it's a fake," Gawain said.

"What do you mean?"

Gawain's wife, Ann, dropped her knitting and leaned forward in the chair on the opposite side of the fireplace.

"The first letter of the first sentence isn't capitalized but the second is. See?" He waved the paper at Matilda.

"What does that prove?"

"They are trying to make themselves sound more ignorant than they really are," Gawain said. "Probably someone with more education than it seems."

"I don't see how that helps us. Both Mr. Bliven and Mr. Majewski are intelligent men."

"Yes, but we can safely rule them out anyway. Tell me, is Izabela literate?"

"Of course," Matilda said. "I've never seen her handwriting, but she read stories to Jacob and consulted Mrs. Beeton's book, read shopping lists."

Gawain made a noise and returned to staring. Ann resumed her knitting.

"Have some more toast, dear," her mother said. "You should try some of the lemon curd. It's from Hatbrook's farm."

"It doesn't matter," Matilda muttered. While normally it behooved all of the family to stock and use a relative's various products, she couldn't care less at the moment who had made the lemon curd. She didn't even want to eat the bloody lemon curd.

Mrs. Miller came into the room. If Sir Bartley had aged ten years, the housekeeper had aged twenty overnight. She looked ready to be packed off to a small cottage in the country.

"Your sister is here, Miss Redcake, with Mr. Courtnay."

Sir Bartley's head came up. "Good, another cool mind on the case."

Matilda's two bites of toast lurched in her stomach. She didn't want to see her happy sister, nor have to feel guilty again about the ruined wedding. Her father, on the other hand, heartily approved of Rupert Courtnay.

Mrs. Miller nodded. "I shall send them in to the breakfast room, then?"

"Must have left Liverpool very early. Probably drove one of Lewis's horseless carriages," Gawain said.

"Yes, Courtnay did say he'd just acquired one," Sir Bartley remarked.

The door opened and Rose bounded in. Normally a rather languorous girl, courtesy of her lung issues, she did not bound, or have pink cheeks. Yet Matilda saw her sister transformed.

Behind her stood the solid, graying form of Rupert Courtnay. A bit mysterious, he nonetheless had the charm to find himself in the lower rank of aristocratic circles. Matilda had thought that Rose took him on not to be a spinster, but as she saw her sister's beaming face now, she would have believed it a love match.

Rose pulled off her gloves and held out her hand. On it was an ornate gold ring. A wedding ring.

Matilda reached for a chair and half-fell into it as her mother pushed her chair back and rushed her youngest child.

"You married without us?" her mother asked.

Rose nodded. "I'm sorry, but I could not wait a day longer." She smiled shyly at her new husband. "Forgive us. We could not make it a ceremony, but at least this way I could talk Rupert into taking the week as we had planned for our honeymoon trip and return to Bristol."

"Are you staying here?" Matilda realized she'd spoken much too loudly when Ann stared at her.

Rose waved her hands. "I cannot imagine there is room under the circumstances. No, we went to a hotel. Mr. Hales is staying there as well. He said he would be here directly."

"Why?" Sir Bartley asked. "Doesn't he have his new duties in London?"

Gawain narrowed his eyes at Matilda, then shared a glance with his wife. Matilda didn't like the direction her brother's thoughts were heading. He saw too much with that brilliant cynic's mind of his. "No doubt he wants to help."

Rupert Courtnay cleared his throat. "I understand there has been a ransom note?"

"On Friday," Gawain confirmed. "I have it here. Let's go out on the terrace so you can see it in the light."

Mrs. Miller reentered the room, followed by Ewan. Matilda was thunderstruck. Her housekeeper hadn't even announced him, or asked permission. What, was he a member of the family now?

Gawain nodded at Ewan, and he followed her brother and Rupert out of the room with scarcely a glance at her. Matilda dropped her forehead into her palm, while Rose took a chair next to where their mother had been sitting. Her beautiful blond mother and beautiful blond sister all but touched heads as Rose shared the details of her simple ceremony in a hushed tone.

Within two minutes Matilda was ready to explode. She pushed her chair back and rushed from the room. Climbing the stairs, she went to Izabela's room and began to tear it apart.

"It would be best to be methodical," came her father's voice from the doorway. He breathed hard from his climb up the staircase. "Let me help you, Matilda."

She turned to her father. Saw his red hair rapidly going white, what was left of it, his homely face that she had mostly inherited, and all but fell into his arms, gasping with unshed tears.

* * *

Ewan leaned on the balustrade around the terrace, listening as Gawain and his new brother-in-law took the ransom note apart and put it back together again. He frowned when he saw Rupert Courtnay rubbing his fingers together after he had held the note. Was there a substance on it?

"What are you doing with your fingers?" he asked.

Rupert glanced at his hand. "Some kind of powder?"

Ewan bent his head over the note and sniffed. "Well, I'll be. Do you smell chalk?"

Gawain stared at him as Rupert smelled his fingers. "I think your friend is right."

Gawain narrowed his eyes, his damaged skin wrinkling around the network of white scars. "Chalk," he muttered.

"The adulterant in the flour," Ewan said, feeling sick.

"You think Douglas Flour had something to do with this?" Gawain asked.

"More likely that Matilda handled this, or Greggory did, after messing with a flour sample," Ewan said.

Gawain rubbed his chin. "I don't think Greggory has ever touched the note."

"Did Matilda?"

"She is more likely to have done so, but I don't think she did. It's an evil talisman to her, you understand."

"I'm not sure who you are," Rupert said, turning to Ewan.

"I was Sir Bartley's secretary in London," Ewan said. "Then Lord Judah's, but now I am the regional director of Douglas Industries."

"Maybe you are behind the kidnapping," Rupert said, his stolid face betraying nothing.

Gawain grinned. "All this to get Matilda's attention? She'd be more likely to kill him when she found out. This is, after all, the sister who refused to marry the father of her illegitimate child when she had the opportunity."

"Ah. You are courting her?"

"It's no laughing matter," Ewan said quietly. "I do want to marry Matilda, even though she won't believe me after the things I've said in the past."

"Whatever do you mean?" Gawain asked.

"I told her that I, the heir of an earl, could not marry her. But you know, I feel that I must. Who says I need to be in Society? I am engaged in trade. I don't have a proper upbringing. Who can blame me for marrying where I will?"

"Marrying money," Rupert said. "No one blames any aristocrat for that, these days. Not enough money in land."

Gawain bared his teeth and chuckled. "Matilda a countess? I love it. I'll throw in my support."

"Thank you," Ewan said, taking his proffered hand. "And the earl is strapped for cash, I understand. But we've got to find Jacob. She won't be able to move forward otherwise. That's where all this nonsense about marrying Bliven came in. She's desperately unfocused."

Gawain nodded. "I agree with you. You can't turn her head with romance now. Let's verify she never touched the note."

"Walk me through the circumstances of it," Rupert said.

Behind them, the French doors opened, and Daisy walked out with a tray containing a coffeepot and cups. "It's chilly out here."

"Thank you," Gawain said. "Put it on the table there."

Daisy curtseyed after she had obeyed and left. Ewan went to pour the beverage while Gawain spoke.

"It was rolled up and pushed between the neck and the collar of Sir Barks, Jacob's puppy. Ought to have smelled like dog, rather than chalk," Gawain mused.

"I think chalk was rubbed into the paper. Maybe the lotion on my skin extracted some of it. Rose is insisting I treat a mild skin condition I have with some potion of hers."

The man seemed faintly embarrassed at this display of wifely love.

Gawain nodded. "She has learned everything my mother knows about treating her lung condition, then branched into other remedies. She loves to make beauty treatments. Something to do in the country."

"I don't mind," Rupert said, almost dreamily. "It doesn't smell bad."

Ewan cleared his throat and passed out the steaming coffee. Gawain took his cup and said, "I held it. It went into a cabinet for the night, on top of a tea service in the breakfast room. I have no idea why I left it there. Yes, we've had it for a few days now, but we could look at it in the cabinet, you see. I didn't take it out again until last night. Now that you mention it, I did see a streak on the paper."

"Chalk?" Rupert asked.

Gawain shrugged. "I suppose. What do we do with that information?"

"I think you should ring the factory and ask Greggory if he touched it," Ewan said.

"And speak to Matilda. Do you want to do that?"

Ewan nodded. They left the coffee tray outdoors and went inside to the telephone room, standing around Gawain as he spoke to Greggory, who verified he had never touched the note.

"Can I speak to Mr. Hales?" Ewan heard Greggory ask.

Gawain handed him the earpiece.

"I understand you've taken over management of Douglas Flour," Greggory said.

"True," Ewan said.

"Are you aware of their warehouse here in Bristol? I didn't know it existed until the manager at Bristol Flour told me."

"It wouldn't have been important. We found chalk in the flour in the London facility."

"I know, but what if someone at Douglas Flour is out to attack the Redcakes? Could they have both ruined the flour and taken Jacob? What if he is in their warehouse here in the city?" Greggory asked, his voice betraying nervous excitement.

Chapter Ten

Ewan wished he'd had his cards ready, but a telephone call from Corwin Vare in Southwark to the nondescript Bristol warehouse belonging to Douglas Industries took care of his bona fides. The local manager, Albert Pigge, had done his best to make Ewan feel unwelcome by placing him in the lower, visitor chair in front of his imposing desk. Ewan made a mental note to check the finances of this warehouse to see if Pigge deserved such an elaborate personal setup. He doubted it, given the utilitarian nature of the Southwark branch. "I was not aware your office even existed, Mr. Pigge."

"Mr. Vare prefers to forget any other part of England exists, Mr. Hales," Pigge said with a snort. The rotund manager hooked his fingers around the armpits of his purple velvet waistcoat, exposing old sweat stains.

"You report to Mr. Vare?"

"Yes, sir, I do."

"Why does the flour for the Redcake's factories come in from London, rather than from your establishment?"

"We mostly deal in rye flour," Pigge said. "We do old-fashioned stone-grinding here."

"So you have nothing to do with Redcake's, then?" He thought he might have wasted a meeting for Jacob's sake. Meeting Pigge was useful for his own new position, though.

"Not here in Bristol, but we do ship down to the London Redcake's. The bakery makes a drop scone with our flour and maple syrup. You knew about Douglas Maple Syrup?"

Ewan shook his head. "Does that fall under my purview, do you think?"

"Oh, yes." Pigge leaned forward, giving Ewan a good view of the man's untrimmed nose hair. "Tapped in Vermont, you know. Very interesting business. Wouldn't mind spending some time in the United States myself."

"I shall keep that in mind. Tell me, who is in charge of that?"

Pigge spoke for twenty minutes on the subject of his favorite part of the business before winding down. Ewan thought he looked too slender for both his overlarge head and his animal appetites.

Eventually, Pigge shook his head. "Still, I'd be sorry to leave Bristol. Land of my ancestors and all that. But the crime, sir." He shook his head mournfully. "Why, that business with Jacob Redcake just sets your hair on fire, don't it?"

"Jacob Bliven," Ewan said, his interest aroused.

"Oh, right, he has the father's name?" Pigge tsked.

"Miss Redcake had hoped to marry the boy's father, and he desires it as well, naturally, but he's on his deathbed. Such difficulties they've had, you know, with his travel to India."

Pigge snorted. "You don't say. Well, that explains the boy's surname, then, if the father has had some involvement."

"Sir Gawain attempted to get them a special license," Ewan confided. "But now it appears to be too late, with the kidnapping. Miss Redcake can't leave Bristol, you see."

Pigge's eyes widened. "Oh, yes, I do see. Such a tragic tale."

Ewan leaned forward, mimicking Pigge. "Tell me, how did you learn about Jacob? I thought the family was keeping the tragedy very quiet."

"Well, you know, sir." Pigge bared his teeth.

"Yes, because I was still employed by the family a week ago," Ewan pointed out.

"It's local gossip, sir. You can't expect a leading family to be running about Gipsy camps and the like without word getting out."

"So you didn't hear anything beyond servants' gossip, then?"

"I shouldn't think so. I do wonder who is trying to destroy the family. First the flour and now the child. Does someone want the family out of Bristol for good? You know, there was a great deal of resentment when old Sir Bartley moved the family to London, a great deal." Pigge smacked his lips.

"Many years ago now. It's been what, at least six years."

Pigge shrugged. "Couldn't say. Now, if you'll excuse me, I always walk the floor about this time. Keeps the workers in line."

"And you get your exercise," Ewan said with a nod. "An excellent notion."

As Pigge stood, his chest puffed. "Thank you, sir. A pleasure to make your acquaintance. And please keep Vermont in mind."

"I will." Ewan stood as well, wondering just how he could discern how disliked the Redcakes were in Bristol, and who their enemies were. It seemed the flour adulteration and Jacob's kidnapping might be linked. Except the flour problem had originated in London.

Matilda felt too agitated to sit, so she'd spent a fair amount of the day pacing around her home. Greggory had been by with a great deal of paperwork to go over. She'd signed the documents without really looking at them. How long had it been since she'd visited the factory or her office? She couldn't find the energy to care. Everything showed on her cousin's face, so if there had been anything important to do she'd have known by his expression.

Her father had paced with her at times, not complaining about her lack of attention to the business, while her mother sat in front of the fire, remarking on a chill that was not actually in the air.

The desolate peace of the parlor was disturbed when Gawain and Ann entered the room at teatime. Her brother slapped a sheaf of papers on the piecrust table at the side of one sofa.

"Your special license," he announced. "If you still want to marry Bliven."

Matilda stopped on the rug in front of the window. Hadn't she called Gawain off? Perhaps not.

"Why wouldn't I want to marry him?" she said, picking up the papers to peruse them. She had dreamed that if she married Theodore, a knock would come at the door and Jacob would be there. Why couldn't she shake the notion that marrying his father would save her child?

"You might want to marry Ewan Hales," Gawain said.

"What?" her father said. Her mother glanced up from the afghan she was worrying between her paint-stained fingers. Not that she had touched a paintbrush since she'd arrived.

"He has indicated he is willing," Gawain said. "He'll be Fitzwalter someday. It's an excellent match. Almost as brilliant as Alys's marriage, and very unexpected for you, Matilda."

"I don't understand," she said.

"Mr. Hales had a chat with Gawain," Ann said in a slow, patient voice. Normally, her voice was quite musical, but Matilda knew she had another style that she used for talking to the patients she sometimes saw in her role as an Indian healer.

Matilda chuckled. A fallen woman, nearly past her youth, with a two-year-old son, had two eligible suitors? Of course, one was dying and the other had recently been her family's employee, but still. How droll. She giggled.

Gawain frowned in her direction, then put his hand on their father's shoulder and bent to speak in the older man's ear. Matilda wondered what he was saying. An instruction to talk Matilda into one suitor or the other, given the fact that she wasn't doing anything to run the factories lately? She laughed again.

Her life had fallen apart, despite having worked so hard to rebuild it after Jacob had been weaned. Suddenly, all that effort seemed the silliest of pastimes. Who had she been kidding? Life had been bound to punish her for those sins. Lady Bricker, whose bad advice on how to obtain a proposal from Theodore Bliven, had helped put her on her path in the first place, had lost her first child to a stillbirth and hadn't conceived again. For a long time it seemed that Matilda had been so lucky; blessed, really. And now, all ashes. Her child gone and her brother conspiring with her father to take her position away.

She found it nothing but funny. She started to laugh, hard enough that she'd have bent at the waist if her tight stays hadn't prevented her. Light-headed from the effort of breathing, she reached for the mantelpiece for balance, then stumbled.

Hands caught her under her arms. She muttered a protest. Her vision failed.

Sometime later, she found herself blinking on the sofa, concerned faces staring down at her.

"You fainted," Ann said kindly, her large dark eyes fixed on Matilda's wrist, where she was checking her pulse. "Have you been eating, Matilda?"

She just giggled, a hollow sound this time.

Ann glanced over her shoulder. "Some poppy syrup, I think, to help her rest, then beef tea."

Matilda attempted to keep her giggles to herself while people moved around, speaking outside of her hearing. She didn't attempt to rise. What was the point?

Eventually, Mrs. Miller came with a little cup full of some brownish fluid and a piece of toast. Ann insisted she drink, then chase the foul stuff with a bite of toast. Eventually, the giggles stopped and her thoughts, hazy and convoluted though they had been, faded into nothing.

That evening, Ewan sat in his hotel's front parlor, reading the local newspapers, which were piled, edition after edition, on a table. He hadn't been invited to Matilda's home or indeed heard anything from the family. Why was he here if they wouldn't let him help? He had expected to hear from Gawain. At least he'd put in a day's work at the warehouse, reviewing the books.

He flipped through the paper, checking advertisements, and then returned to the front page. On page three, something finally caught his attention: the Redcake name.

He frowned as he read the article. It appeared that Redcake's had been buying up wheat fields. Odd, when he didn't think they had any flour factories, but maybe that was next on Matilda's list. She must have been planning to eventually cut ties with Douglas Flour as a supplier, just as the London bakery had. Had one of his subordinates decided to punish her for that decision by adulterating the flour, thereby destroying her business before she could ever use her wheat?

How did Jacob's disappearance fit into this?

He threw down the paper and ran his fingers through his hair, then went to the window. It was full dark out now, much too late to make any use of this information. Why hadn't Matilda told him about buying the farms? He supposed the kidnapping had come so fast after the flour problem that she hadn't thought the possibilities through before being distracted.

He had to wonder, though. Could Jacob be imprisoned in a Douglas Industries building? If he was even alive.

Ewan went directly to the Redcake home after breakfast the next morning. Much too early for a call, but he didn't care. They needed to take some action, and he wanted to be involved.

"She isn't well," Mrs. Miller confided in the front hall.

"What do you mean?" Ewan asked.

"Sir Gawain's wife is keeping a close eye on her. She went a bit hysterical yesterday."

"How can that be a surprise? She's lost her child." He handed her his gloves.

"It became worse, Mr. Hales. I'm not sure what was going on, but Sir Gawain bustled out of the parlor late in the day, demanding I bring the poppy syrup. I think the poor lamb had fainted."

Ewan frowned. "The last thing a fainting woman needs is poppy syrup."

Mrs. Miller sighed. "Lady Redcake is all but a physician. She must know best."

"Maybe last night, Mrs. Miller, but not now. I have discovered some new information and I must see Miss Redcake."

Ewan looked up as he heard footsteps on the stairs. Sir Bartley came down. Ewan nodded his head respectfully, then plowed forward.

"Did you know about the wheat fields, sir? That Matilda was buying up local farms?"

Sir Bartley glanced up at the ceiling. "I am not involved in the operations anymore."

"This is long-term planning, sir. If her suppliers thought she was going to cut them out of business, they might have taken action."

"Like Douglas adulterating our flour."

"And taking Jacob to distract her," Ewan said.

The cast of Sir Bartley's mouth became grim. "Who knew about this?"

"I was looking through a weekly paper last night. A local. The news was a couple of weeks old."

Sir Bartley nodded. "Anyone would have known, then. I'll speak to Matilda."

"I'd like to talk to her myself. I'm working for Douglas now. I need to understand, so I can reassure my people. A word in the right ear might make all of these problems go away."

"You can't see my daughter. She's in Ann's care."

Ewan stared his former employer directly in the eye. "I have to insist, sir. The situation is much too important. I cannot imagine your daughter not wanting to explain herself if it will help her cause."

Sir Bartley shook his head, then pointed a gnarled finger toward the stairs. Ewan nodded, then went up. Social niceties didn't matter much to him right then.

He went to the door that led to a bedroom over the front of the house. It appeared to be the best room, so he knocked, then entered. The room's decorations were an older style, some kind of busy, red-and-black–patterned wallpaper, red velvet drapes, dark heavy furniture.

A log cracked loudly in the fireplace, the noise drawing his attention to the armchair pulled in front of the fire. There sat his Matilda, in a dressing gown, an afghan of riotous blues and oranges pulled over her lap. She clashed terribly with the room, between her copper hair, her blue wrapper, and the afghan.

"You don't belong here." He'd spoken aloud before he meant to, but his lover scarcely moved her head. Frowning, he went to her and knelt at her side. Her eyelids weren't closed precisely, but they weren't open either. When he put his hand on hers he felt cool skin. He reached for her wrist and felt her pulse. He didn't know exactly what he was feeling for, but when he tried his own, he found it much stronger. Was that the difference between a man and a woman, or was hers more subdued than it ought to be?

"Matilda," he said, rubbing the afghan over her right thigh. "Matilda, I need you to pay attention to me."

Her head tilted at a strange angle. She licked her lower lip, very slowly.

"Matilda, it's Ewan. In your bedroom."

She blinked, her eyelids stopping again at half-mast.

"I'd like to ravish you," he said in a conversational tone.

She didn't respond.

He pulled the afghan off her lap, then put his hands on each wrist. "Come, we need to get you moving."

She made a sound of inarticulate protest as he pulled her to her feet. Her knees buckled slightly, and he put one leg between hers, attempting to shore her up.

"Oh, sweetheart, this isn't good. You need to stand up for yourself, refuse the medication. Did they dose you with laudanum?"

"Poppy s-s-syrup," she slurred. "After I fainted."

"Have you eaten anything?"

"Toast, yesterday. Toast after every dose." She giggled.

He realized Gawain probably hadn't been exaggerating about her hysteria the day before. She might be stronger than most women, but she wasn't immune to the stresses she was under. And where had he been? At the hotel, sulking over old newspapers.

That thought reminded him of his purpose. He gave her a little shake. Her eyes opened, but her eyes didn't seem to be focusing. He tugged her through the room to the window and pulled back the heavy curtains, then unlatched the window, letting in fresh air.

"Breathe deeply; it will help you come back to yourself. Do you know when that woman last dosed you?"

"She was trying to help."

Ewan looked at his lover's slowly blinking eyes and felt savage. "How dare she? I won't have her or anyone else do this to you."

"You aren't in charge here."

"Neither are you."

She smiled sleepily. "Then who is? My father?"

"I'd say it's Sir Gawain's wife. And who is she?"

"A princess's daughter. A healer to Queen Victoria herself."

"The queen hasn't done anything worth noting since Prince Albert died," Ewan said with a sneer. "That doesn't impress me. She might spend all day dosed with poppy syrup, for all I know."

"Ewan." Her tone was too soft, but he understood her censure.

"Yes, that's my name, and thank you for remembering," he snapped. "Look, I read that you've been buying up wheat fields. Is that true?"

"Land is still cheap," she mumbled. "I bought a couple of farms. The owners had died and the children were looking to sell."

"Are you going to buy up flour mills next?"

"I think there is a small one on one of the properties," she said slowly. "Why?"

He gripped her upper arms, forcing her to look at him. A gust of cold air breezed between them, making them both blink. "Because that might be the motive we've been looking for. The adulterated flour, Jacob's kidnapping. Maybe this is all about business, trying to destroy Redcake's over the wheat farms."

"What? Why?" Matilda's head went loose on her neck again.

"Why not?" Ewan demanded. "I'm irritated, and I only just took over Douglas. Why would the Redcakes buy wheat farms if they weren't looking to make their own flour? And London is buying elsewhere, at least experimentally."

"I don't know what I'm planning to do. I merely purchased the land at an excellent price. Greggory's younger brother Dudley is writing me a report about what I really purchased. He is interested in farming."

He turned her to the window and let her breathe in the crisp air with its hint of spring buds for a couple of moments. "You bought the farms to keep a cousin occupied?"

"Yes," she said softly. "Dudley doesn't like the factories. Why are you here in my bedroom?"

"The manager at Douglas's local warehouse, Albert Pigge, knew Jacob was missing."

That snapped her attention into focus. "We've kept it all quiet. With Izabela being involved, even the servants are too frightened to gossip. I'm sure of it."

"Then how did Pigge know?"

Matilda breathed hard for a moment. Color swept over her cheeks, then faded again. "I'd like to know the answer to that."

Then, as he held her arms, her knees buckled again. He caught her in his arms and carried her to the bed. When she was safe on her velvet coverlet, he found a bottle of eau de cologne on her dressing table and soaked a handkerchief in it, then pulled the bell pull in the corner.

He touched the handkerchief to her temples and wrists.

"I hate that scent," she murmured.

Mrs. Miller came into the room.

"She nearly collapsed," Ewan reported. "She needs proper food, and no more of that damned medicine."

"Yes, sir," Mrs. Miller said. "I quite agree."

"I'm going to confront Sir Gawain and his wife now," he said. "I trust you to take care of Miss Redcake."

"I can't follow your orders, sir," she protested.

"You can soon enough. I'm going to marry your mistress." Ewan fixed the housekeeper with a purposeful glare. "I'm going to be an earl someday. I'll outrank them all in the end. It would be best to stay on my good side."

"Yes, sir. I'll do whatever you wish, as long as you bring Master Jacob back safely to us." The housekeeper's eyes glittered with tears.

In that moment, Ewan lost his anger. But after the grief came wrath. He would fix this, fix Gawain and his bloody wife, and this entire damned mess. He'd beat the truth out of Pigge if he had to, but first he needed to see if the earl himself was involved. And he'd best tell the man he was getting married.

When he reached the parlor, he found Sir Bartley inside, along with Gawain and his wife. From Gawain's wretched expression, he knew his former employer had just finished sharing the news about the farms.

"Would the earl truly be so vindictive?" Gawain turned to Ewan. "When did he learn that his heir was employed by the Redcake family?"

Ewan winced. He hadn't thought of that angle. "I cannot say, but I do not find that relevant. Besides, I do not believe the earl is that involved in the day-to-day workings of one aspect of his empire."

"So you think all of this has been concocted by some underling?"

"I aim to go to London and find out. I will telephone the earl's solicitor and have an interview as soon as I arrive. Perhaps I can shake something loose."

"An explanation," Ann said.

"My grandson," Sir Bartley added, his bushy eyebrows coalescing into one gingery unit.

"It isn't going to be so simple," Gawain said.

"What will be simple is aiding Matilda in returning to reason," Ewan said. "I cannot understand why you are dosing her with poppy syrup, madam, but it must end."

"It was a temporary measure, I assure you," Gawain's exotic wife said.

"See that it doesn't happen again."

"Who are you to order around my wife?" Gawain snapped. "You aren't an earl yet."

"I am going to marry your sister," Ewan said. "It is clear that she needs my support."

"I have a special license that says she is going to marry Bliven," Gawain countered.

"Is it possible to change the name to mine?"

"Certainly not."

"Fine. Then I shall acquire my own." Ewan went to the table where the papers lay and snatched up the special license. "Bliven cannot help her now and Matilda knows that."

"Do you think there is any chance poor little Jacob is still alive?" Ann asked.

Ewan pressed his lips together. When he caught Sir Bartley's eye, he saw true pain in the face of his former employer. "I will be proud to marry Matilda under any eventuality."

"She will keep her position?" Sir Bartley asked in a low voice.

"I will not have the time to assume her duties," Ewan said. "But when I become earl, she will have to move on. You had best plan for a successor."

"She might not want to marry you," Ann said. "After what she has been through with men."

"Just one man," Ewan said. "Not me. You will see when she is restored. Do you have any medications to help her that will not put her into a stupor?"

"A pot of tea and a good meal is what she needs now. And her son back."

Ewan closed his eyes for a moment. Her son back. Yes, Matilda certainly needed that. But while he could give her his name—and needed to, because he had bedded her—he could not give her the child back. If only it were that easy.

That evening, Ewan sat in Shadrach Norwich's office. The earl had agreed to meet him there. He had dragged Norwich from his office to help him straighten out the mess with the special license and now had one with his name and Matilda's, not Bliven's. Norwich had taken a copious gulp from his brown bottle upon their return and now dozed in his chair. The earl was late.

As Ewan fingered the rustling papers in his coat, the door opened behind him and the earl appeared in the doorway. Norwich blinked and stood. Ewan followed his lead.

The earl gestured for them both to sit and took the chair next to Ewan. "Explain yourself, sir. I expected you to be taking up the reins of Douglas Industries, counter to my original plans, not gallivanting about in train stations, visiting the Redcakes."

"I severed my employment with them, my lord, on schedule. I had my initial meetings here, but then discovered we had a warehouse in Bristol."

"Why is that so important?"

Did the earl know nothing about his company? "Because we are having trouble with Redcake's, which you must know is an important customer of Douglas Flour. There is a lot of money involved. And we are in danger of losing that business. I am unsure of the sequence of events."

"What events?" the earl asked in a bored voice. He flicked a speck of ash off the checked sleeve of his coat.

"The London bakery is experimenting with new suppliers. We have sent adulterated goods to Redcake's. I have also learned that the Redcakes have bought wheat farms. I do wonder if the flour was adulterated in retaliation for Redcake's appearing to plan to cut us out of their supply chain."

"Are they?"

"I do not know. Miss Redcake has been distraught over the kidnapping of her son."

"I see." The earl tapped his chin with a long bony finger.

"I have a plan," Ewan said.

"You do?" Norwich leaned forward, almost knocking over his bottle.

"Yes. I'm going to marry Matilda Redcake," Ewan announced. He thought to appeal to the earl's self-interest. He could secure his own heir and marry a wealthy woman. "That will keep our most valuable customer in line. We'll have to fix the problems that led to the adulteration, whatever that might be, of course."

The earl sat upright, his voice rising in a thunderous roar. "You will not marry that . . . that loose daughter of a tradesman!"

Chapter Eleven

"I will not see you sullying the line of the Fitzwalters with such a woman. Why, we are descended from Charles II," the earl snapped.

"One of the bastards," Norwich said, the contents of the brown bottle clearly warring with his common sense.

The earl snarled. Norwich giggled once, sharply, then subsided.

Ewan ignored the comments and the absurdity. "I need to marry her."

"Why?" the earl asked, nearly as loudly as before.

"I have compromised her." He crossed his arms over his chest.

The earl snorted, then coughed for a minute before he recovered. "You, sir, are a fool, as was your father before you. She was already compromised. You can't compromise a woman twice."

That made no sense to him. "She could be carrying my child."

"Then she's carrying your bastard, just like the bastard she carried before. Not my concern." The earl licked a trace of spittle from his lips.

"Her sister is a marchioness," Ewan said. "She has good connections. Her father and brother have been knighted. Her sister-in-law is descended from Indian royalty and her youngest sister just married Rupert Courtnay, the dye manufacturer whose daughter married the inventor Lewis Noble."

The earl sniffed. "The Redcakes have done well for themselves on the marriage mart, I'll give you that. But I won't have you marrying a whore."

Ewan stiffened. "I assure you she is not that. She's a good woman, and I take full responsibility for compromising her when she was distraught."

"She should marry the father of her child."

"She had planned to. She even had the special license, but I had it changed to my name. I'm going back to Bristol in the morning to marry her."

"If you do so, I will cut you off," the earl said. "I will not allow it."

He changed tactics, preferring the offensive. "Did you tell the flour factory to give the Redcakes an adulterated product?"

"Of course not. I'm not that involved. I didn't even know the Redcakes were buying land. Even so, they might want to use our mills. We might still do business with them." The earl ground his teeth. "I understand that much."

Ewan appraised him. His great-uncle had a temper. Was he liable to act on it, or just use words? "What about little Jacob? Did you have anything to do with the kidnapping?"

"Certainly not." The earl drew himself up. "I could have assumed a Walter would be the sentimental sort. The last thing I would have done was create unnecessary romance in the Redcake family just as I was moving you into position as my heir."

He ignored the insult. "So their misfortune has nothing to do with you."

The earl shook his head.

He attempted to assess the man's innocence. "That doesn't mean that the business has nothing to do with it, however. If you aren't particularly engaged, others are taking all the responsibility."

The earl stood. "That's your responsibility now. You asked for it."

"I'm going back to Bristol to marry Miss Redcake."

The earl puffed out his chest and stared across the desk. "Norwich, take a memo."

The solicitor blinked. "I'll get a clerk."

"No, you do it."

Norwich sighed and pulled a piece of paper and a pencil from his desk. "Yes, my lord?"

"To the managers of Douglas Industries: Ewan Hales is no longer the managing director. Return to your previous chain of command. That is all." The earl put one ankle across the other and neatly pivoted, then walked out of the room, slamming the door behind him.

Ewan leaned back in his chair, stunned. Of course he should have seen the threat coming, but he'd thought the earl, as a gentleman, would have understood that he'd compromised a vulnerable woman and owed her marriage.

Now, he was unemployed. And he'd used up much of his savings bribing the clerk to alter the special license. What was he going to live on?

The next morning, Daisy trotted into the parlor, looking quite flushed. "A note for you, Miss Redcake."

Matilda had been dozing in an armchair by the fire with Ann at her side. Gawain's wife was taking her pulse and muttering to herself, something about adverse reactions.

"Give it here," Gawain said, snatching the note from the maid.

Matilda wanted to snap at him but couldn't find the energy. Ann released her hand and poured yet another cup of tea. She'd sworn tea would counteract the poppy syrup eventually.

"It's another ransom note," Gawain reported.

Sir Bartley rose from the sofa and went to the window with Gawain. As Matilda struggled to alertness, he bent over the note. "Any smell of chalk this time?"

Gawain sniffed, then frowned. "No. Here, I'll read it aloud. 'you must want yer baby something bad. He crying for you. You goin to pay for the littl one. 5000 pounds in the park at dusk. Come alone, Matilda Redcake.' "

"Tonight?" Sir Bartley frowned. "Good thing we have the money sorted."

"I don't like this," Ann said. "There's nothing about where to put the money. Or what to put it in. She's meant to meet someone."

"I'm not sending my daughter into that park in the dark to meet some blackguard," Sir Bartley said stoutly.

"Of course not," Matilda's mother said. She went to her husband and patted his arm, looking frail and stooped. She'd aged a year for every one of the nine days Jacob had been missing.

Matilda tried to push the gray fog, the torpor, out of the forefront of her brain and into some dusty back corner. She needed to focus. "We know it is a note from the same person, at least. Some of the same wording. The same amount, the same park where Sir Barks was found."

Gawain nodded. "Good points, Matilda."

The door opened, and Matilda saw Ewan enter the room. He looked exhausted, too, careworn. His shoes were scuffed and his coat had dark stains. Why hadn't Mrs. Miller removed his coat? He still wore his hat as well. He needed a woman's care, and far fewer trips on the train. She wanted to smooth that hair off his brow, force it back into the tidy slickness, and return him to his office at Redcake's Tea Shop. Turn back time, basically, to the moment they had kissed and none of this had happened yet.

She rose, trying to ignore her weak limbs. The maid was still standing just inside the door, riveted by the new ransom note. "Daisy, please take Mr. Hales's things and fetch us some sandwiches and fresh water for the tea."

The maid bobbed a curtsy and helped him with his coat. Ewan frowned at the girl as he handed her his hat, then stared at Matilda. She felt the force of his gaze.

"What took you to London? I didn't hear the details."

"I wanted to speak to the earl. The end result, before you have to ask, is that I am no longer regional director of Douglas Industries."

"He's going to send you to manage one of the farms after all?" Matilda put her hand to her stomach. Why had he returned, instead of fighting for his position? What did he want from her? Couldn't he understand she had nothing to offer him?

"No, he's cut me off." Ewan shrugged. "No position at all."

"You're his heir," Gawain said. "That's outrageous. Whatever for?"

"It's all right, my boy," Sir Bartley said, coming to stand next to Ewan. "We've plenty of land for you to practice managing."

Matilda winced as she thought of the wheat farms. She'd forgotten entirely about that project. It had been an idea of Greggory's, to use up some excess capital and interest his younger brother in the family business. She'd agreed with alacrity, knowing how her father liked to own land, but she'd never even taken a look at what she'd bought.

"Thank you, Sir Bartley. I appreciate that." His grin was too practiced for her taste. "What else is going on?"

Gawain held out the note. "No chalk smell this time, just a new demand."

Ewan took the paper and read it. "You aren't going to go through with this."

Matilda straightened. "You know I have to."

"They might kidnap you, too, or kill you," he said. "I cannot allow that."

Matilda ignored her brother's look of significance. "I can allow exactly that. I need to take any chance possible to ensure my son's safety. What if it is Izabela waiting for me in the park? I might be able to reason with her. I thought she genuinely cared for Jacob."

"We could say you are indisposed. Send Mrs. Miller," Ewan suggested. "She knows Izabela."

"The two women together?" Gawain said. "Mrs. Miller wouldn't be seen as a threat."

"The kidnapper might not even enter the park if he sees two figures in the dusk," Ewan said. "It's gated. They can survey the entire place before coming in."

"I'm going alone," Matilda said. "We'll have men from the factory come into the area around teatime, walk the entire area, keep an eye on the square. If they are there for hours, the kidnapper might not spot them."

"We'll be there," Gawain said. "I won't let them take you, too."

His grim cast reminded Matilda of Gawain's military experience. She wished she'd had the same, instead of years in a finishing school.

Ewan spoke up. "They might recognize you, but probably not me."

"I'll stay closer to the house," Gawain said, agreeing easily. "You are in residence at that hotel on the other side of the park, so you have every right to be walking by."

"Frequently," Ewan agreed. "I like the idea of the factory men, Matilda, if you are sure they aren't involved in any way."

How could she be certain of anything? But she had to press on, for Jacob's sake. "If you think the adulterated flour and Jacob's kidnapping are related, we've proven the flour came from Douglas in London. Therefore, my men ought to be innocent."

"Oh, they could be involved with Douglas in some fashion," Gawain said. "I wish we knew who Izabela's mystery follower was. Has Mrs. Miller had any luck with that?"

"I am sorry I have not had more time to learn about Douglas's companies," Ewan said. "I don't know if it employs spies or believes in information gathering. Redcake's is far more moral than many concerns."

"It doesn't matter now, my boy; you are with us," Sir Bartley said.

"Until the earl dies," Gawain added.

"That will be years from now," Ewan said. "Meanwhile, we need to get word to the factory men you trust, Matilda, and put them in place in a few hours."

She sighed. "I'm going to go over there myself and walk the factory floor."

"Wouldn't it be best to speak to the managers about who can be trusted?" Ewan asked.

She straightened her shoulders. "I care more about who I can trust, which isn't many. I want to see faces, expressions. Are they concerned about me? Condescending? Will they mention their own children and shudder? Those are the men I want. Family men."

Ewan nodded. "Who do you want to go with you?"

Matilda glanced around the room, then smiled tentatively at her father. "You, Papa. Will you come?"

Sir Bartley smiled. "Of course, my dear. I will remember some of the men. Has it really been six years since we left Bristol?"

Her mother came to her father and rubbed his arm. "I'm glad we didn't leave Bristol behind entirely. I've missed the old house. So many memories here. It brings Arthur back to me."

Matilda's brother had died here, in a bedroom down the hallway from the nursery. No one had slept there since. She sent a prayer up to her brother, hoping he didn't have Jacob in his trust quite yet, up in heaven, but was keeping an eye on him here.

A cloud moved away from the face of the sun, and a ray of light burst through the window sharply, illuminating the parlor. Matilda felt the heat on her face and smiled. Perhaps Arthur had sent her a sign. She gathered hope's strength into herself.

"It brings Arthur back to me, too, to have you both here in this house with me," Matilda said, taking her mother's arm. "He was a brave lad. Papa, we should go now, so the men can move into the area slowly."

"I'll check back into my hotel," Ewan said. "I wonder if I should return to the Douglas warehouse, before they discover I've been sacked."

"Does the earl know you were inclined to return to Bristol?" Sir Bartley asked.

Ewan nodded.

"Then don't do it," her father advised. "You don't want them to think we're focusing in on them until we have more information."

"We need to learn more about Izabela's follower," Gawain said. "Have we talked to the mother again?"

"Mrs. Miller has added visiting the woman to her daily duties," Matilda explained. "There's nothing."

"We should put men on that house," her brother muttered. "This is where Dougal Alexander, the private inquiry agent, would come in handy."

"Let's just get through tonight," Matilda said. "I've given up on the Gipsies and Izabela's family. I don't think we'll find Jacob through them."

"What's left?" Gawain asked.

"This ransom note," Matilda said. "Following the money."

"There is no way to do that," Sir Bartley said.

"You must follow whoever meets me," she said.

"I will," Ewan said.

Gawain swore. "It will be every man for himself at the opportune moment."

"We have good men at the factory. Someone will get them," Matilda said. "We'll find my son."

Ewan gave her a sympathetic smile. She turned away, not wanting to feel soft or enamored.

It rained. And rained, the sky a puddle of dark clouds and moisture. Dusk came early, about three P.M., thanks to the weather. Wind gusted lustily through the trees. Everyone scrambled, grateful that they couldn't be seen any better than the kidnappers. Six men from the factory were in the streets. Gawain and Sir Bartley walked on a wide circuit along with their wives. Even Mrs. Miller went to the main road to see if anyone she recognized climbed down from the bus.

Hours went by, and everyone became weighed down by the water. They needed a change of clothes and hot tea. Ewan couldn't even say for certain if the six men had stayed. Who could tell under hats and umbrellas? He wondered if the money had stayed dry in the valise Matilda held. She was nothing more than a dark shape under a tree when he passed by the gate of the park once more, about six P.M.

He kept walking as he heard a harness rattle, fiddling with the whistle in his pocket. It was Jacob's, and Gawain had given it to him, to blow for help from the others if he saw anything. Gawain had one as well, as did one of the factory men, but no one had blown them all evening. A carriage click-clacked down the street behind him. Turning to look at it, he saw a black old-fashioned park coach with four sturdy horses, possibly a decommissioned mail coach from fifty or more years before. He had looked at the cost of such things for Sir Bartley, who had wanted them for his new country life. The coach might cost five hundred pounds, the horses another thousand. What was a member of a driving club doing in Bristol? For the owner of such a coach could be nothing more than a member of such a group as that, and most likely based in London.

He peered closely, increasingly confused and concerned. The coachman wore the clothing of an eighteenth-century man, right down to the wig underneath his tricorn hat. A long coat covered him to his boots. Ewan stared hard, thought he saw a handkerchief over the man's lower face, in the manner of a highwayman. As Ewan goggled, he heard a gasp.

He whipped around, grabbing the closest iron fence posts, and peered into the park. Someone was standing next to Matilda. He cursed the dark and the rain. Surely that was a tricorn as well, a wig and a long coat? Expecting her to hand over the valise, he was shocked to see her bend at a strange angle, then start to move alongside the figure. He forced himself to remain quiet, though his instinct was to call out. What was going on? Another shadow detached from a tree: a second person. Not eight feet away from him, the park gate opened.

Matilda coughed, and he could see she was being held by her scarf, wrapped tightly around the figure's gloved hand. She was being choked. Did the figure have a knife in the other hand, right up against her temple?

He stepped closer, gaining a foot. Yes, it was a knife. A streetlight caught it weakly, but he could see the metal's shine. What could he do? He gained another foot as the other figure passed out of the gates. To his shock he saw that person had a small sword strapped to his side. An honest-to-goodness sword. What on earth?

"Matilda!" he called, unable to help himself, as she passed under the faint illumination of the streetlight with the first figure.

Her head turned slightly, then was stopped by the grip on her scarf, the knife against her face. While her lips moved, he could hear nothing, though he saw her anguished expression.

Oh, God, he had to do something. He put his hands in his pockets, hoping for a sharp pencil, something. All he found was the whistle. Matilda cried out. Could he persuade these men he had a gun in his overcoat?

But then, the second figure pulled the sword from his scabbard and swung it playfully in Ewan's direction, just four feet away, a mad grin stretching his larger-than-usual mouth. White paint covered the lower half of his face, and black was painted around his eyes. No handkerchief here, yet the disguise was just as effective. Ewan could not say if he had ever seen the person before.

He stared at the sword, then at the man, his hand fisting in his overcoat pocket. Matilda's face tilted toward him, her face contorted with fear, her eyes huge in her face. He could not let her go. He lunged forward, putting the whistle to his lips.

The painted man laughed, a high-pitched, banshee wail. He lifted his sword as Ewan kicked out, aiming for his knees. The sword came at him, ripping down the fabric of his left coat sleeve. He felt nothing, kept moving, blowing the whistle, trying to get around the man, take him down. The rain-soaked cobbles slicked his shoes and he slid, careening into the man. The whistle fell from his mouth. Ewan caught the swordsman's free arm and they capered in a crazy dance, a half-circle of twisting, bending movement, the man trying to get his sword up as he lost his own footing.

Before Ewan knew it, occupied as he was with his macabre dance, Matilda had been pulled into the coach. He heard people running. Help, at last. If there was just one more person, he could attack. As it was, he'd be cut down by the swordsman before he ever reached Matilda. The coach door slammed closed and the swordsman tugged away from his grip and dashed across the cobbles. Ewan's shoes slipped as he attempted to follow, and he went down on one knee, screaming invectives at the man. The whistle crunched under his foot.

As he struggled to his feet, he saw the running people were not the men from the factory, or Redcakes, but two men dressed like the footmen of a bygone era. They jumped onto the back of the park coach, hauling the painted swordsman with them. Another figure, dressed similarly, came out of the park, carrying the valise with the money, and threw it through the coach's open door before flinging himself inside. Ewan reached the door as the moneyman pulled it shut, almost trapping his fingers between the door and the coach.

The coachman yelled something and took the reins as Ewan attempted to pry the door open again. The four horses began to move down the street, splattering rain and mud all over him as he fell back.

And no one, absolutely no one, was present to watch the coach move away, but Ewan. When the coach had vanished down the street, he felt the first pangs of pain from his arm and saw the thick red blood dripping down his glove.

Chapter Twelve

Matilda tried to stop crying, holding out faint hope that her child, or the nanny, Izabela, or someone she recognized, would be inside the coach. Instead, the musty-smelling, black-as-pitch interior appeared to be empty. Her kidnapper pushed her face-first into the squabs, then sat on her, his heavy coat covering her head. She fought for breath, aware his knife must be painfully near. His coat smelled chokingly of stale body odor, which was even worse than the old coach's mildewed atmosphere.

No one had protected her from these men. She had seen the berserker light in Ewan's eye when they had left the park enclosure on the way to the coach. Her lover had not deserted her. Where had everyone else been? Had all her factory men been bribed? Her father and brother subdued somehow? She knew Gawain would fight to the death for her, a warrior trained and tested in battle, even though he had a wife and child to protect at home. He wouldn't even think of them, though, when he fought.

For that reason, she was glad he was safe, hadn't seen her go. She liked the idea of little Noel, a cherub a year younger than Jacob, safe in his nursery in Battersea, with two living, doting parents. Perhaps she and Jacob, her tiny family, were both to be annihilated. If her baby were truly dead, then she wanted to be as well. Just let her die.

Her parents would mourn, but they had survived the loss of Arthur. They would survive her, too. Ewan would fall in love with someone else, marry her.

The thought struck her, that of Ewan's love. She almost smiled, and wondered if the coach fumes were affecting her brain. Maybe it was still the side effects from the poppy syrup. Why did she think he loved her? Yes, he watched her continually with a careful, silent regard, but that wasn't love, was it? No man had ever loved her before, so how would she know?

Faintly, through the heavy wool of the overcoat, she heard the sounds of unsnapping and paper rustling.

"It's all here," a man growled.

Another man, with a posh voice, snickered. "Didn't doubt it. The Redcakes have a reputation for being honest folk."

She felt a hand, most likely attached to the man sitting across her middle, move down her flank, find her bottom, and pat it familiarly.

When she wriggled, he chuckled. "Three of us and one of you, missy, and I hear you're no better than you should be. What do you say you give us a good time?"

"Stop it," said a third voice. "That isn't our orders."

"Oh, who is going to stop us? You weren't supposed to take her."

"Had to, or that fellow on the street might have fought harder. He was trying to call for help with that whistle, too. Not risking my neck for what we're being paid."

The carriage whipped around a turn. The side of Matilda's head smashed into a wooden handrail, and she saw cracks of shiny red light across the backs of her eyelids. She lay in a stupor for the remainder of the journey, focused on the motion of the coach, not sure what the men were saying.

Eventually, the journey ended with a sickening, swaying stop. Wind and rain swept in as the coach door was opened. More men began to talk. Matilda was dragged from the carriage, then pulled roughly over someone's shoulder, her upper body hanging down his back. The overcoat was tossed over her before she could see anything but the tail of the man's coat.

She was carried through a yard smelling of wet earth and privy, then into a dark room with a stone floor.

"Wot's she doin' wi' you?" asked a woman.

"Had to bring her. It's Plan B."

"Bleedin' fools. You can't have her in here, for when we're done," said the woman in front of them.

"Where do you want her, then?"

It struck Matilda that these men, while sounding coarse, did not actually have uneducated accents. It was as if they were playing at being low kidnappers.

The idea of them acting was enhanced by their ridiculous clothing. Either way, they were still criminals. They'd taken her at knifepoint, and for what purpose? They had the money. Even if they killed her, someone would run Redcake's. Her father would return to Bristol and train Greggory, probably. Gawain, though in full protest, would help as well.

"Bring her in here," the woman said.

"We'll use her to get more money from the family. No point in killin' a rich woman," said a man.

The man behind her pushed. She stumbled forward. He pushed again, and she moved through a low doorway, following the woman's voice. Then the overcoat was pulled from her head. She squeezed her eyes shut, then opened them cautiously. Not much light illuminated the room. A small fire burned, and a couple of candles flickered. She could see a rocking chair by the fire. A cupboard on the wall hung open. It had a stack of stained but clean clothes on it. Clouts? She could smell milk in the air, and unwashed infant. A baby must have just been taken from the room, for no one was here, not even the woman who had spoken. She whipped around, suddenly wondering where the man who'd pushed her had gone, but no one was there, and the door swung behind her.

Somewhat hysterically, Matilda hoped no one had kidnapped her to be a wet nurse. Her milk had dried up when Jacob was only five months old. Too much anxiety, her mother had told her, and had revealed that her milk had done the same when Arthur was a baby. This led to fears that Arthur had been unhealthy as a result of being weaned early, and Jacob might suffer the same fate. So far, however, he'd been a hale and hearty boy.

When her eyes had adjusted to the light, she moved closer to the fire and warmed her hands. Her entire body felt clammy and damp from standing in the park for so long. The tree she'd been under hadn't protected her entirely. Her skirts had soaked up moisture from the ground and her leather boots were dark with water. She pulled off her gloves with her teeth and put them on the fire screen, then held out her pale, bloodless fingers to the coals. Somehow, the thought that they were holding her for more money made her calm.

As her fingers warmed, she noticed the door leading out of the room was covered in green baize, indicating a desire to keep noise and smells from this room separate from the rest of the house. Why?

What couldn't she hear, or what was going to happen to her that the rest of the household shouldn't hear?

She went to the door, putting her ear to it. Could her son be on the other side? Nothing; she heard absolutely nothing. She wondered where the money for Jacob was going to end up. It hadn't come into this room with her.

She tried the door, but it was locked. Out of pure, foolish curiosity, she went back to the room door and pushed it open. However, no one was in the space, and the air was freezing besides. She closed the door and cursed the cold air that had reentered the room. When she touched her gloves they were still soaking wet, of course, so she tucked her hands into her somewhat less damp pockets and began to pace, trying to warm herself.

She walked along the featureless walls, noting uneven plaster, a lack of decorations. The candles were fresh and threw interesting shadows along them. She was standing behind one candle, trying to decide what the shape of its shadow was, an angel or a tree, when a key rattled in the lock, and she saw the baize-covered door open.

Her heart, so chilled, thudded in her chest. Was she about to be saved? Or be told her fate? Or her son's? Her knees all but buckled when she heard fast, light footsteps, and a blur entered the room at the level of her hip and launched itself against her skirt.

"Mummy!" shrieked the familiar and beloved voice of her son.

Her knees betrayed her completely, and she sank to the ground, reaching for him. Jacob flung his arms around her neck and burrowed his head into her shoulder. She could smell him, her boy. All the usual scents of shampoo and familiar food were gone, but that faintly spicy scent of his skin was the same, and the oily scent his hair developed when not washed a couple of times a week. She didn't recognize his shirt, and it smelled musty. She could see a repaired rip on one arm. Secondhand or worse. Who had dressed him?

His small arms all but strangled her, and she took on his full weight. She struggled to her feet and headed toward the back door, resolved to walk home if she must. Could she remember the way? It didn't matter. She merely needed to find some main thoroughfare and hire a hansom. No one would pass a well-dressed woman and a child in this beastly weather.

She hoped the overcoat that had been thrown over her head was still in the room. She could use it to cover Jacob. Otherwise, she'd have to button him into her own coat somehow. She unwound her muffler, which was still dry in the parts where it had been tucked into her coat, and wrapped the dry bits around her son's torso.

"Where going, Mummy?" Jacob asked, lifting his small face.

"Home."

He kissed her cheek with a smack and tucked his cheek against her neck again. She smiled for the first time in what felt like years as she turned her back to the swinging door and began to push her way through.

The door hit her back and she stumbled forward. Someone had been coming through behind her. She growled in protest, moving out of the way, then headed back toward the door.

A figure came in through the green baize door, moving quickly, and grabbed for Jacob. He cried out, trying to hold on, but the figure wrenched his arms from her neck. Matilda screamed his name, grabbing for the muffler ends to try to keep him close even as he was pulled away. Something came down over her head, a burlap bag. She raised her hands to strike, to scratch, to rip, but a sweet, heavy odor filled the air, and when she opened her mouth to scream again, she got a lungful of the stuff. The room spun and she stumbled, going to her knees again. She only vaguely felt her head hitting the floor. The bag had blackened the room, but now everything, even her baby, swirled away, out of reach.

A cat's hiss woke her. She felt a tail brush her eyelashes, smelled the odor of wet feline, then felt raindrops hit her face. Wind sent the remains of last fall's leaves rattling.

Blinking, she tried to turn her head, to see something more than rain, but the insides of her head rocked in a liquid fashion. Instead, she rolled to her side and then to her stomach, then tried to get up on her hands and knees. Heavy, sodden skirts trapped her legs until she tugged the fabric away, sluggish in her movements. At least her hair was taking the rain now, instead of her face. She'd lost her bonnet and could sense most of her pins had gone, too. Her hair swung in a wet rope across her shoulder, the braid still intact.

She coughed, wondering if she was ill. How long had she been unconscious? Was it still the same night? It felt like the same rain, the same spring night that reminded one of autumn more than the coming summer.

She sniffed and sneezed, realized her neck was frozen stiff, re-membered where she'd last seen her muffler. On *Jacob*.

Her lips opened in a half scream, half yawn, and she started to cry uncontrollably, deep, racking sobs that made her chest hurt. She couldn't even feel her tears on her half-frozen, soaking-wet face.

A thought struck her, and she began to scrabble on the ground, searching for a small body near her. Could they have dumped him, too? Was she in the courtyard where the old coach had pulled up? She picked up her skirts and crouched, then rose uneasily to her feet, swaying like a drunkard. Moving tentatively, slowly, she searched the area with shuffling steps and outstretched arms, but there seemed to be nothing but grass, unlike the dirt of the courtyard she'd seen ear-lier. As her vision cleared, she noted trees, just starting to bud. They looked familiar. She turned, noting the configuration of fruit trees, and realized she was in her own garden, behind the Redcake house.

A door opened, probably her own tradesmen's door. She stumbled forward, forgetting caution, calling out. "Hello? It's Matilda."

"Matilda?" A woman rushed forward, heedless of the rain and slippery grass.

Matilda moved forward and all but fell into her sister Rose's arms. She felt the slender bones of Rose's arms as she closed them around her coat. Her sister exclaimed, and a warm shawl was dropped over her head and shoulders. She was towed toward the house.

Her sister only said one word. "Jacob?"

Only the most important thought came for now. "He's alive, Rose."

"You saw him?"

She nodded, feeling her wet hair snake up the back of her neck, then drop again, a ticklish sensation. "Yes, in a house somewhere."

"I don't understand," Rose said, pulling open the door and push-ing her in.

As the door shut, Matilda said, "They etherized me. How did I get back here?"

"We didn't hear anything, but the back garden is quite large. They must have brought you in through the mews, and the sound of the storm muffled everything." An oil lamp flickered over her sister's flushed face.

"That coach wouldn't have fit through the mews."

"Maybe they left it on the main street and carried you." Rose cupped her cheeks, her hands feeling hot on Matilda's frozen cheeks.

"How long?" Matilda asked.

"Three hours, darling. You were missing three hours."

They could have taken her anywhere in the city, then. But she had been in that room, waiting, for quite a while. She had warmed up twice: once before she went exploring, and again after she'd closed the swinging door. She'd been there for at least an hour, she estimated. Still, that gave the kidnappers plenty of leeway. The coach ride had been sickening, she recalled. So many turns, as if they had been going about in circles. Had she actually been nearby, the ride intended to confuse her? She knew she'd never been in that home before, though.

Rose closed the door behind them and latched it, then started to unbutton Matilda's coat. Matilda grabbed her sister's hands.

"We need to search the garden," she insisted. "What if Jacob is there, too?"

The door to the corridor leading into the house opened, and Gawain poked his head in. "Rose?" His eyes widened when he saw her, as light from the hallway illuminated the room. "Matilda? Oh, thank God."

She let him hug her for a second, then stepped back. "Find some lanterns. We need to search the garden."

He nodded and disappeared.

"We'll search," Rose said, her voice strangling into a cough. "You need a bath. I'll have Daisy start one for you."

"I need to find him."

"You're shaking, and we need to know everything that happened. A quick bath and a change of clothes, while we search the garden and the mews. There might be tracks that will be obliterated by the rain soon."

The door opened again, and their parents burst in. Their mother gave a cry of joy and threw her arms around Matilda.

"I'm soaked to the bone," she protested, but her mother held her close anyway.

"Jacob?" her father asked in an unsteady voice.

"They brought him to me, then knocked me unconscious," she said. "I don't think they meant to take me. But he's alive and well. I was hoping he was outside, too."

"What happened?"

Rose shook her head. "She needs to warm before she becomes ill."

Gawain came in with two lanterns, Mrs. Miller behind him. The housekeeper took one look at Matilda and wrestled her away from her mother and bustled her down the corridor and upstairs to tidy up.

She could hear the sounds of voices in the garden while Mrs. Miller helped her undress. The doors opened and closed in the house. She only allowed herself ten minutes in the bath, wrapping a towel around her hair to soak up the moisture rather than wash it, then Mrs. Miller helped her into dry clothes. The shaking had stopped, though she still felt icy to the bone.

"A hot bowl of soup will do wonders," Mrs. Miller said. "Let's go downstairs so you can share what happened while you eat."

Matilda passed the clock in the hallway as she followed her housekeeper into the dining room and was shocked to discover it wasn't quite nine P.M. While it had been a good six hours since she had left home for the park, it seemed like so much longer.

By the time she had eaten half of her soup, the family had gathered around. Daisy and Mrs. Miller ladled out more bowls to the searchers, but before Gawain took his first bite, he shook his head with regret at Matilda.

"I didn't really think they'd sent him back with me," she said, setting down her spoon. She still felt cold, but her mind had the kind of quiet that came before exhausted sleep.

"You saw him, though?"

Matilda watched her father's hand shake as he picked up his spoon. She felt a surge of affection for him. "Yes, Papa. And then they ripped him out of my arms and etherized me. They'll want more money, now."

"What do you mean, they won't see me?" Ewan asked Mrs. Miller, cradling his aching arm.

Gawain had asked him to stay on the streets after Matilda was taken, leading the search for signs of the coach along with the factory men. He'd done that for half an hour, but then he'd circled back to Gawain. The former soldier had seen the blood on his arm and had sent him to Mrs. Miller for repair. The gash had been bad enough to require some sewing. His knee had only been scraped, though his trousers were tattered. He'd taken a glass of brandy to help with the pain, but that had been hours ago.

His arm throbbed, but he had returned to the street, walking a circuit that allowed him to interact with the men who moved farther into

Bristol, reporting back any findings to Gawain. Nothing the men had seen had helped. The old-fashioned coach had vanished into the storm, like a hallucination.

A few minutes before, he'd heard voices shouting and run toward the Redcake house, realizing that the noise had come from the back garden.

Daisy, meeting him at the front door, said Matilda had been found, but not Jacob. He'd told the factory men they could go home, distributing the money Sir Bartley had handed him earlier so he could thank the men when appropriate.

Now his duties were complete, and he expected to be welcomed into the family home to see the woman Gawain knew he wanted to marry.

"I'm sorry, Mr. Hales, but she was drugged and so frantic about Jacob. She made us search the back garden just in case they'd left him as well."

"I hope Gawain's wife didn't drug her again." His physical exhaustion had him all but beyond emotion.

"No, but she is dizzy enough from the ether. She's had a rough night, if you don't mind me saying so. And you lost a lot of blood. Go home and return in the morning. You need your rest as much as she does."

He nodded and turned away, half-forming plans like throwing rocks at Matilda's window, above the front door, in the hope she would come to it, or going to the back garden himself. If he did that, though, Gawain might shoot him by accident, assuming it was the kidnappers returning.

So, he went to his hotel, wishing he'd brought a flask or bottle of his own. Despite the throbbing of his arm, though, he fell asleep almost instantly, and slept until the sun had risen. When he opened the curtains, he saw sluggish rays of light between clouds. So far, this day appeared to be an improvement over the previous one.

Still, they were missing one small two-year-old boy. As he dressed and shaved, he wondered what the kidnappers would do next. Demand another five thousand pounds? Would they expect the Redcakes to follow through, or imagine their refusal would make their choice to kill him easier? Who could think like such an outright villain?

As he walked over to the Redcake house after breakfast, he wondered about those men at the coach. The factory men had admitted sheepishly that they had not been watching the park because bewigged and costumed associates of the men who'd actually taken Matilda and the money were doing a performance down the street, juggling and tumbling and that sort of thing. Very well calculated to keep people away from the park and distracted.

Too clever by half.

But that coach; where could it be hidden? The exterior was anonymous enough, but the old-fashioned nature of the conveyance made it not so easy to hide. Still, Bristol was a big city. If it hadn't been for the rain, they might have spoken to people on the street, costermongers and the like, and followed the coach's path to somewhere, but in that rain, there hadn't been many out of doors.

He reached Matilda's home and knocked. After a minute, Daisy opened it, and with a roll of her eyes she allowed him to pass inside.

"Rainin' out?" she asked pertly.

"Not right now. You haven't been out at all?"

"Run ragged with all the people in the house. We need another maid if they're going to stay much longer."

"They will stay until we have some resolution," he said.

Daisy sighed. "I could box Izabela's ears for all this nonsense. If I'd had any idea what she was up to, I'd have tattled to Mrs. Miller."

"Tattled about what?"

"She had men in her room, a couple of times. Miss Redcake didn't mind Jacob creeping downstairs into her room, so Izabela was alone sometimes."

"How did Izabela let her followers know she was free?"

"With candles in the window."

Ewan stared at the maid. Could they call the follower to the house using the same system? But no, the follower was probably the kidnapper and would know Izabela wasn't in residence. "How did the man get inside the house?"

She shrugged. "She'd go down and let him in through the tradesmen's entrance."

"No one heard the footsteps?"

"Miss Redcake wouldn't. She's over the front of the house. Mrs. Miller sleeps like a hibernatin' bear. You can hear her snoring."

Ewan struggled to understand how this information could help them at all, other than to show how utterly immoral the nanny was, and to make it all the more obvious that her lover would have known about the Redcakes' wealth. He would have seen the art, furnishings, and fixtures, known he could bite deep for ransom money. "Thank you, Daisy. I appreciate your telling me."

The girl nodded. "Everyone is in the breakfast room."

He took off his coat and hat and went upstairs to a room in the back of the house, overlooking the garden, where the food was sent up by dumbwaiter.

When he reached the door of the room he hesitated, looking at the tableau before him. *Picture of a family in distress.* Everyone was assembled. Possibly they had planned a regrouping, a family meeting. Matilda's hand trembled as she lifted her teacup. His poor darling. Whether from traumatic stress or the aftereffect of the ether he did not know, but she did not look well. Her skin was so pale that her freckles stood out like they'd been pasted on, beauty marks on lead-painted skin. Sir Bartley's skin looked almost gray, and he could see the skull underneath Lady Redcake's drawn face. The younger Redcakes and their spouses did not look much better.

How he wanted a seat at the table, to be welcomed as an equal in their pain. His hand went involuntarily to his coat, where the special license was contained in a pocket. He had hovered on the periphery of this family for six years, watching marriages, births, knighthoods. From the outside, it had appeared that everyone in the family went from strength to strength; everyone but Matilda, that was. Even asthmatic, fragile Rose had found her happy ending in Rupert Courtnay. But Matilda had only had a miserable excuse for a man, Theodore Bliven, and her bastard child.

Now, all that was left was as it had been at the beginning. She had her family, who had never deserted her. He, who had been deserted by his parents by misfortune, had no one to love him, wanted a part of this Redcake bond, this family, who had held close even their most imperfect member.

He wanted Matilda, and he wanted her family, for his own.

Rose glanced up and gave him a shy, welcoming smile. It hovered on her lips for a moment, then disappeared, as if she had just remembered the occasion. Gawain looked up next and gave him a cool nod, and pointed to a chair next to Sir Bartley.

Ewan figured this was the closest to a welcome he was likely to get and took the spot.

Dash, the boot boy, who seemed to have been promoted to footman, passed him a plate of the remnants of the hot plates and poured tea. Ewan had already eaten, but he took what was offered, thinking he might be spending a long day outdoors and would be grateful for the hot food.

"How is your arm?" Matilda asked. Her voice sounded hollow, as if some of her spirit had departed.

Still, he was touched that she even realized he'd been hurt on her behalf. "I don't notice it much," he lied. He made a mental note to procure a bottle to numb himself before attempting to sleep that night.

"You are holding it strangely," she observed. "I wish you hadn't been hurt."

"My first attempt to be a man of action did not end so well," he admitted, forking up a sausage. "I am so sorry I let them take you."

Her expression was tender, but Gawain interjected before she could speak. "They had knives and guns. If we'd known that, we might have brought an army." He dropped his crust of toast onto his plate.

Ewan could understand the ex-soldier's disgust. "Cutthroats and tumblers; what a strange assortment of villains."

Matilda stared at her plate. "At least they aren't murderers, not yet. What will happen next? Will another ransom note come soon, or will they let us stew for a while?" She glanced up, her gaze inquiring of her father.

His plate of hot food suddenly looked greasy and unappetizing. "Miss Redcake, could I have a word while your family sorts out their thoughts on the events of yesterday?"

She turned to him. "Of course, Mr. Hales."

They both rose. She led him out of the room, then upstairs. When they walked into a large room, he recognized it as the nursery.

"I spend as much time here as possible," Matilda said.

"I can't blame you. It must make you feel close to your son."

She twisted her hands into her skirt. A serviceable garment, though well cut and of good fabric. Gray was not her color, however. She should wear green to offset her beautiful hair. "What did you want to say to me that my family couldn't hear? Something you observed last night? Some clue?" She glanced up, capturing him in her nut-brown eyes.

Instead of responding, he pulled the special license from his pocket and handed it to her. "As I stood in the doorway, I only knew one thing, Matilda. That I wanted a seat at that table, the privilege of sharing your sorrow, your hope. Please, will you marry me, so that I can be at your side through this, whatever the outcome might be?"

Chapter Thirteen

Matilda stared at Ewan, then slowly sank into the nursery's rocking chair. He watched the emotions flash across her face. Incredulity, shock, anger. Was it wishful thinking that he thought he saw a moment of longing? But then, her lips firmed, and the skin around her eyes tightened.

"You could not have suggested this at a more inappropriate time. You know I'm to wed Mr. Bliven."

He lifted the paper so she could see it. "If you had truly meant to, you'd have done it by now. I've had the special license changed. It's in our names now, yours and mine. Please, let me be a part of this as your affianced husband."

"You said you could not wed me." Her voice was calm, but she was twisting her hands together, betraying her unease.

"That was before we made love."

"You were not a virgin any more than I was." Her lips trembled.

He reached for her, ashamed that he'd forced her to say that, but she turned away. "Matilda."

"You do not have permission to call me that."

"I don't need to, not after all this. Your family is in favor, at least those who know I wish to wed you."

"They'd be happy if I married Mr. Bliven. Or anyone, even poor old Ralph Popham at the bakery."

He changed tactics. "As a future earl, I have a great deal to offer you."

Her fingers went white as she pressed them against her ribs. "I don't need some flower of aristocracy to make my life complete."

"I know. You just need Jacob. And believe me, if I could find him, I would. I risked my life for you last night, and I would do it again. Doesn't that prove anything?"

He could see tears in her eyes, like rain on glass. "It tells me that you're a fool. I don't care if I survive this, if Jacob does not."

"He will survive." This time, when he reached for her hand, soothing the mistreated digits, she didn't stop him. "He will, Matilda. You have to believe that. We all do."

"It's so hard to keep believing." Her voice broke before she righted it. "Even after I saw him just last night. He didn't smell the same, you know, not like our soap, our house. Yet I could still smell his skin, his hair."

"They couldn't have fooled you? Low light? A child the same size?"

"No, it was Jacob." She forced a smile. "I held him, I heard his voice. He knew me, screamed when they pulled him away. I know it was him."

"Good." He smiled back. "It's confirmed that he's alive. We just need to grab him next time. Not be distracted by their sophisticated techniques."

She nodded.

"I have the sense that there are too many people with strong opinions and not enough is getting done," he told her. "If I am going to marry you, that gives us the primary voice. Maybe we can accomplish more."

"Gawain is going to call Dougal Alexander in," Matilda said. "He'll be in charge then."

Ewan had only met the man once and hadn't liked him or his superior attitude. Another sprig of the aristocracy. "Please say you'll marry me. I know I don't have the polish to do this the right way, nor even to be a good earl, not right now, but we'll muddle through. I promise. Say you'll agree to be my wife?"

She pulled her hand away as the door opened. Gawain poked his head in. "Dougal will be here this afternoon. He's suggesting, before the rain begins again, that you try to figure out where they took you. Do you want to go on foot or by carriage?"

Matilda looked blank for a moment before rallying. "I was inside the coach. I couldn't hear a thing."

"You must have a general sense of how long you were in it, what turns you took."

She straightened her shoulders. "Then we need a carriage. I'll try anything."

"Good girl," Gawain said. "I'll have the brougham brought around, so you have that sense of enclosure."

"I had a heavy coat over my head," she said.

"You can use mine," Ewan offered.

"No, it smelled really bad." She forced a smile. "You're much too much the dandy to have a foul-smelling coat."

"Why did it smell so foul?" Gawain tilted his head.

She blinked. "Sweat, of course. Gin, I think. Some heavy tobacco. Turkish?"

"None of that is anything out of the ordinary," Ewan said. Gawain nodded at him.

Matilda squinted. "Manure. I think it had manure on it."

Gawain sighed. "Not of any use, then. Probably got manure on it when they harnessed the horses to the coach."

"Sorry."

"Should we put manure on the coat?" Gawain asked.

"No," Matilda said severely. "Let's not be that perfectionistic about this. I don't want to be sick."

"At least it shows how much you really do remember," Ewan offered.

She nodded slowly. "I know this area very well. I think, once we were out of the square, we went straight for a long way, right out of Clifton. And then we did go over a bridge. There is no way to mistake that."

"Excellent." Gawain rubbed his hands together. "I'll just get the carriage, then, and off we go."

Matilda let Ewan hold her hand as she lay under the coat in the brougham. Gawain sat up front with the coachman as they drove southwest, then more directly south.

"Yes, I remember this," Matilda said. "All these twists and turns made me feel quite ill. Then the bridge."

"After that?" Ewan asked.

"It felt like we were going back the way we came. I did wonder if we were traveling in circles, but now that I remember the bridge it's obvious we didn't."

"So, northeast then, you think?"

"Must be."

The coach drove into Southville. As they went past warehouses, the light began to dawn on Ewan.

"Men shouting," Matilda said. "I remember men shouting. Oh, it seemed like the drive took forever."

"About what point in the journey did you go over the river?"

Her voice was muffled by the coat. "Halfway, maybe? I have no real idea."

Ewan leaned to the window to speak to the coachman. "We want about the same amount of distance northeast from the bridge."

"That's less than three miles from home," Gawain said. "Not a very long trip."

"She was disoriented by the stench, soaked to the bone from the rain," Ewan said. "Besides, the Douglas Flour warehouse is near here."

Gawain turned as fully as the seat allowed. "But Jacob can't be at a warehouse. Matilda was in a home. A back room, a parlor, a muddy yard."

"Could be an inn, could be a house. But near the warehouse," Ewan argued. "Isn't that telling?"

Gawain threw up his hands. "Who can say? It's a theory."

"The warehouse is near the river, a ways past North Street."

Ewan watched out the window as the carriage stopped. The coachman spoke. "This is about the same distance from the bridge."

"We're two blocks from the warehouse," Ewan said. "And there are houses here." He pulled the coat from Matilda's head.

"What?"

"I don't think we're going to do any better than this. Does it feel right?" he asked.

"It was a house with a large, damp back garden."

"Row house? Free-standing?"

"I have no idea. I think it was brick, but the room had a stone floor." She sat up straighter. "I think that's what the man meant about not leaving me in there. He knew they were going to give me ether, and if I'd fallen in there I could have hit my head on the stone."

"We'll never find it," Gawain said.

"We could start at the warehouse and work our way around. We might see the coach. You never know," Ewan said.

"We can't expect Matilda to walk the streets for hours. She's not well."

"Your leg was troubling you today, Gawain. The damp, I would imagine," Matilda said. "I am probably in better shape than you are."

Gawain grunted in response.

"I think Ewan and I should stroll the area. You never know what we might see. Meanwhile, you can drive around, Gawain. Meet us here in an hour?"

Her brother nodded. "We don't want to be away from the house for too long, in case another ransom note comes."

"Surely they won't risk that today," Ewan said. "Not when we'll be extra vigilant."

"And exhausted," Gawain pointed out. "Do not forget that part."

"Do you think we'll see another ransom note?" Ewan asked Matilda.

Her eyes were dark hollow pools in her face. She glanced out the window. "It's going to rain again soon. And yes, I expect they'll send another demand. They've kept him alive this long. But at some point they will become nervous."

"We'll find him before that," Ewan promised.

"I just wish I was certain we were in the right part of town," Matilda said. "I can't be sure."

"We've done our best. Let us walk for a while."

She nodded, and he helped her from the carriage. "Do you remember seeing any trees behind the house, like those that line the river?"

"It was dark and it was raining. I didn't see anything. I'm amazed I noticed the house was brick."

He sensed a whiff of hopelessness in this endeavor, but he had to be strong for her. "Let's walk to the warehouse and see what is around there."

They walked the two blocks slowly, Matilda holding his arm like they were a proper couple. He couldn't help striding proudly, thanks to her being next to him. She stared closely at each house they passed on the street.

Soon, they came to the edge of the residential area and saw the first warehouse. Matilda hesitated, then looked back over her shoulder.

"We turned through narrow streets at the end," she said uncertainly.

"Like a warren of old houses?"

"Yes. I'm sure I wasn't in a warehouse."

"Very well. We'll go back. The Douglas Flour warehouse is three down, as a point of reference." He gestured.

She nodded, then they turned around. "Is it coincidence, do you think?"

"I don't want to see a pattern that isn't there, but . . ." He shrugged.

"I take your meaning. I wonder if I should make a plea to the Earl of Fitzwalter myself."

"He had put me in charge of the businesses, no matter how temporarily. I cannot imagine, if he had planned the kidnapping of my former employer's grandson, he would have done so."

"Unless he thought you were our natural enemy?"

"I believe they investigated me. They must have known I was a loyal employee."

She smiled faintly but squeezed his arm. He remembered their initial meetings, before Jacob was stolen, how much he had enjoyed simply talking to her. Stopping, he pulled her under the overhang of the last roof on a row of houses.

"You know I was genuine in my proposal." He touched her cheek. "I really do want to marry you."

"I believe you; I just cannot think about that right now, and whatever the truth is with Mr. Bliven, I am his fiancée. I agreed to marry him, so I am not free to say yes to you."

"Surely you must have some sense of what you want, even now." His hungry gaze roved her unlined forehead, her wispy, arched ginger eyebrows, her fine brown eyes, slightly reddened with exhaustion, her faintly hooked nose and soft, plump lips above a stubborn chin. Her usual rosy complexion was white with fatigue, but she was so lovely despite that. He wished he could paint, or even sketch, so he could capture her for himself.

She put her hand on his chest, lightly stroking down the buttons of his coat. "You are the sweetest, bravest man, Mr. Hales. How I wish I'd seen you clearly four years ago. Things would be so different for both of us."

"If I'd known who my family was, I'd have had the nerve to court you."

She smiled. "I'd have been honored. I should have been honored either way, but even Alys didn't want to marry one of our father's employees. I, in my foolishness, always thought I should do better than her."

"You've learned, but it made you, Matilda." He took her stubborn little chin between his thumb and forefinger. "Strong, in the face of everything. You may have made mistakes, but no one could fault you for how you've risen to the occasion."

"We are the same in some ways," she said with a little frown. "We're both outsiders anywhere we go."

"You aren't an outsider in your own family," he argued. "They love you. Look how they've rallied to your side."

"But you're the only one who was hurt. And I find it very interesting somehow that I was with you when I discovered Jacob was taken."

He was afraid she meant it was his fault somehow, but then she went on, placing a finger to her mouth, drawing his complete attention to those plump lips.

"Do you remember that kiss, Ewan?" Her eyes fluttered closed. "So delicious. It had been so long since a man touched me with any sort of passion. I've had so little of that, because of my foolishness. In that moment, I wanted you more than I've ever wanted anything, even a slice of Alys's best wedding cake, with all those soft, luscious fruits and that rich, silky buttercream."

He hardened instantly at the longing, knowing tone in her voice. "It was a splendid appetizer for what was to come for us."

"Can you marry just for passion?" she asked, opening her eyes. The whites seemed brilliant now, all redness gone. "Just for the sake of having a lover?"

"Would you choose me as a lover?"

"Oh, yes," she said shakily. "I hated you for it at the time, but you made me forget everything, for a little while. I desperately needed that. I haven't been coping well."

"No one could have done better." He glanced around to make sure they were alone and slid his arms around her slim waist. "I am so impressed by your courage."

When her lips touched his, he heard her moan. He hadn't even realized he'd closed his eyes, but they'd come together beautifully, instinctively. His mouth slid against hers. Her lips parted slightly, and he tasted her with his tongue, stroking into her mouth. She was cool, but the way her hands gripped his back set him on fire. She moaned softly again, then pulled away, breathing hard.

"I think it was a row house," she said. "Not a small one, because the coach came through what could have been the back garden, but I think there were fences on either side. I feel like the garden was enclosed."

He fought his arousal in an attempt to make sense of her words. Hazy with lust and longing, he tilted his mouth toward her again, but she moved her hands from his back to his chest and pushed gently at him, forcing him to listen.

"It wouldn't be a house on the end, but in the middle of a row. Somewhere around here, I imagine."

"That was the entire point of the exercise, to figure that out." He swallowed hard, still tasting her on his tongue, his lips.

"We should keep looking, before it rains."

"Yes, of course." He nodded sharply but wished quite desperately that he could somehow get her back to his hotel and have her naked underneath him again. They both would be more focused after. If only time was not of the essence. A niggling thought at the back of his brain made him wonder if the kidnappers would move Jacob after last night, however, in order for them not to find him by just this means.

He breathed in, smelling the river and smoke, and garbage, and offered his arm to Matilda again. She took it with her most businesslike nod. What strength she had, this woman. She would rise to any occasion with the heart of a warrior queen.

"If you are right about Douglas Flour," Matilda said, as they walked through malodorous mews, "then it would be best if we had someone inside."

"Pity they sent me packing."

"I agree," she said, chewing on her lower lip. "I think you have to return to London."

"Why?"

"You need to apologize. I need to see Mr. Bliven. It's Friday, and the kidnappers will know we can't get any more money until Monday at least. So this is the time to go back to London."

"You can't marry him now. I've had the special license changed."

"I will have to break our engagement."

Ewan's heart gave an extra thump as he thought of what that might mean. "We can take the train this evening. I will attempt to meet with the earl tomorrow and apologize, while you see Mr. Bliven. Do you want me to come with you?"

"Of course not; it isn't your place." She glanced around, her head drooping. "I wish we could have found the house."

"We'll set the factory men on the case. Have them document every house not on the end of a row, made of brick, that has a back garden with just mud and obvious fencing. Then we'll go to each one when we return."

"I wonder how many that will be," she said as they turned back toward the main road to find Gawain.

"We'll find out when we return from London." He wished he could kiss her again, but from his height and present vantage point, her hat was in the way.

Shadrach Norwich had sighed when Ewan telephoned him from Bristol before boarding the train, and told him to present himself at Fitzwalter House at two P.M. the next day. Ewan was surprised he'd be allowed to pay a visit with so little fuss, but he supposed he was the man's heir after all.

The house's stone edifice impressed him as he climbed the stairs to the front door. A liveried footman opened it, and he was ushered up the stairs into a study. He felt like a boy called on the carpet by his father. After about fifteen minutes, the earl entered from another door and sat behind his desk, steepling his fingers across his expensively attired chest.

"Come to apologize, have you, Ewan?"

Ewan pushed all thoughts of Matilda's passionate kisses of the day before out of his mind. "Yes, my lord, of course. I was out of bounds."

"Lust will make a young man do the strangest things," the earl observed with an air of malicious satisfaction. "Come to beg for your position back? You know, I should send you to one of those farms, far away from the Redcakes."

Ewan had discussed his approach with Matilda on the train. "She has thrown me over, sir, agreed to marry another man. I have learned a valuable lesson." In saying this, he hoped once again to uncover any relationship the earl had to the misdoings.

The earl smirked. "Sir Bartley has found another victim, has he? Money has spoken, and he has plenty. Not only that, but Lord Hatbrook has gone from strength to strength financially, and there's the son to account for as well. Gawain, is it?"

Ewan nodded.

"We old guard cannot sit back on our laurels anymore, Ewan. Money speaks almost as much as position. I'm told you are the competent sort, despite your poor taste in females, so I will give you another chance."

As if the earl really had a choice. He'd be talked about in clubs all over town if he mistreated his heir, regardless of who he was. Ewan had lived a respectable life, if not a fashionable one. He thought he'd have supporters if he needed them among the higher classes.

"Thank you, my lord."

"See that you don't fail me this time."

Ironically, Ewan had not failed the earl in any way, but he kept that thought to himself. At least his business had been a success. He hoped Matilda had let her dying Mr. Bliven down easy. They had to return to Bristol as soon as possible.

He had agreed to call on her at the Redcake home on St. James's Square around teatime that day. He had never been invited there in all these years and looked forward to seeing it.

Chapter Fourteen

Matilda walked into the house on Grosvenor Square, dreading the meeting with Theodore Bliven as any person would, an encounter with a fellow being so close to the grave. To bring him bad news was deeply unfortunate.

As she walked behind the silent servant up the stairs, she argued with herself. How much should she tell? The stench of the sickroom had changed. While the camphor, lavender, and laudanum were still present, along with coal and smoke, the human reek seemed to have diminished.

She thought Theodore Bliven had looked bad before, but now his tongue rested on the corner of one gray lip. How this emaciated figure needed peace. She sank into the chair at the side of the bed and bowed her head.

Unbelievably, Mr. Bliven spoke. "Did you find him?"

She felt tears prick her eyelids. "I am so sorry I didn't return. We had trouble with the special license."

"My son?" he rasped.

"Then we had Jacob and I couldn't leave him, or travel. I am so, so sorry," she lied, the instinct of a moment.

"Safe?"

"Yes, you poor dear," she said, touching his hand, which looked more like a claw. Almost all his hair was gone now. She could see a scar on the side of his skull and remembered him telling her about a cricket match gone wrong at school, all the blood.

"Safe," he repeated.

She noticed his breathing, a rattle in his chest. "I did want to marry you."

"I cannot help," he wheezed.

"It is fine. We'll be fine. He's a strong boy, and he has your name."

"The will." His chest rattled again.

She stood, as his eyes popped open, sunken. His hand clutched her, spasmodically, then his grip loosened.

"Jacob," he said, a soft, keening moan, then nothing more.

The attendant came up on the other side of the bed and touched Mr. Bliven's neck. "He's gone."

Matilda tore her hand away from his, then felt ashamed of herself. She bent, kissed his brow. Even as she watched, his features seemed to relax. He was still warm.

"Only sleeping," she murmured. "You're only sleeping."

"Yes, ma'am."

"He was just thirty-two years old," she said.

"At least his line won't end with him." A new voice came from the doorway.

She turned and saw a man with Mr. Bliven's curls. A clerical collar showed under his coat. This must be the vicar. "You are too late. He is with God now."

"I heard part of your conversation. Is your son truly found?"

"We paid a ransom and I saw him, alive and well, but then we were separated again."

"How dreadful." The man's eyes were full of sympathy instead of Mr. Bliven's dancing humor.

"I assume we'll receive another demand on Monday," Matilda said. Already, she sensed the encroachment of death in the still air. She had an animal's keen desire to escape this horror.

"I hope you have better luck," the man said. He went to his cousin's bedside and seated himself in the chair Matilda had vacated. She wished he had offered her some useful words of comfort, but she supposed to a vicar, she was nothing but a lusty sinner.

She left the room and went down the stairs, meeting the footman in the hall. "I'd like to give you my direction in case the family needs any assistance with Mr. Bliven's burial."

"He's passed?"

"Yes."

The footman nodded his head solemnly as she found a pencil and paper in her reticule and wrote her information for him.

"Please, will you make sure his son is mentioned in the death notice? He would have wanted that."

The footman nodded again, and Matilda asked for her carriage. She considered walking, to clear her head, but she wasn't dressed for it, nor did she have an umbrella. In that moment, she wanted nothing more than to be exactly what the vicar thought of her, a lusty sinner. Ewan would arrive at her parents' house soon. She needed to see him, see his healthy, hearty self, touch him, taste his love. Those strong muscles, lovely skin tone and color; hear his voice, rich and deep. With a desperate hunger, she wanted to drink him down like a perfect cup of Earl Grey tea with cream and sugar.

When she reached the mansion, she called for tea in the front parlor, and settled down to wait for Ewan. She hadn't even poured it when he arrived. He stood in the doorway, his smile crooked and endearing.

"Theodore Bliven died today," she said as she poured them both tea. The scent of citrus normally cheered her, but today it did not have the power.

He nodded and seated himself. "I am terribly sorry."

"Is it wrong of me to say that I'm not unhappy to have avoided being a widow? Mr. Courtnay's daughter lost her first husband after one month. He was ill the entire time, and then she had to spend eighteen months all but locked up in her father's home, wearing deepest mourning." She shuddered. "I do not want that."

"Of course not. I do not entirely understand our nation's customs. Of course we grieve our dead, but what good does it do to lock away widows? Especially under such circumstances. She was probably quite young as well."

"Rose's age," Matilda agreed. "Now, we need to get back to Bristol and see what the factory men have found."

"I think we should wait until tomorrow." He set down his teacup and took her hand. "You must be exhausted."

She squeezed his hand. "I feel an odd sort of levity, as if I must celebrate being alive."

"What do you want to do?"

She lowered her voice. "Things we should not do here."

He matched her tone. "Such as we have done before?"

She nodded, scarcely believing her own audacity. Yet the man was all but her affianced husband. She knew he would marry her as soon as he could. "Please, Ewan."

His other hand reached for her. He stroked her palm with one hand. The back of her hand rested in his other palm.

In the doorway, someone cleared his throat. Matilda snatched her hand away. "Yes?"

"The stables wanted to know if they should keep the carriage ready, or if you will stay in for the night," Pounds, the family butler, said.

"Have it brought around. We are going out again, I am afraid."

The butler nodded and left the room.

"Where are we going to go?" Ewan asked.

She smiled at him. "Your rooms, of course. I have never been in a bachelor establishment."

His gaze was incredulous. "I live in a single room, Matilda. It is not luxurious. I am ashamed of what I have to offer you, in fact."

"I need to know more about you." She leaned forward to touch his knee, then picked up a slice of seed cake and fed him one end. "Have you eaten since the train?"

"No. And I should tell you about my conversation with Lord Fitzwalter."

"Eat." She watched him take another bite of cake, feeling very maternal. "You need fuel." Was someone feeding her son?

He allowed her to finish feeding him the slice of cake without protest, then drank the contents of his cup. "What about you?"

She pressed her hand to her stomach. "I don't think I could."

He kept his gaze on hers as he took another slice of the caraway-studded cake and broke off a piece. "Open your mouth, Matilda."

Mesmerized by the way his full lips moved when he said her name, she did as she was told. He placed a fragrant bite on her tongue. She chewed and swallowed, staring into his eyes. Her nipples, taut and sensitive, rubbed against her chemise, and she could feel heat pooling between her thighs.

"The carriage is ready, Miss Redcake." Pounds had appeared in the doorway again.

She swallowed a second bite of cake, then nodded. "Shall we go?"

Ewan folded the rest of her cake into a linen square and tucked it into his hand. "Drink your tea. I've often noticed that not drinking sufficiently at meals leads to an aching head later."

"A topic Gawain would be pleased to weigh in on, given that he is in the tea-selling business." She tilted her cup to her lips and drank the contents.

"No doubt, but I would prefer not to think about your family for the remainder of the evening," he said, his mouth making that funny half smile again.

She quite agreed. "They would have telephoned if anything had occurred."

"Exactly."

A maid stepped forward in the front hallway with their coats and hats and they were soon on their way to Ewan's single room. Matilda wondered how mean it would be. Did his clothing hang on pegs on the wall? Did he have a comfortable chair? To think how he'd worked alongside her father, who came home to a large mansion once owned by aristocrats, while Ewan just had the one room.

She could not be displeased by what she actually found, however, when he ushered her inside. The space smelled like him, which instantly put her at ease. While not large, he had a bed with sufficient soft blankets, an armchair, and a table with two straight-backed chairs, along with a chest and a washstand. Tidy and clean, she could find no fault with his housekeeping ability, and no scent of food fouled the air.

"I would have thought Redcake's paid you better," she said. "But I suppose you spend a lot of money on clothes."

"They are expensive," he agreed, "but I've always made an effort to save because I had no family. I'd hoped to buy a cottage, be ready to support a wife. It was no harm to live simply for now."

"I see. Very sensible of you."

His smile seemed tinged with sadness. "Not what you expected?"

"Much nicer," she said quickly. "And very clean, given that you had no idea I would come here."

"Ever," he muttered. "I admit I thought you came from humbler surroundings. I had never seen the family home in Bristol before."

"My father built that house when I was a girl. I don't think the previous house was as nice," she assured him. "He had turned around the family finances by then."

"Do you remember the earlier house?"

"It smelled like the factory," she said, frowning as she tried to remember. "Sweat and flour. Alys and Arthur and Gawain, they worked at the factory, as did my father, of course. Our family was fairly humble not so long ago."

"One would never have known it from you."

"Finishing school." She stared into his eyes as she unbuttoned her coat. "It sanded off all my splintery edges."

"You had any?"

"You know I still do." She unbuttoned her coat next, leaving her in a blouse and skirt. "I do not think like a lady. I am too impulsive."

"No, you think like a Redcake, and as someone who has allied himself with your family for my entire adult life, I do appreciate that. Plus, I like your impulses."

He took her hands and pulled her toward him. His mouth met hers, and she opened eagerly for him. They went to work on his buttons, then hers. Fabric dropped to the spotless floor next to his bed as they wrestled each other out of their clothing, their mouths never separating. His hands tunneled into her hair when they had finished with their clothing, knocking pins askew.

"I love your hair," he said. "Is it a crazy nimbus of red in the morning?"

"I'd look like a lion if I didn't keep it in a braid," she assured him.

"You don't get to braid it when we are wed. I want to see it." His gaze on her intensified.

"You will soon regret that, when I make you brush it smooth." She tucked a stray lock behind her ear.

"I would be honored to brush your hair. And undress you. But I shall leave the dressing to someone else. Too depressing."

She ran her fingernails lightly down his chest, following the thin line of dark hair, marveling at the contours of his body. To think she could marry this man, have all of this heat and muscle in her bed each night. How could she have reconciled herself to a life without passion? It didn't suit her at all. She fairly ached with pulsating lust.

He seemed to know what she was thinking. Instead of reaching for her breasts or hips, his palm went to her mound. Then, as she gasped in pleased surprise, he feathered his fingers through the ginger hair that covered it. Pulling her to him with one arm around her waist, so that her side touched him, he spread her inner lips open with the other and stroked through her silky heat. She arched against his hand as it moved in tantalizing circles, her open mouth on his throat.

As she suckled a tiny patch of skin there, her thoughts wandered between the pleasure of leaving a visible mark on his body—the ownership of such a gesture—and the glorious feelings he was firing in her most intimate place.

He sat on the edge of the bed, his hands continuing their soft, heaven-sent strokes inside her, along her flank. But then, his mouth found her right breast and closed over her nipple, sucking hard enough to draw a moan from her, a wriggle of pleasure. One of his fingers slipped inside her channel and he moved it in and out. She wanted to collapse against him, but he might stop.

"I want you inside me," she whispered.

She heard his breath catch. "Matilda, you're killing me." His mouth moved to her left breast, suckled there, too.

Her nipples were distended, aching. She would never get enough of this man, ever. Losing all sense of decorum, she straddled him, his hand still between her legs. She put her palms on his cheeks and slid her thumb along his lips, then kissed him so hard that their teeth clicked together. He chuckled and tilted his head.

She felt his penis against her belly, thick and deliciously hot, and moved a hand down to stroke the tip, spreading the bead of his own precious moisture across the broad head. Amazing to think something so large could fit her so perfectly, but it had and would again.

"Are you ready for me?" he whispered.

"Yes, please."

His lips tilted up. He filled his warm palms with her bottom, lifting her off his thighs so he could fit himself inside her. Her eyes opened wide as she smelled her own arousal, felt his head, too big. But her own juices lubricated him, and slowly, he worked himself inside her.

She was only halfway down and he was shaking. Stopping, confused, she lifted her face from his shoulder. "Are you all right?"

"Oh, God, stop moving."

She froze, horrified. Was she hurting him? Doing it wrong? His arms were corded strength along her sides. He still held her bottom as his head dropped into her hair. She felt his heavy breaths, heard him moan.

"So good," he said into her hair. "I want to last long enough for you to enjoy this, too."

One of his hands left her bottom and found a place just above where they were joined. He began to stroke her there. Just a few times, and she had to move against his hand. The acute pleasure, the scent of their bodies mingled together, it all made her head swim. The movement of her hips fueled the fire between them.

"Now," he moaned, and pulled her down, seating himself completely in her depths. She thought she'd taken all of him before, but she'd been wrong. He showed her how to move against him, to slide along him as he thrust upward. Soon, they were both crying out, then shuddering together as they found bliss.

He lifted his feet onto the bed, then lowered himself onto his back, helping her relax against his chest, still inside her. She had quivers from the aftershocks of their passion and her mind felt utterly, blissfully blank. When the first prickles of chill hit her exposed back, he pulled a blanket over her. His fingers stroking through her hair were paradise.

"We cannot go on like this. We have to be wed, Matilda."

"Mmm." She rubbed her nose against the soft spot under his shoulder blade.

"What if you conceive a child?"

"I don't want to talk about children. It's too painful."

"Why? Did something go wrong with Jacob's birth? Will you have trouble with another birth?" He struggled up slightly, and her body lost its grip on his softening penis. It slid out of her, bringing a rush of moisture in its wake.

"No, I just don't want to think of Jacob right now. He's frightened, alone, maybe cold and hungry, while I'm safe in your arms."

"You need comfort, too."

"I don't deserve it while my child is in danger."

"We've done everything we could, sweet girl. Everything."

"I can't agree with you. If we'd done everything, he'd be home now."

He slid his hands up and down her back. "We can disagree on that. I know what a devoted mother you are. You didn't deserve this and you are not at fault."

"I could have stayed in my parents' home in Sussex. Lived quietly, cared for my child. Instead, I was restless, and my father taught me the business. He didn't even encourage me. I was as hotheaded as always, insisted on it."

"You are good at your work. There is no shame in that."

"I'm an unnatural woman," she insisted.

He stroked down her back again and cupped her bottom in both hands. "Not from my vantage point. You are an entirely natural woman, with a good mind and a stout heart. Who else was going to run the business?"

"Greggory," she said. "Once Gawain didn't want it, my father would have trained Greggory."

"But he's not your father's son."

"No, but he is my grandfather's grandson, and the first factory was founded by him, John Redcake."

"I see. Does this other branch of the family resent you?"

"Not at all. My Uncle Arthur is a painter, and was happy to be bought out by my father so he could pursue his art. Greggory is his oldest son, and he's more interested in his fiancée than the business. For now, at least."

"Then you are what the family needs. Don't feel unnatural for that. Every family is different."

"What will ours be like?"

"Are you going to marry me now, for sure?"

She nodded, rubbing her face against him. "How could I say no to this? But everything has to end well, Ewan, or I will be completely broken."

"It will, darling. Now rest for a little while, and then I shall embrace you again, before we get you home."

"I'd like to sleep in this little bed." She yawned.

"No, that would be a scandal. I shall take you home, then call on you quite properly in the morning for our return to Bristol."

"I should go now. What if we receive a call from Bristol this afternoon?"

"You know there won't be any news. Not on a Saturday evening. It became obvious on Thursday that this kidnapping scheme is complex. They will act carefully."

"Do you really think Jacob will have been moved?"

"I think the place they took you to was carefully chosen for complete anonymity. I don't know that we'll ever find it, so he might very well still be there. You have an unusually good sense of geography. I'm amazed that we came as close as we did."

"I could have been wrong."

"I don't think so, not with the warehouse so close by. It will be their undoing, if anything is."

"I hope you are right."

Ewan tipped her sideways, and she found herself flush against his body on her side. He bent his head to hers, giving her a gentle kiss on the lips. "Relax, rest a little. I shall trouble you again, madam, when I am restored."

"How long does that take?" she asked, curious.

"I don't know. I am an old man of twenty-seven now, and you are my first lover of the year."

"And the last, I hope." She poked him in the side.

"The last forever, I hope." He mimicked her. "No, Matilda, if your face is the last I ever see, on that final morning of my life, I shall count myself a lucky man. And never think to stray from you, as so many men do."

"We can take comfort in each other." She whispered this, feeling vulnerable.

"With a family as strong willed as yours, we shall have to promise to always put one another first. Otherwise one or another of your relatives will run roughshod over us, as we have already seen."

"I know it, Ewan; I do know it. But you are going to be an earl, and power will start coming more naturally to you. For now, it is a little hard to see yourself as more than a secretary. I feel that myself, having gone from a younger, pampered daughter to a woman of business. I do not have much in the way of role models. Alys is one for me, somewhat, but she is so involved in the marquess's estates and her own reproducing. I'd honestly never thought I would marry or think of having another child."

"She still owns the tea shop."

"I don't think she'll ever sell it, nor do I think Lady Judah will stop dabbling in cake decorating, but neither of them do more than dip into their interests. They have too much else to do. Whereas I left far more of the child rearing to staff." She swallowed hard. "And paid the price for it."

"Most women of your class have nannies," he said. "You did nothing unusual, and I will not allow you to feel you've done anything wrong. I am proud of you for doing something constructive with your time, instead of spending endless hours in society meetings or embroidery, like so many do."

"Some of it is worthwhile," she said. "You do not really know very many women like me. Our lives are more useful than you might expect. We aren't entirely decorative."

"I'm sure you are right. I have a great deal to learn."

"We both do. We must promise to never argue at bedtime, so we can wake up happy with each other."

"Agreed." He kissed her head. "And now, as for the rest, I do believe I am quite restored."

She giggled, feeling his manhood nudge her meaningfully. It had grown again, and she was eager to put Ewan through his paces before he deemed it time for her to leave for St. James's Square.

After church services the next morning, Ewan presented himself at St. James's Square. He hadn't listened to the vicar at all, too busy castigating himself for agreeing to an engagement he couldn't sensibly keep. How could he want something so dangerous to Jacob's well-being? The earl did not see Matilda as the future countess, and he would lose his restored position if he announced their intention to wed.

He was convinced a connection existed between that warehouse and Jacob. They would be back in Bristol that evening. Tomorrow, he would confront Albert Pigge again and get to the bottom of this.

He heard a flurry of slippered feet when Pounds ushered him into a cheery back parlor looking over the garden. Matilda crashed into him, wrapping her arms around his waist.

"I missed you last night. How I wanted to wake up in your arms," she said, squeezing him close.

"It makes me very happy to hear that," Ewan said, stroking her hair. "I look forward to waking up that way every morning."

"I don't want to wait. Let's have the banns called right away. I have to believe that we'll find Jacob over the next week. Something is going to change, I can just feel it."

"Yes, it has to," he agreed, hoping that event wouldn't be finding the child's little body. But the Redcakes had handed off money once before without proof the boy was alive. They would do it again, even if it beggared them in the process, as long as any hope existed.

"At my family's church, then, in Bristol? We could be married in

May. I'll make all the arrangements; you won't have to do anything but arrive on time."

"I wish I could agree," he said, as gently as he knew how.

There was a moment's pause, then Matilda released his waist and stepped back. "What do you mean? Not May?"

"May might be fine, but we must find Jacob before we even announce our engagement."

"Why? As you said, I could be expecting already, and that isn't suitable for an earl's heir. You need to secure the succession."

He closed his eyes for a moment. He hadn't thought of that. "Of course you are right, but Lord Fitzwalter will terminate me again when he finds out I'm to marry you. You've forgotten all about the special license. We can be married any time. No need to call banns."

"So we find Jacob, marry, and then the earl will wipe you from his businesses again."

"Correct, but meanwhile, I'll have access to the properties. I mean to search the warehouse, every inch of it."

She swallowed. "I see what you mean, but Ewan, if there is any hint that I'm increasing—anything at all—we must deal with that for the future's sake. Oh, dear, I really am the most inappropriate bride for you."

"I can live with that because I do not want to live without you. Do you know how many years I longed for you to so much as notice me?"

"No, I didn't know you then. I'm not even sure when you saw me first."

"It was in 1884. Right when Redcake's opened in London and I came to work for your father. You and all your sisters were at the staff party to celebrate a successful first week."

"You found me attractive? I'm so like Alys, and Rose is so much more beautiful."

"It was a long time after that before I saw you again, but I never forgot you."

"I was such a romantic when I was younger," she said reflectively. "If you had wooed me, I wonder what might have happened."

"You are still a romantic." He smiled at her. "You simply take more persuading than you used to."

"I cannot comprehend that Mr. Bliven has died," she said. "I'm sure my mood has something to do with that. Oh, Ewan, life is so terribly short."

"We will make the most of it," he promised. "It will be fun to have a delicious secret for a few days."

"It will be much more delicious if you sneak into my bed at night." Not that he would dare.

He chuckled. "No possibility of that. Your father is sleeping in the house. I am not romantic enough to risk my life."

Chapter Fifteen

"Mr. Hales, this is entirely irregular," Mr. Pigge protested from behind his oversize desk in the Douglas warehouse office on Monday morning. "To the best of my knowledge, you have no position in your uncle's business interests."

"That is a lie," Ewan declared. He stood from the low visitor's chair to give himself more authority. "I know you received a telephone call this morning. I spoke to the solicitor, Mr. Norwich, myself."

"Well," Pigge said, snorting and wiping his nose with a handkerchief. "Well."

"I do not care to employ a liar," Ewan said in measured tones.

"Please, Mr. Hales, you understand I must be cautious, with you in and out of favor with the earl in such a manner."

"Mr. Norwich is the earl's particular mouthpiece. It is not for you to have an opinion on my relationship with my uncle. Be assured I am the authority of this enterprise."

"How am I to know who Mr. Norwich is? Most communications come to me through Corwin Vare in London. These telephones leave me quite flustered." He wiped his forehead.

"Perhaps you would do better in Vermont," Ewan said. "Although I would prefer to have a trustworthy man in a position so remote."

"Come now, sir," Pigge said, standing as well.

Ewan stared at the man. Matilda had recommended he stand during the interview, when he'd shared how Pigge's desk and chair seemed to be on a dais compared to the visitor's seating. How would she unlock the reason behind Pigge's choice to stand? Was he trying to assert authority over Ewan, who was undeniably his senior and the heir to the earl besides?

He could not waste more time. He did not want this man following him around the warehouse. Five handpicked men were waiting at a pub down the street, ready to search the warehouse for Jacob. "Please return to your home, Mr. Pigge. I will consider the conditions of your future employment further, but I cannot tolerate looking at you and that ghastly nose hair one more moment today."

Pigge puffed his cheeks until he looked like a balloon about to pop. "I am outraged, sir!"

"I do not care. We will both have the rest of the day to consider our tempers. Do I need to call a constable?"

"Of course not." Pigge put his hand to his waistcoat and marched out, leaving his overcoat behind.

"Good riddance," Ewan muttered. He hadn't liked the man's attitude toward Matilda anyway. He rustled through the man's desk for five minutes, looking for financial records, a list of employees, anything that might be of use. Finding nothing of value, he stepped into the outer office, told the astonished secretary that he was not to allow Pigge into the office for the rest of the day, and went to the pub to gather Matilda's men.

The warehouse was a long dirty rectangle a couple of blocks from the river. When Ewan came back with the men, he assigned them each about 20 percent of the cavernous space to search and took the offices for himself.

"We don't know anything about where he's being kept, only where he was on the one night," he told them. "Don't be flashy about your search. Tell the employees that you are here to learn the operation. Maybe someone will let something slip. But if you see any evidence of a child—clothes or anything—come find me."

Given the time of year, it seemed the warehouse was stocking barley and wheat seed, as well as peas and beans for the spring planting. Rows of feed sacks stretched the length of the warehouse.

When the first man returned to him, having completed his task, Ewan sent him to search the property outside, looking for outbuildings. Then he returned to the offices, searching for any documents that might relate to Jacob. Despite Pigge's clear knowledge of the kidnapping, he and the men found nothing. Had he retaken control of Douglas Industries for nothing?

Eventually, he telephoned Matilda's house.

"Have you found anything?" she asked, hope in her voice.

"Nothing. I'm so sorry."

"I didn't really think he was there. I think they are keeping him where they took me."

Privately, Ewan had his doubts. Why make it easy for them to find the boy? "We are so close to where you were taken, though."

"There might be a connection through the men who work there. A wife is keeping him, something like that."

An excellent notion. "We need to interview the men here. That is an excellent point."

"Will you come for dinner?" Her voice broke, then strengthened again. "It has been a long day for you."

He didn't know if he would have the chance to hold her, but even seeing her would be enough. "I would like that very much, thank you."

"I will need to return to London tomorrow, I'm afraid."

"Why?"

"I know it is ridiculous, but I'm going to help with Mr. Bliven. Gawain is coming with me to pay for a cemetery plot. What if Jacob wants to be buried near his father someday? I need to choose somewhere nice."

"Why would Jacob want that?"

This time he heard an actual sob. "I'm never going to tell him the real story. It's going to be a romantic one, about a man who went away to sea, never knowing the truth." She sniffed.

"Oh, Matilda. If you must, you must." Gawain must think it was a good idea if he was going along. He would go as well. They'd have more freedom in London. "I will see you soon."

As the warehouse shift ended, he gathered his five men together.

The tallest man spoke first. "Nothing out of the ordinary here that I can see. They bring in beans down the river, transport them here in wagons, then repackage to individual farms."

"Some flour moving through," another reported. "They supply bakeries in Bath from here."

"Just barley and oats, barley and oats," said a third, in a sing-song voice.

"No outbuildings at all," said Barker, the man sent to look outside. "It's a small operation."

"I found nothing in the offices, no correspondence that seemed telling," Ewan said with a sigh.

The last man spoke. "I thought a couple of the men in my section were shifty-eyed, if you know what I mean. They kept an eye on me and the other men. Don't know if they are involved, or just doing something like stealing."

"Tomorrow we need to interview everyone who works here. See if anyone will tattle on another's wife or someone like that, watching a child. Miss Redcake reminded me that she seems to have been brought very near here to see her child."

"You think whoever has him has a connection to the warehouse?" the tall man asked.

"It makes sense. Once we learn something from the interviews, we can have a private inquiry agent follow the most suspicious men and see if it leads us anywhere." Ewan rubbed his aching scalp. Had he been tugging at his hair all day?

"Has the family heard anything more about the kidnappers?"

"I'm afraid not," Ewan reported. "A great pity."

The five men shook their heads. "We'll be here tomorrow. Do you want us to talk to the men casual-like, or do you want us to haul them, one by one, into an office?"

"I'm not sure. What do you think?"

"We don't want to scare them off," said Barker.

"Very well. Each of you take the men in your area aside, one by one. Tell them the new director wants a private word to discuss safety issues. Learn about the families and especially find out where they live. I'm going to send Barker here around the neighborhood with the list of addresses I've received from the foremen."

"What you want me to do with it, guv?"

"You remember the other search? A brick row house with a fence, same description? That's what we're looking for. You find it, take the omnibus to the Redcake home, and find Sir Bartley. But make sure there aren't five of them exactly the same first."

"Don't want to raise the family's hope, like," Barker said.

"Exactly. They've been through enough. Today was the day we expected things to change and it hasn't happened. Tomorrow needs to be that day."

The men nodded.

"I will not be able to be here tomorrow. I have to be in London. But I will have Greggory come by at the end of the shift so you can keep us informed. Hopefully, they won't recognize him as a Redcake. Anything else?"

"We need to return to our own jobs," the tallest man said. "How long do you expect us to be here?"

"Just through tomorrow, I hope. If you can talk to all the men, we're done here. We already know Jacob isn't about."

"Poor little mite." The speaker stopped and hummed. "Wish we could have found him for Miss Redcake."

"For his own sake," Barker said. "Let's get home to our own families, and hug our wee ones tight."

Ewan nodded and led them out the door as the night watchman entered.

Ewan followed the Redcakes into dinner that evening, feeling underdressed. He hadn't thought Matilda kept a very formal home, but now he saw evidence to the contrary. His suit, perfectly fine for work, had obvious dust stains, and a streak of white paint had embedded itself into the fabric atop his right knee. Dougal Alexander, on the other hand, lean and dark-haired, had dressed appropriately for his first night in Bristol.

Thankfully, though, Matilda's mother was no stickler. She gave him her usual kind, vague smile as her gaze passed over him.

"That's a very fine mural," he said as he held out her chair so she could seat herself at the dining table.

"I painted it myself. Arthur helped me with some of the bigger shapes. He had promise," she said.

"He was named for my father," Greggory said from across the table. "He is a painter as well."

"Your father introduced me to Sir Bartley," Lady Redcake said. "We met when we were both painting the Avon Gorge. That was long ago, before the railway was built."

"I didn't know that, Mother," Matilda said, then thanked Mrs. Miller as she poured wine.

"I thought your father's name was Charles," Ewan said to Greggory.

"No, it's Arthur," Lady Redcake said, holding up her glass. "Though he likes to style himself *A. Charles*. Artistic temperament, you know. Such a pretty yellow, isn't it?"

"Yes indeed." Ewan smiled. "Tell me, what is the mural meant to represent?"

"The grounding of the steam tug *Black Eagle*," Lady Redcake said. "In the gorge. It's not easy to navigate through."

If Ewan squinted, he could almost make sense of that: the shape of the gorge, the small tugboat puffing steam in the middle. She'd painted it in abstract fashion, with a bird's-eye view. Matilda's mind ran along far more concrete lines than her mother's.

"I've been waiting patiently to hear what happened at the warehouse today," Sir Bartley boomed. "Obviously nothing of import."

"No, sir," Ewan confirmed. "But we haven't ruled out some kind of participation from an employee's family. We're going to interview everyone tomorrow, and I hope we can get a look at the homes of those who live near the warehouse."

"An excellent notion," Dougal Alexander said from his seat. "I'll come with ye tomorrow and search the area."

"I had hoped Mr. Hales would come to London with Gawain and me tomorrow," Matilda said. "He'd be such a comfort to me."

"He's needed here to interview the men."

"That will be done by the Redcake's factory foremen who are assisting."

"I can manage well enough without him," Dougal told Sir Bartley. "Even if another ransom note comes tomorrow, they'll have tae give ye a day or more tae collect the funds. If they go across tae London for just a day, they will not miss much."

Sir Bartley's eyes narrowed. "When has Mr. Hales become such a comfort to you, daughter?"

Gawain coughed as his swallow of wine went down the wrong way. His wife patted him on the back, serene in the face of his distress.

"I shall come as well," Gawain's wife said. "It is time I visit my own little one."

Sir Bartley's expression didn't change. "I asked you a question, Matilda."

Ewan cleared his throat, and as the Redcakes' gazes turned to him, he stood, lifting his wineglass to shoulder height. "I hope you will congratulate us. Miss Redcake has agreed to become my wife."

Matilda knocked over her wine. Her mother's eyes went wide. Gawain chuckled, and Dougal Alexander's sharp investigator's gaze went to each of the family in turn, assessing.

"I-I thought we had agreed," Matilda said, in a much breathier voice than usual. She didn't finish her thought as her mother leaned over her and patted her hand.

Ewan felt like the *Black Eagle*, foundering in a twisty river. "I am sorry, I merely meant to explain your remark. It would be an honor to be of comfort to you either way of course."

"Will this engagement not cost you your position with Lord Fitzwalter yet again?" Gawain said.

"Not if we keep the information within the confines of this house," Ewan said, more sharply than he meant. "We'll see this dastardly business through to the end, and not marry before that. I'll do what I must, as we all have."

Gawain nodded. "This does not, of course, come as a surprise, but you are not much of a love wallah, are you?"

His wife shook her head ruefully. "He's doing his best, my dear. Such a difficult time, with poor Mr. Bliven dying in such a fashion, and Jacob missing. But love will out in the end. It always does."

"A short engagement?" Sir Bartley mused.

"It depends on so many factors," Ewan told him.

"It is best to share happy news, even in hard times," Lady Redcake said. "Life must go on. I imagine Jacob will be so excited to have a new addition to his little family."

Matilda's eyes went wide, which clued Ewan in to the import of her mother's words. Did Lady Redcake think Matilda was expecting his child?

Across the table, Gawain openly grinned. His wife had a secretive female expression on her face. Ewan couldn't speak in his defense, given that they were lovers, though of such a short duration it would hardly matter if they wed soon.

He cleared his throat again, wishing he could down his glass of wine in one long gulp. "I would hope we could wed soon. I have a special license. But there's no need to be so fast about it that we draw talk."

"No?" Sir Bartley said.

"No, sir," Ewan assured him.

"Hmph," his former employer said in response.

Matilda had gone scarlet. Ewan felt awash in sympathy, especially given this was not her first time having embarrassing news disseminated through her family. Never again. She'd be a respectable married lady soon enough, and a countess someday.

Soon, her time of shame would end, once and for all. If he couldn't offer the woman he loved some happiness, what good was he? He wasn't much of a man either, if he allowed his desire for physical passion to risk a premarital pregnancy. No, he would not attempt to make love to her again, not until they were wed. He must be a gentleman with her, even if her blazing cheeks reminded him of the way she looked in passion's sway. Her shallow breaths plumped the soft rise of her breasts over the top of her dinner dress. How he wanted to bury his nose between those soft, scented mounds. He wondered if he could tease her nipples from behind their hidden prisons of whalebone and linen and suckle her until she moaned.

Gawain raised an eyebrow at him. Ewan shook his head ruefully.

"I am sure Ewan is too well trained in his habit of respecting our family to overstep his bounds with Matilda," Gawain said, tapping his index finger against the dinner table. "I am sure his courtship has been a model of propriety."

"Really," Matilda muttered, just audible enough to hear.

"After all, dear sister, you did learn your lesson the last time. As much as we've all been pleased to have little Jacob, what led to his appearance in our family was regrettable," Gawain said.

Gawain's wife turned her head to Ewan. "Are you aware, Mr. Hales, that our own dear son Noel was born out of wedlock?"

Ewan choked on his wine. Really, he didn't think he'd ever hear a conversation like this taking place around an earl's table. "I may have been aware of that, but it's long forgotten, Lady Redcake."

She smiled serenely. "I just want you to be aware that, all teasing aside, any Redcake child will be welcomed by all of us, with no trifling worries about the baby's birthdate. As a midwife, I'll be more than happy to see to Matilda when the time comes."

Matilda pushed back her chair and stood, trembling. "There is no child. The only child that should be of anyone's concern is Jacob. Just Jacob, my missing son." She turned and ran, the blue silk half cape attached to her dress fluttering as she moved from the room.

The men stood automatically. Ewan reached her before she fled and tucked her against his chest.

"Ann, my dear," Gawain said mildly. "Most ladies do not care to discuss the mysteries of reproduction at the dining table."

"I was merely attempting to generate a little enthusiasm and reassurance," his wife said serenely.

"Please do not," Matilda said. She let Ewan reseat her.

Ewan sighed and sat again. They spent the next half hour listening to Lady Redcake, who planned and replanned Matilda's wedding three times. Ewan refused to make any comments. The wedding was the bride's affair. All he needed to do was be available with the license. Dougal Alexander, however, was quite enthusiastic on the topic, sharing details of his Heathfield Farm wedding with his wife, Lady Elizabeth.

Gawain's wife made a point of asking after Dougal's foster daughter, careful to ensure Ewan recognized that Lady Elizabeth had taken in a foundling herself, yet another out-of-wedlock child embraced by kin of the Redcakes. Yes, they were a veritable tribe of bohemians.

No wonder Lord Fitzwalter was so skeptical of his alliance with the family, after his experience with Lord Ritten and the eccentric Walters. Yet Ewan had never felt so at home. He would have a family for the first time since early childhood. This band of outspoken, even outré Redcakes felt more like his clan that the Douglases ever could. He could admire no one any more than he admired Sir Bartley, Gawain, and his sisters.

As the conversation wound to an end, Ewan took Alexander aside. "Mr. Alexander, please do everything in your power to find Jacob. I am convinced he is in a house near to that Douglas warehouse."

"He was recently," Alexander agreed. "I will go door-tae-door if I have tae."

"Thank you." Ewan sank into his chair, wondering what they would do if he was wrong.

Matilda rang for Daisy once dinner was done, eager to get out of her confining evening dress and into a nightdress. The dress had seemed much too tight around the bosom. All that talk of matrimony and babies had her remembering the signs of early pregnancy. Of course, even if she had conceived, it could not matter yet. Ewan would marry her before she would have any suspicions at all. She could trust him. Detecting deception was a skill she'd worked hard to earn after her experience with Mr. Bliven. Mr. Bliven, who would be buried tomorrow. She wondered if he'd had any premonition of disaster in 1887, when he'd boarded that ship for India to escape from her. Had that supposed fiancée waiting for him there even existed? Gawain had been insistent over the years that Bliven had his good points, but Matilda had decided the man was quite mad. Unlike Ewan, who had been a positive rock in her family's employment for years. Why, she'd never even seen him with a lock of hair out of place until Lord Fitzwalter had entered the man's life. Between the earl and her, Ewan had experienced a sea change, yet he still seemed controlled, at least most of the time.

She climbed into bed and twisted her head into her pillow, breathing deeply of the lavender Mrs. Miller tucked around the linens, and tried to make herself relax.

"There, miss, you are all packed for tomorrow," Daisy said. "Poor lamb. Would you like some hot milk?"

"No," Matilda said. "That will be all. Go and help Mrs. Miller."

"Yes, miss," Daisy said, not moving.

"What is it?"

"You're ever so lucky to have a nice beau," Daisy said. "I feel sorry for that Izabela sometimes. All those men panting after her, but the silly chit couldn't tell who the good ones were, and who were the villains. Makes a body wonder if she had a brain in her head. Why, to hear Mrs. Miller speak, that Gipsy trader is quite a man. And the butcher boy has prospects, you know. A nice butcher's shop. I wouldn't mind that."

Matilda sat up. "Obviously you know something about the bad men Izabela chose. Have you remembered something about the most recent bad choice?"

"I think his name started with *W*," Daisy said, after a moment of reflection. She shrugged. "I knew he was a bad one. It goes without saying."

"Anything else?"

"No, miss. Nothing else. I am sorry. I just remember the name from Izabela saying her prayers."

"Could I have missed any mail today?" Matilda asked.

"No, miss, you went through it all. You are most particular."

Matilda stared at the ragged cuticles on her right hand. "There should have been a ransom note by now."

"Maybe they won't write again until they spent the first money. It was a lot of money, miss."

She tucked her hands against her heart. "They won't keep Jacob alive that long."

"You never know. He's an important boy, and such a dear. Why, I'm sure even an evil snatcher couldn't help but fall in love with him."

Daisy's stouthearted faith made Matilda smile a little. "Thank you, Daisy. I very much appreciate that." Matilda leaned back on her pillow.

Daisy turned down the gaslights and left the room. The door closed with a soft snick, leaving Matilda alone with a lamp and a softly glowing fire. Any woman would be lucky to have a man like Ewan. He had her best interests at heart, would make an excellent husband and father. Not to mention his status as an earl's heir. But he deserved love, and she felt so utterly drained, incapable of passion or affection right now. She could not move forward without knowing her son's fate. If she were Roman Catholic, this would be about the time at which she'd throw herself in the Avon Gorge, or join a convent to spend her life helping humanity with silent prayer. Anything more was quite beyond her.

Tomorrow, she'd have to watch as Jacob's father was laid to rest. Theodore Bliven would have more tears shed over him than he quite possibly deserved. But the tears would be for all he'd lost, all that potential. His lost dream of an earldom, his marriage, his health.

"You were able to go blessedly to sleep, Mr. Bliven, while I lie here and suffer," she whispered. "I suffer completely, while that beautiful man is downstairs, willing me to love him. How can I ever be worthy of Ewan Hales?"

Chapter Sixteen

It might not be seemly for a woman to attend a funeral, but it had been a long time since Matilda followed convention, and Gawain's wife, Ann, Lady Redcake, had never been the type to follow rules either. Therefore, they arrived, in suitable black gowns, attended by Gawain and Ewan, in time for the Theodore Bliven viewing.

Mr. Bliven's cousin, Hiram, patted Matilda's hand sadly at the door. "You should have been his widow, Miss Redcake. I know he wanted it that way."

"Yes. I underestimated the severity of his final illness," she said, holding back a sneeze at the overwhelming scent of mixed lilies and amaryllis.

"All that trouble with poor Jacob cannot have helped matters any. Have you had any word?"

"Not since I was here last." Her voice sounded tremulous and her eyes burned, but whether it was from emotion or the flowers she wasn't sure.

Hiram Bliven patted her hand again. "You poor dear. I am so glad you have your family here to support you. The Marquess of Hatbrook is already inside."

"I am glad he was able to come."

"I do have something for you." He turned to a small table and plucked a box from it, handing it to her.

"What is this?"

"A lock of hair and a photograph." He saw her look of alarm and hurried to explain. "Not postmortem—I've always thought that a gruesome custom—but one from his university days. My brother and I thought you might like it for yourself. And his signet ring, for Jacob."

Her hand shook as she accepted the box. "How kind of you. I'm sure Jacob will treasure these things. I'll make the hair into a brooch or something."

Gawain patted her shoulder. "Very decent of you, Bliven. Your brother was a good employee of mine, and I'm sorry India had such a dreadful effect on him."

"He was never strong," Lord Hatbrook said, coming to stand next to them. His austere face, never very full of expression, did not change, but Matilda sensed a certain softening around the eyes. "Measles, mumps, every chill and cold that came through school."

"So he never should have gone to India?" Gawain said tersely.

"It was his choice," Hatbrook said. "Matilda, I'm so sorry for your troubles and my family's inability to be there for you."

Hiram cleared his throat. "After the burial, our solicitor will read the will in his office. Miss Redcake, may I request your attendance?"

"Of course." She forced a smile and nodded, then, carrying her box, went to sit in the back of the room, as far from the overpowering flowers as possible.

After half an hour, the coaches came and men closed the stout oak coffin, then carried it to the hearse. The family had paid for quite a nice funeral, with a procession on the way to the cemetery. Matilda and her family, plus Ewan, were taken to Hatbrook's carriage to follow the official mourning coaches out of town. The procession went at a snail's pace due to all the pages, though when they were out of town, the walkers climbed onto the coaches to speed up the trip.

Then they went to a chapel for the funeral service. Mr. Bliven was interred after that, but ladies were not allowed to be present for that. Matilda didn't mind. She felt quite upset enough without watching the coffin of her one-time lover being lowered into the ground, and the morbid imaginings it would engender, that of a tiny coffin being buried next to Mr. Bliven's sometime all too soon if they couldn't find Jacob.

She couldn't hold back her sobs any longer. Ann gripped her arm and stuffed a black-edged handkerchief under her veil as emotion racked her already exhausted body.

"Would you like to go to St. James's Square, or even to Hatbrook House?" her sister-in-law asked, as the few other ladies in the chapel whispered in sympathetic murmurs.

Matilda shook her head and snuffled. "There's the feast back at the house, and then I need to go to the solicitor's office for the will reading."

"A very long day for you, with the train back to Bristol tonight."

"It can't be helped. It's those flowers. Irises always make my nose itch and my eyes water."

"Why don't we go wait in Hatbrook's carriage?" Ann suggested.

Matilda nodded assent and rose, her still dripping eyes and nose hidden under her veil. For once, she understood the appeal of mourning garb.

After another half hour of waiting, staring blurrily out the window, Matilda saw the first men returning. Top hats bobbed down the dirt lane as the men walked between monuments, urns, and the occasional statue of a weeping angel.

Feeling as claustrophobic as if she were enclosed in a coffin herself, she rose and opened the carriage door, climbing awkwardly down the steps by herself just as the first men walked by.

"Had a son, you know," the first man said to his companion.

Matilda wasn't surprised Jacob was being gossiped about, but the knowing smirk on the man's face confused her. She climbed back up the two steps, sheltering in the open doorway of Hatbrook's carriage.

"Still missing?" said the second man in an arch voice.

The first man laughed openly. "Of course. Can't have made Bliven's final days easy."

The second man chuckled and pulled a cigar case from his pocket. "Poor bastard."

"Didn't have nearly enough bad habits, if you ask me. Lost his health in India. His nerve, too. Really, despoiling just one Society miss?"

Matilda's eyes opened wide at the insult. Behind her, Ann peered over her shoulder. Matilda put a firm hand to her sister-in-law's shoulder and pushed her back.

"Don't imagine those upstart Redcakes will find their bastard offspring anytime soon."

"Not if I can help it." The first man accepted a cigar as the two strolled out of earshot.

Matilda stepped back and carefully closed the carriage door, unbelieving that she'd managed to overhear as much as she had. Her mind spun as Ann opened her mouth. Who were those men? Had Jacob been taken to punish Mr. Bliven for something? And yet, venom had been directed toward her family, quite specifically.

"Did you hear?" she whispered.

"Some." Ann nodded emphatically. "We have to find out who those men were."

"Do you think they really know something?"

"I would consider them nothing more than nasty gossips, except for those final words."

" 'Not if I can help it,' " Matilda repeated. "Oh, Ann, what did he look like? Help me remember."

Keeping their voices low, they catalogued the man's appearance. Between them, they decided the man's hair was straight and ash brown. He had an upturned nose and thin lips, which would be recognizable, but his height and weight were very average. They had much less to say about the second man.

"His clothing was expensive," Ann said.

"I agree. We have to hope those men return to Hiram Bliven's home."

"Could you see what carriage they entered?"

"I don't even know if they came by carriage," Matilda admitted. They continued to fret, peering through the carriage's windows as the mourners returned.

Within ten minutes, the coachmen were back in place and the procession returned to its place of origin: Hiram Bliven's home. Matilda and Ann spent the time explaining to Gawain, Hatbrook, and Ewan what they had overheard.

"I think you've given us enough description to find them, if they return," Gawain said, his expression grim.

"What if they do not?" Ewan asked, his glance at Matilda sympathetic. They shared a long glance.

"At least we know someone at the funeral is likely to have been involved in the kidnapping. It's one step closer to the answer," Gawain said.

"I can't believe Theo wanted his son kidnapped," Hatbrook interjected. "I understand, Matilda, that this was your original theory, but Theo was much too ill to plan anything."

"Then what is your idea?" Gawain asked.

"London Society is small. It doesn't signify that the kidnappers were at the funeral."

"Oh, it signifies," Ewan said. "It means someone in fashionable Society is involved in this kidnapping business."

"Like Bliven's family. Who's that, then? An earl, right?"

Hatbrook nodded, rubbing the back of his neck. "Lord Barstow."

"How is he related?"

"Another cousin. He's the one who remarried at fifty to a twenty-two-year-old cit's daughter. Has an infant heir now."

"Doesn't seem likely he would care about Jacob," Gawain mused. "But then there's Fitzwalter. We keep circling around him."

"It must go back to the wheat farms I purchased, and Fitzwalter," Matilda said. "He doesn't want me to marry Ewan either. Doesn't think I'm good enough, and I don't blame him."

Ewan leaned over and took her hand, surprising her. "Never say that, Matilda. Never."

She smiled sadly at him. "If you have family ruthless enough to kidnap my child over some silly wheat farms, then we are not worth the risk. You must never indicate a continued preference for me in public. It's too dangerous."

"We are in an enclosed carriage."

"In the middle of a funeral procession, with enemies about," Gawain said. "Matilda's right, Ewan. I understand your desire to show possessiveness, but this is not the time."

Ewan sat back, his jaw working. He stared out the window. Matilda wondered how they could ever make their relationship work under such circumstances. And if she conceived a child, pure disaster. She had to pray she had not, however much she wanted Jacob to have a brother or sister.

At Hiram Bliven's home, ham and game pies were served in the room adjacent to where the viewing had been held, along with a tasteful assortment of desserts from Redcake's. Mr. Bliven was probably having a hearty laugh at that from wherever he was now.

"Look down upon us and find Jacob. Send me a sign, something. You know we haven't much time left." She blinked back tears. "Lead me to those men, at the very least."

No sign ensued. She continued to scan the crowd, walking through the fairly crowded rooms. The ratio of men to women was at least six to one. Every few minutes, she and Ann crossed paths and shook their heads at each other.

"Should we try upstairs?" Ann whispered.

"No one should be up there."

"We have to hope they are here somewhere. We can't give up our search."

Gawain walked by with Ewan. The women consulted with them. The men promised to keep searching the main floor while the women tried upstairs.

They went up together, planning to say Matilda felt faint if they needed an excuse. In truth, she did feel woefully overheated in her heavy black dress and pushed her veil back as soon as they were out of sight of the main crowd.

"Stop." Ann held out her hand. A beautiful sapphire ring adorned her glove.

Matilda saw a man appear in a doorway. She bent over the ring, exclaiming her admiration. The man passed by. In shock, she tightened her grip on Ann's hand. It had been the second man; she was almost certain of it.

She let go of Ann and crept down the staircase slowly, to keep the steps from creaking. At the bend, she saw the man clap his top hat on his head as a footman opened the door. She glanced around the front hall and spotted Hatbrook, just inside the first parlor. Gesturing frantically, she pointed to him, then to the door.

Hatbrook frowned, rubbing his neck, then his eyes widened as he caught her meaning. He went to the footman at the door and whispered in the man's ear, then straightened and shook his head at Matilda.

The footman must not have his name. She rushed down the stairs, holding her skirts. When she reached the tiles, she saw Ewan coming from the opposite direction. Moving as demurely as she could, she reached him an age later.

"The second man just went out the door. We still don't know who he is. You have to follow him!"

Ewan nodded and pointed a finger behind him. Gawain appeared in the doorway, limping slightly. It must have been a difficult trudge for him through the muddy cemetery.

"We'll follow him," Gawain said.

"But your hats?" she fretted.

"Tell Hatbrook to get our things and join us," her brother said, walking out the front door without a backward glance.

Matilda stared at his and Ewan's backs as they walked down the front steps and crossed the path to the main street. They must have seen the man to the left because that was the direction they took. She turned back to Hatbrook.

He nodded. "I'll get the hats and coats. They'll keep him in sight. Stay here."

"The first man might still be inside."

"Keep your distance," Hatbrook advised. "We don't want the kidnappers to feel they are under any kind of threat. Something could happen to Jacob if they do."

Her stomach lurched as she considered the possibility and knew Hatbrook was right. Her brother-in-law made sense, as usual.

She and Ann wandered through the Bliven home for another hour, but never saw the first man. "Do you think he left before we spotted the second man?"

Ann twisted her ring. "Possibly. He may never have entered the house at all."

"Ladies?" the vicar said, appearing by their side in the second parlor. "We are ready to leave for the solicitor's office now."

"Very well," Matilda said. The vicar went to collect his brother.

By the time they were back in Hatbrook's carriage, headed for the solicitor's office, she had a pounding headache. Heedless of the discomfort, she kept a close eye on the streets as they passed, just in case she saw either of their family members, Ewan, or the suspicious men, but men dressed so similarly she would not have had much luck recognizing them even if it had been a clear, sunny day.

Ewan held the hansom door as Gawain climbed in, then went to speak to the coachman. At least his quarry had been joined by a second man a moment ago, probably the other fellow they were looking for. "We need to follow those two men ahead. You see them? Pull over wherever they stop."

"Owe you money?" the man asked.

"Five thousand pounds," Ewan said.

The coachman's eyes widened. "Get in then, guv. I've driving to do."

"Thank you," Gawain said. The scars on his face seemed more evident than usual. He leaned back against the squabs, wincing, and massaged his hip.

The walking stick he'd borrowed from Hiram Bliven clattered to the ground. Ewan stepped on it to hold it in place.

"God, I'd kill for a drink right now," Gawain said. "Or some pills."

"At least we're off the street," Ewan said, not without sympathy. Gawain should be far more disabled than he was. He'd fought hard against his battle injuries and usually had them mastered. Marrying a healer had been one of his more intelligent strokes. Hiring Theodore Bliven to find him eye medicine from India had helped him restore his vision, as well. Another good move.

"Yes, I'm glad you thought of this. Those two blackguards can't see us, and we can follow them in comfort."

"I hope these are the men your sister saw outside the chapel. They seem to match both descriptions. Any thought as to where they were heading?"

"After a funeral? I expect they were going drinking somewhere. A public house if they are not gentlemen, a club if they are."

Gawain was correct. The hansom had driven them less than two miles before pulling over in front of a hotel on Leicester Square. Ewan jumped down from the hansom and went to pay the coachman.

"They went in that door to the left, guv," the coachman advised. "It belongs to the Blair Club, I believe."

"Never heard of it. Can you advise me?"

"Young gentlemen. Heavy drinkers. Picked up a couple of fares outside that made a mess in my cab." The coachman shrugged as Ewan tossed up his coins. The hansom rocked as Gawain exited.

Ewan came to his side as the coachman spoke to a potential fare. "The Blair Club," he said.

"Think we can get inside?"

"I don't know that we want to. We just want to know who the men are, right? It's not as if Jacob is being held in a men's club."

Gawain rubbed his nose. "I'd have preferred if they'd gone to ground in a pub."

Ewan patted his shoulder, for the first time feeling truly comfortable with his future brother-in-law. "I second that, but no luck. Let us talk to the doorman. Got any guineas on you?"

Gawain fished in his pocket, then poked through some small coins. "Ah, here's one."

"Let's hope it's enough." Ewan pasted on a friendly smile as he approached the doorman.

The man bared rabbitty front teeth at him as they approached. "Gentlemen?"

Ewan put his hands to his lapels and struck a confiding pose. "A friend of mine just went into the club. I've forgotten the name of his companion, and I do not want to look a fool in front of my friend, as you can imagine. The short man. Bliven, is it? Or . . . ?"

The doorman tucked his lower lip underneath those alarming teeth. "Now, sir, you cannot expect me to reveal confidential information."

Gawain tossed him the guinea. The gold coin flashed through the air, and the doorman had it hidden in a pocket before Ewan could blink.

"Such fine gentlemen as yourselves could certainly not be a threat to Mr. Wyld. His friend is Hulk. Augustus Hulk."

"Mr. Wyld; that is, Mr. Richard Wyld?" Gawain said. "He still lives on Charles Street? We don't want to interrupt him at his club."

Ewan's hearing sharpened. Clearly Gawain had recognized the name. Of course, Gawain had been a high-flying bachelor around town not too long ago. He'd even claimed one of the most notorious mistresses in the fast set for a short time.

"Yes, sir. I believe so."

Gawain nodded. "Good man." He turned away, tapping his cane on the pavement.

Ewan followed him back to the hotel's entrance. "What was that about?"

"Richard Wyld was a tutor to Lord Murchie's younger brother years ago. Oldest son but had no money."

"How do you know him?"

"I can't say I do, but Lord Murchie is a Redcake's customer. I believe Wyld used to come in with the lad before he went to Eton. That was probably four years ago."

"I fail to see the significance of any of this."

Gawain leaned back against the stone edifice of the hotel. "Wyld is from a good family, obviously, to get such a post, also well educated. Familiar with Redcake's. No idea what he's been doing since."

"Why would you?"

"Exactly. No reason." Gawain grimaced.

"What about Charles Street? Where did that come from?"

"Lord Murchie's address. I never expected to hear that Wyld still lived there, or nearby."

"I see."

"Let's stop in at Ye Grapes, shall we?" Gawain asked. "Just a couple of minutes from here, and I could use a pint to wet my whistle."

Ewan raised his eyebrows at the idea of visiting the racy pub, right in the middle of Shepherd Market, a hive of prostitution. "Really, Gawain, I'm about to marry your sister."

"Did I mention women? No, I assure you I'm quite happy with my wife. I simply want a comfortable spot to sit before we venture off to Lord Murchie's home."

"Are we going there?"

"You know we have to."

Ewan sighed. "Lead on. I wonder how long they will be at their club."

"I don't know if it's them we want to speak to," Gawain mused.

By the time they exited the pub, Gawain looked more relaxed. His hip seemed to have ceased troubling him. He led the way to Lord Murchie's home, a warm yellow brick structure on the exclusive street. Gawain and Ewan both gave their cards to the footman who opened the door. They waited in the entrance hall for a few moments, then were led into a parlor.

Less than five minutes later, Lord Murchie entered, a slender figure of about thirty years. Ewan knew he was soon to be married.

"Sir Gawain," the lord exclaimed. "And Mr. Hales; I believe I have heard your name at White's recently."

"He is Fitzwalter's heir," Gawain explained.

"Ah, yes, the secretary who will be earl someday," Murchie said, only his lower lip showing beneath his bushy mustache, which looked distinctly oversized on his long face.

Ewan nodded, wondering if his future equals would be kinder if he'd been elevated to manager of Redcake's Kensington before Fitzwalter had found him. Most likely not. It was still trade.

"I believe you know Richard Wyld," Gawain said, as Lord Murchie gestured for them to be seated.

"Oh, yes, lived here for years."

"I remember he tutored your brother."

"All three of them," Murchie said. "Children of Father's second marriage, you know. Much younger than me. Youngest just went to Eton last fall. Not sure why Wyld is still here, but he's an institution, you know, old thing. I believe he's giving Millicent geography lessons."

"Your half sister?"

"Yes; she's twelve." Lord Murchie made a face. "Impossible girl. Best to keep her busy. Africa fascinates her, what?"

"Still receiving a salary, then?" Ewan asked, thinking perhaps the tutor had entered into a kidnapping scheme for money.

"Oh, yes, but he's in arrears. Always asking for an advance. Horse racing, you see. Likes to visit Newmarket, that sort of thing. Not enough to keep him busy here."

Ewan and Gawain shared a glance.

"What's this all about?" Lord Murchie asked. "If the man is involved in something truly unsavory, I'd best know about it. Child to protect and all. Innocent young bride about to live under my roof."

"He was at Theodore Bliven's funeral today, with an Augustus Hulk," Gawain explained. "He made a remark that my sister overheard, sounding like he had a hand in my nephew's kidnapping."

"You have a kidnapped nephew?" Lord Murchie exclaimed. "Terrible business that must be."

"Yes. He's only two. We've paid a significant ransom. He was alive last week. My sister saw him, but they got him away again, and now, nothing."

"Which sister?"

"Matilda."

"Doesn't live in London," Murchie said, rubbing his fingers down his mustache.

"Bristol. Her nanny disappeared, too, presumably part of a plot. We think she had a follower. Maybe he talked her into it."

"You think that's my Mr. Wyld."

Gawain shrugged. "It's his own words that damn him. But curse it if I've any idea why. I know he admired Comtesse Valery, who I was once acquainted with, which is why I recognized his name at all."

Lord Murchie licked his lower lip. "Ah, yes, the lovely Marie. Who could not admire her? You know, I think Wyld had prospects once upon a time, but I've heard nothing about it for years. Can't remember what."

"So he's merely a tutor in debt due to a gambling addiction."

Lord Murchie nodded. "I must suggest gently that he find a new post. Given his debt, it seemed easier to let him entertain Millicent. But now, given this troubling information, I'm not sure that's wise."

"We'd like to speak to him."

"Of course, of course," Lord Murchie said heartily. "But he ain't here now, what?"

"Can we wait?" Ewan asked.

"He's off duty this afternoon. Usually has Thursdays to himself, but he especially wanted to attend Bliven's funeral. Old school fellow. Didn't see the harm in it. Not much for him to do here."

"Of course." Matilda had been kidnapped on a Thursday.

"Come back tomorrow," Lord Murchie suggested. "Can't say when he'll return. Hate Thursdays. Millicent always underfoot, you understand."

They nodded and stood. When they left the house, Ewan hesitated on the street outside. "You'd think if he had an afternoon off he'd have gone to Bristol to check in there."

"He probably has access to a telephone. Besides, his employer might have heard gossip if he hadn't turned up at the funeral."

"Maybe he ordered a new ransom? He could be too busy any other day."

"We should check in at St. James's Square soon," Gawain agreed. "In case there is news."

"We need to go to the train station so we can return to Bristol at a reasonable hour. It's been a stressful day for Matilda."

Gawain nodded assent, then clutched Ewan's sleeve. Ewan looked at him curiously, thinking his hip had seized up again, then saw the direction of Gawain's gaze. Wyld and Hulk were coming down the street, moving directly toward them. Wyld was tossing shillings in the air, juggling them with proficiency in one hand.

Chapter Seventeen

Ewan swore softly. Were they about to come face-to-face with Jacob's kidnappers or, at the very least, part of the ring? What was the tie to Theodore Bliven? It made him sick to think Matilda had been correct all along.

Gawain's face had transformed into a tight mask, a battle-hardened warrior's expression. Ewan relaxed his shoulders and widened his stance, ready for whatever came.

The men walked forward, Hulk swinging his walking stick, chatting animatedly. He saw Hulk clap Wyld on the shoulder, for all the world like two sporting men coming home from a hot day at the races, rather than mourners returning from a funeral.

He smelled the heavy scent of an orange-flavored liquor before they reached conversation distance. At that instant, Wyld saw Gawain. His coins vanished into his fist.

"Blimey!" the man cried, grabbing the shorter Hulk by the shoulder.

"Eh?" Hulk said, clearly not the more intelligent of the duo. He stepped forward menacingly, brandishing his cane.

Gawain bared his teeth and tossed his own cane into the air. He caught it in the middle, then turned it across his midsection, making it a striking weapon with two points.

"Where is Jacob?" Ewan said, raising his fists. "We just want the boy."

Wyld sneered and leaned toward a house. As Ewan watched, confused, the man turned and began to run. Hulk, equally baffled, brandished his cane for another moment, then ran after his friend, his coattails flapping.

Ewan took off, knowing he couldn't wait for Gawain. He chased them through St. James's Square, then lost them in the Piccadilly crowd. Half an hour later, he walked back to the Redcake house on the square, where he assumed Gawain had returned to wait for him.

He was correct. Gawain had a carriage standing by. They both climbed in, not speaking, defeated.

"Didn't expect me to get them, did you?" Ewan said.

"No. Either they'd have lost you or beat you to a pulp, unless you had a crowd involved."

"Wish I had your background. I'd have had them."

"Found yourself dead or beaten, more like. But you've done well. Worthy of my sister."

Ewan tossed his hat on the bench and tucked his head into his hands. "Thank you. Now what do we do?"

"Need to have them arrested," Gawain said. "Luckily, we are on our way to a solicitor's office. We'll have them take care of it."

The Bliven family solicitor's office was a far cry from the dingy environs Ewan had told Matilda that his great-uncle's solicitor operated under, so much so that she wondered if the Blivens overpaid for legal services. But the results of the will reading were what she expected. Not surprisingly, the deceased had left all his worldly goods to his son, Jacob, under the care of his mother. Additionally, she saw no sign of shock or distress in Hiram Bliven when she glanced at him.

"Luckily for you, there isn't much in the way of material goods, because he didn't reside in London. I believe he disposed of his Indian possessions, knowing he would never return. He'd led the life of an itinerant traveler these past few years."

Matilda nodded.

The solicitor continued. "But his personal effects are your son's now."

Matilda glanced at Hiram again. "I think you should give his clothes and intimate items to your servants to do with as they please, in thanks for their service to him."

Hiram nodded.

"I will take everything else as keepsakes for my son. Can you arrange to have the items sent to my family home in St. James's Square?"

Hiram nodded. "Of course. He had some artwork, Indian in nature, books, cigar cases, that sort of thing."

"I'm sure Jacob will eventually treasure those items."

"I will transfer the bank accounts to your son's name. There were two," the solicitor said.

"Please forward the information to my family's solicitor," Matilda requested.

"He did have savings," the solicitor said. "He didn't spend a great deal, or his expenses were covered by his business. There will be enough to send your son to school when the time comes."

She would never send Jacob away to school, at least not until he was of age to attend university, nor did he need a penny of his father's money, but it wasn't important. Mr. Bliven had wanted to provide for his son and he had done so, quite admirably and correctly. She thanked the solicitor and exited his office as quickly as she could. It had still taken an hour to listen to the will, her head throbbing in tandem with each tap of the solicitor's finger on the relevant documents.

Outside, Hiram and his brother took her hand briefly. The vicar seemed mournful. She wondered if he had expected something to go to the Church.

"I am glad you were there at the last," was all he said.

"As am I." She saw movement out of the corner of her eye. Gawain and Ewan entered the outer chamber of the office and came toward them. She saw her brother had acquired a walking stick somewhere along the way.

"In a way, I am glad you didn't marry him," Hiram said frankly. "I hate to see a pretty woman in dull black."

Ewan took her arm, perhaps judging correctly the gleam of Blivenish female appreciation in the man's eyes. Hiram lifted his eyebrows at the proprietary gesture, but Gawain appeared at her other elbow.

"We need to return to Bristol now," Ewan said. "Jacob, you know."

"Of course," Hiram said. "I do hope you find our young cousin soon. If there is anything we can do to help, please let us know."

"Thank you," Matilda said.

"Actually," Gawain said, "we need to have a couple of men arrested. They are involved in the kidnapping, though they obviously don't have custody of Jacob. Think your lawyers can take care of it?"

Hiram frowned. "Of course. Young Jacob is our family."

Matilda grabbed her brother's arm. "What? Did you find those men?"

Gawain nodded. "Sort of. They are definitely involved. We just have to find out how, and that is going to be a job for the police."

Matilda sat dumbfounded in the law office for another hour, while

Gawain explained to the lawyer what they knew. She'd never heard of Richard Wyld or Augustus Hulk, though she now suspected they were part of the gang that had kidnapped her.

"Wyld made it sound like he was in charge," she protested.

"I think he was boasting to Hulk," Gawain said. "I know enough about him to think he couldn't possibly be the master kidnapper. Not with just one day a week free. It makes no sense."

"I question whether he really had only one day a week free," Ewan said. "I didn't get the sense Lord Murchie would know where Wyld was much of the time."

"Either way," the lawyer said, "we will speak to the superintendent of the St. James's division on your behalf. Hopefully his men can run these criminals to ground."

"Thank you. We need to return to Bristol," Gawain said. "Still no word on a ransom and we need to continue our search."

Her brother stood. Matilda noticed how heavily he was leaning on his walking stick. They were all suffering the effects of Jacob's long disappearance. Ewan had a tear in the arm of his coat, and he'd lost his hat somewhere along the way. He noticed her perusal of him and smiled, but he looked exhausted.

How many men would chase two villains through the streets of London for her, risk their lives in a fight? She had chosen wisely in her future husband. If only she could tell him how much she appreciated him, but it would be hours before they had the opportunity to be alone.

Eventually, they made it into the Redcake's carriage and were on their way to the train station. Ann glanced at Ewan, then frowned. "Is that blood on your sleeve?"

"It might be from my cheek. I caught a branch."

"But your sleeve is torn. Did your stiches reopen?"

"I think it is just my jacket, not my shirtsleeve. I don't think my arm is any worse."

When the carriage stopped at an intersection, Ann changed seats so she could look. "No, you were cut all the way through." She held his arm up to the light. "Minor wound, though; nothing like the first one. Should be fine. I'll wash and bandage it on the train, if you will allow."

Ewan tilted his head toward her. "I hope you don't think I consider you to be a bad healer, Lady Redcake. I am sorry I was so harsh with you when I was concerned about Matilda."

"She was hysterical."

"That is not her normal state of being. She's very levelheaded generally, and she did not seem to react well to the syrup."

Ann nodded. "That I will agree with, and I should have kept a much closer eye on her while it left her system. I was worried about her, too."

"We both want the same thing," Ewan said. "Matilda's well-being."

Matilda smiled at them both. She had forgiven Ann, knowing enough about medicine to be aware that people reacted differently to treatments. She'd never had poppy syrup before, so how could anyone have known she would react so? But she'd never take it again. Ironically, she'd done better with the ether with which the kidnappers had assaulted her. "There now, is everyone friends again?"

Ewan and Ann nodded as Gawain rolled his eyes. The carriage stopped. "Here we are. We're going to have to run."

"As if we ladies can run," Ann said with a glare at her husband.

As it was, they were not even seated by the time the train pulled out of the station. The first-class car was full of cigar-smoking businessmen, two to a seat. Ann made a face and they went into the corridor.

"It's funny. Having been out of the inn business for a while, I can no longer tolerate cigar smoke."

"Is that new?" Matilda asked.

Ann smiled. "Afraid I'm expecting another little one? I don't think so. Perhaps."

Gawain put his arm around his wife and kissed her on the temple. "Noel would like that."

"A tentative congratulations to you both, then," Ewan said, nodding his head at the beaming couple. "I wonder if we can find somewhere else to sit."

"I noticed a couple of private cars attached to the train." Gawain gestured over his shoulder.

"That won't do us any good unless we know the owners," Matilda pointed out.

"Let's go and see."

They discovered the first private car was inhabited by Lord and Lady Burnham, longtime patrons of Redcake's who were also in business with Lord Judah. The couple invited the foursome in, and they spent an hour chattering while Ann cleaned and bandaged Ewan's arm. Eventually, Lord Burnham suggested they repair to the dining car because they hadn't laid in supplies.

Ann and Gawain agreed readily. Ewan, with a glance at Matilda, declined.

"Stay here, then, Miss Redcake," Lord Burnham said. "Might as well rest in comfort. Understandable why you don't want to be out in public with such goings-on. Have a bit of quiet with your young man."

Matilda smiled and rested her head against the back of the gilded settee facing one set of carriage windows. As the compartment door closed, she said, "Heaven. Peace and quiet."

"We don't get much of that," Ewan said, settling next to her.

She opened her eyes lazily. "I never did. Ewan, you've lived alone for years. How are you going to cope with a household? A wife, servants?"

"And a son," he said. "A busy boy running through the house."

She reached over and squeezed his hand. "Yes. I cannot believe we identified some of the kidnappers, and at Mr. Bliven's funeral no less. I don't know what it means, but I'm so glad. I feel Jacob will be home very soon."

"I think so, too," Ewan said, pressing up against her. He winced as his arm met hers. Standing, he took off his overcoat, exposing the smaller rip in his coat.

"Let's remove this as well, so I can see the extent of the damage. I couldn't ask to take a look with everyone else here," Matilda said, unbuttoning his coat. Gently, she helped him take it off, then took a critical look at his arm. "You've taken a beating for me, haven't you? Eight stitches and now this, plus your knee."

"The latest is just a deep scratch. I slid against a potato seller's cart when Hulk took a sharp turn to the right."

"You're lucky you weren't burned." She kissed the bandages with a featherlight brush of her lips. How brave he had been.

He shrugged, putting on a heroic pose. "All in a day's work for a secretary."

She chuckled and kissed an unblemished spot on his forearm. "My hero."

"I would have liked to slam my fist into Richard Wyld's self-satisfied face," Ewan reflected. "I'm not usually a violent man, but under these circumstances I feel quite elemental."

She ran her hand over his ripped sleeve, feeling the same way. "Can we bend your lust for violence into some other kind of passion?"

He blinked, staring at her, then his lips curved. "Why, Miss Redcake, I do believe you just made an improper suggestion."

She smiled back and unpinned her hat. Her hair had been done in a rush, and some of the strands came down with her hat, tumbling around her face. He wrapped his hand around the back of her head and pulled her close, angling his face for a kiss.

She met him openmouthed and heated, suddenly burning for his touch. Pulling at his tie, ripping at his shirt, grabbing for his suspenders, she had his trousers open before he'd even finished unbuttoning the frogs closing her black velvet coat.

"Tiny buttons," he said.

"Not trying hard enough," she said against his mouth. "How much time do we have?"

"It's never enough, but it will have to be." He pulled her coat from her body and turned her to tackle her blouse next, then her corset, after he took her skirt down.

"You are smiling like you managed something miraculous," she observed.

He went to the door and locked it, then stalked back to her, his wild black curls making him look dangerous. His trousers hung low on his hips without the support of suspenders. He looked mouthwateringly delicious like this. She felt her breasts swell, her nipples harden, the heat surge between her legs.

"Oh my." She put her hand to her chest.

"You are all mine. I'd undress you completely, but it's going to be hard enough to get all this kit back on you again."

"And here I thought I dressed so simply."

He shook his finger at her.

She pulled at her chemise, lifting it up suggestively, exposing one leg of her combinations. Cocking her hip, she continued to raise the fabric. Her lover's mouth opened as he began to breathe harder, his gaze fixed on her hips. When she leaned back against the arm of the settee and parted her legs, she could smell her own arousal. She separated the linen between her legs and touched herself. Moisture coated her fingers and she gasped as she brushed her sensitive pearl.

"God, Matilda," Ewan whispered. "Do that again."

She brushed her fingers lightly against herself. Her hips arched into the gentle pressure. His mouth closed on her lips and his hand pressed over hers, deepening the pressure. She rotated her hips, gasping into his mouth. He bit her lower lip and groaned, moving the heel of his hand in circles, making her fingers underneath do the same. His lips trailed down her neck, licking and biting, tiny gentle stings. Then he found her collarbone and the slopes of her unfettered breasts.

She cried out. He soothed her with gentle whispers, telling her how beautiful she was to him. His words and hands sent her over the edge and she tumbled into orgasm, her hips jerking against the pressure. While she lay there, panting, her legs spread wide apart, he pushed down the rest of his clothing and knelt between her legs.

His cock jutted starkly away from his body, moisture beading on the tip. She'd never seen anything so masculine. Still half out of her mind with pleasure, she reached for him, wrapping her fingers around his hot flesh, and pulled him between her legs. Her body bowed as he entered easily, like he'd been born to fit her in perfect union.

He groaned as he seated himself fully, then began to move. She could tell he felt confident with her body now, and she craved the feel of his strength surging against hers. Her hands slid along the slick surface of his back, kneading his long muscles before she clutched at his buttocks as the heat began to coil again. Lassitude vanished. Desperate to move with him, she tucked her feet against his legs so she could pulse her hips against his strength. When she broke again, he followed her down, shuddering and tucking his head into her shoulder. She soothed him, whispering words of adoration into her ear, wishing they had all night to be together.

"This will be a frequent event soon, I promise," she whispered.

"I know." He kissed her neck and pushed back. "But we can't rest now. We'll be discovered."

He pulled up his trousers and fished out a handkerchief for her. Blushing, she thanked him and did her best to tidy herself.

"And so the messy aftermath," he joked.

"Ahem," she said, holding the handkerchief. "I don't know what to do with it."

He took it from her and opened one of the compartment windows, then tossed the linen out. "I'm an earl's heir now. I can afford to consign one handkerchief to the countryside."

"He's going to cut you off again, not that it matters. We'll have plenty of work for you."

He pulled up his suspenders. "One thing I'm getting with you, for certain, is a modern woman."

"Is that so bad?"

"No, but I'm going to be an earl. I don't know that we can avoid Society completely, and neither of us is going to fit in."

"I've had the training to do so," she said as she attempted to fix her hair while he unlocked the door. "We're hardly going to be the first couple with some scandal attached to us."

"Do you really want to be whispered about for the rest of your life?"

Her hands dropped from her hair. What was he trying to say? "That would happen either way, Ewan. I think you're telling me you don't want to be whispered about for the rest of *your* life."

He tilted his head. She could see a hint of dark beard on his chiseled jaw. "No, I'm just thinking aloud. I need to be able to say painful things to you without you panicking that I want to end our engagement."

She put her hand on his arm, careful to avoid the bandages. "I want you to be able to say anything you need to, no matter whether it hurts."

He bent his head and kissed her forehead. "Nothing is going to stop me from loving you or marrying you. Nothing at all. We'll face the consequences together. But I do wish things were different."

She nodded, blinking back tears. "I can accept that. I wish for that as well, but mostly, I just want my son home safe."

They stared at each other. Matilda noticed the rhythm of the wheels underneath them. She heard the clackety-clacking, felt the vibrations, wondered how she could have ignored all of it while they made love. He took her to another world when she completely concentrated on him, one where none of this reality, this harshness, this pain existed.

She had to do that for him, too, because someday, his problems were going to be larger than hers. She might be running a few factories, raising a couple of children, but he would have hundreds or even thousands of people depending on him. He'd be part of the government, a member of the House of Lords, one of the senior men of the kingdom. She had to be able to support him in his work. At least she knew he was fully capable of it. Her father and Lord Judah had never done anything but sing his praises.

He'd put his focus on her now, damaging his relationship with Lord Fitzwalter to support her. To have all that competence and energy focused on her was exciting and alarming. She'd never had that before, didn't know how to accept it. In time, coming to him with her problems would feel normal; it would be her ordinary, everyday life. Now, though, it all felt tentative and uncertain.

He squeezed her hand. "Jacob is safe. I know it. We'll have him back soon. I cannot wait to meet him. I never have, though I did enjoy seeing his portrait at your home. I feel that I would recognize him."

"Children change so quickly. Even being away from one for a week gives you enough distance to notice certain changes."

"What did you see?"

"He'd lost weight. His cheeks were thinner. I think he grew a little bit. His legs were longer. It's funny how the body parts don't all grow at the same rate. I'll think his head looks bigger on his pillow, then his cheek will line up against mine in a new way. When he stands next to me, he bumps against some different part of my hip. He's never the same."

The door of the private car opened and the Redcakes appeared, along with their hosts. If they noticed anything amiss, they tactfully avoided mentioning it. Half an hour later, the train pulled into the station.

Matilda yawned as Ewan helped her step onto the platform. She hoped they could quickly find a hansom because they hadn't called for her carriage to meet them.

"Sir Gawain."

She recognized the Scottish accent and peered through the steam wafting from the train to see Dougal Alexander's lean body coming toward them. He wore a stern expression that flattened his lips and heightened his cheekbones.

Gawain moved toward him. They clasped hands. "I take it there is news."

Matilda stopped still. All of a sudden she understood the possible import of Mr. Alexander's appearance. But if the news was bad, wouldn't her father have come, too? Greggory? Ewan wrapped his arm around her shoulders, ignoring etiquette completely. Though grateful, she held herself stiffly.

"Yes, sir, there is." Mr. Alexander cleared his throat. "Ah, Miss Redcake, couldn't see ye before."

A porter pushed a laden cart between them. When the man had moved away, Matilda stepped forward. "Tell me," she urged.

Ann clutched protectively at her arm. Matilda remembered that Ann had lost a baby long ago, when her first husband was murdered.

"You should take your wife away," she said to Gawain.

Ann shook her head sharply. "I'm fine." Her voice trembled. "Did you find little Jacob?"

"Nay." Mr. Alexander shook his head. "It's Izabela Pickett."

"What?" Ann gasped.

"The nanny," Alexander clarified. "A steeplejack found her body at St. Vincent's Rocks on his way tae the Clifton Suspension Bridge this morning."

Chapter Eighteen

Ewan groaned. "Poor soul. Where's that?"

"It's below the Observatory. Lots of painters go there: photographers, people who are interested in rare plants. It's not an obscure spot," Gawain explained.

Dougal Alexander nodded. "She hadn't been there long."

Matilda gasped, overcome by the disturbing news. Did that mean Jacob's body was somewhere nearby, too? She hadn't seen Izabela at the house to which the kidnappers had taken her. Had she been hiding or imprisoned in a room nearby, not knowing that her death quickly approached?

Ewan and Ann clutched her arm on either side, keeping her stable. Her neck didn't seem to be able to hold up her head. It hung to her chest.

"Take deep breaths," Ann urged. "They didn't find Jacob. Just the nanny. The nanny who took your baby. She deserved to die."

"We don't know if Izabela and Jacob were together for long after they left your house that day," Alexander said. "We have evidence she was in town, alone, the day after. We can't even know if the two situations are even related anymore. I cannot believe she wasn't part of the original plot, but time has passed."

"Where is the body?" Gawain asked.

"The police have her. An autopsy will be done tomorrow morning. We'll know more then."

"Are the police searching the area? I remember there's a cave. And, oh God, the river." Matilda's belly clutched.

"It's too dark tae search now," Alexander said. "The search will continue tomorrow. I'm so sorry for all the pain this must cause you, Miss Redcake."

She pressed her hand to her chest and straightened her body, praying for strength. "I am very sorry, too. I cannot imagine whatever brought Izabela to her end, however it happened, especially while expecting a child. Surely she did not expect taking my son to result in her death. I have to believe Jacob is still alive."

"He is," Ann said. "I know it."

Matilda tried to smile at her sister-in-law, but her lips trembled and she ended up clutching the other woman and sobbing. Ewan stroked her back. They stood together for a long time, swaying, until Gawain insisted they enter a cab and go home.

The next morning was a flurry of policemen from all levels of the force, gathering information about the kidnapping and looking into the life and death of Izabela Pickett. Eventually, Matilda had had enough. Ewan could see she wasn't able to pay attention to the men anymore. He went to Mrs. Miller and asked to have the carriage brought around.

"Miss Redcake needs air," he told the superintendent, who was sitting with the family, explaining the extent of the search around the bridge.

"The fact that it may have been a suicide doesn't help us any," the man said frankly. "She may have been thrown on her beam-ends with guilt after what she had done."

"She would have been given money," Sir Gawain said. "What happened to that? Where was she staying?"

The superintendent shook his head. "We are interviewing her mother, her associates."

"We've done all that," Ewan said.

"I want to go back to the flour warehouse," Matilda said. "Look at the neighborhood some more."

"I've already had the carriage brought around," Ewan said.

Dougal Alexander stood. He'd somehow been lounging undetected in a corner. A trick of his trade, Ewan supposed. "I have a list of the houses that match your description."

Matilda held out her hand. "Yes, that's what I need to be doing."

"Give it to me," the superintendent ordered. "We'll look into it."

"I'm the only one who will know which is the right house," she said. "So no, that won't be possible." She swept from the room, a regal vision in striped black and jade silk.

Ewan followed her with Alexander on his heels, wondering why she'd chosen to dress like a fashionable lady today, instead of her usual conservative clothing. To impress the police? To help her mood? Either way, she was a vision.

In the front hallway, she took a shawl and parasol from Mrs. Miller and patted her arm before going down the front stairs, where the carriage awaited. Ewan and Dougal Alexander climbed in.

"Should we bring in more men? From the factory?" Alexander asked.

"No, we want to do this quietly," Matilda said. "How many houses are there?"

"Five within four blocks. Go out eight and there are another fourteen. We did our best."

She nodded. "I will assume it is one of the five, based on where we were when we tried to retrace my steps." She tapped her half boot nervously on the carriage floor. "I do wish we'd heard something from the London police. Have they found those two men?"

"I would assume not," Alexander said, then muttered something in Gaelic.

Matilda turned away and stared out the window. Ewan resisted the urge to touch her in front of the other man. She went so far away from him sometimes. In those moments, he was never sure how to get her back. He hoped she would break the habit of so much silent contemplation when they were wed. He wanted her love to be constant and open, not drifting.

Matilda stopped the carriage on the outskirts of the four blocks, and Alexander pulled out a sheaf of papers with the information.

"The first house is down the mews there," he said, pointing. "It's the backs we want, not the front."

"We'll follow you," Matilda said, frowning as her skirts almost touched a pile of dog excrement on the cobbles.

They investigated the first three houses the factory men and Alexander had found. Matilda found a reason not to recognize any of them. Ewan could see the fourth, however, gave her pause. They were to the south of the warehouse, in an area they hadn't visited when they had gone to the neighborhood the first time.

Matilda paced back and forth along the low, wide gate, ignoring the rubbish piles on either side, though the smell was appalling. Washing was stretched between two posts.

"Clouts," she muttered. "Not there before, but this is the first house I've seen with that overhang, and everything feels right."

Without asking, Alexander opened the gate and they stepped in tentatively.

"Are you sure this is wise?" Ewan asked, attempting to keep Matilda behind him.

"I'm armed," the private inquiry agent said in a low voice.

When they reached the back of the house, Ewan could hear crying. Matilda pressed up against his back, then relaxed.

"It's a baby, not Jacob."

"What do you think? Is this it?"

Ignoring the question, Matilda walked to the back door and rapped smartly before Ewan could protest. Alexander lifted his eyebrows and tucked a hand into his coat, probably ready to draw his weapon if necessary.

Ewan went to stand next to Matilda at the door, with an idea of pushing her out of the way of danger if it presented itself. But no one answered.

She sighed. "Let us go around the front. I wish we could find a window."

"They probably chose this place because it has so few," Alexander said. "None at the back at all, except on the upper level."

They left through the gate and went to the front of the row houses. The refuse piles were absent on the street, but Ewan guessed, from the smell, that there were problems with the sewers.

Bristol was holding true to form with another weather change. It had been cloudy and windy before, but now the sun poked through the clouds. On the upstairs level, he could see someone—a young girl perhaps—pushing curtains open.

"She's holding a baby," Matilda said.

"Two babies. One on each hip."

Curtains covered windows on the main level, but they were able to hear an infant's cry again.

"It's not coming from those two infants upstairs," Alexander said, shielding his eyes with his hand.

"I know what this is," Matilda exclaimed. "A baby mill."

"It makes sense that Jacob would be held in such a place."

"But they often have such dangerous practices, dosing the babies with laudanum to keep them quiet. They die sometimes," Matilda said.

"You didn't think Jacob had been harmed."

"Not drugged, but he was thinner," she said.

No fence blocked the front of the house. Matilda marched to the front door and knocked on it. To Ewan's surprise, a slatternly woman with a stained apron, smelling of sour milk, opened the door.

"What?" she asked. "We ain't takin' any more."

Matilda squared her shoulders. "I am here to retrieve my son. He's two and a half, with thick brown hair."

"We ain't got any chillens that old. We have wet nurses here." The woman slammed the door shut.

Repeated knocking did not bring her back to the door.

Matilda swore. Alexander didn't react, but Ewan felt his eyebrows rise.

"I know this is where I was," she said.

"Ye are absolutely convinced?"

She nodded grimly, giving Ewan a rare chance to see her resemblance to Gawain. "Oh, yes. I cannot say if he is here now, but over all that infant wailing, who would worry about hearing a slightly older child? We've got to get inside."

"We can have the police raid the place," Alexander said.

"I have a better idea," Matilda said. "Please, Mr. Alexander, would you keep an eye on the front? Ewan, go and watch the back? I'm going home."

"What do you have in mind?" Alexander asked.

"We need a fresh face," Matilda said. "Someone who will fit in, a servant."

"Who?"

"You'll see." She winked at Ewan and set off down the street.

Ewan and Alexander shared a glance. "Best do as the lady orders," Alexander said.

Ewan nodded. "She's got the right idea. If that woman recognized her, they could try to move Jacob if he's still inside."

Two hours later, Ewan was watching the back of the house, pacing the mews like a bobby on patrol, and seeing no movement among its inhabitants, when Dougal Alexander appeared at the street crossing and gestured to him.

"What's going on?" Ewan asked.

"The brilliant Miss Redcake brought her housemaid Daisy in and sent her tae the house with a pillow under her dress, saying she was an expectant mother who needed tae get back to her millwork as soon as the baby came. The slattern at the front door let her in."

"And?"

Alexander smiled. "She asked for a proper tour and they gave it to her. She saw Jacob."

Ewan felt his jaw drop. "I saw no sign of any activity from back here."

"She must have done an excellent job of acting because she came out again, calm as could be. Didn't even tell us until we were down the street."

He wanted to clap and caper about in a mad dance. "So he's still there. Where are Matilda and Daisy now?"

"In the carriage. They are going to fetch us some fish and chips so we can keep an eye on the house. Soon as it's dark, we'll be getting the lad out of there."

Finally, good news. Jacob would be saved and they could start their life together as a family. He'd have his Matilda forever. "Is she going to tell the police?"

Alexander shook his head. "Not until the lad is safely out."

He couldn't wait for that moment. "What is the plan?"

"Men will arrive as soon as we reach twilight. We'll block the street and the mews with carriages." He shrugged. "Then we go in."

He wondered at the man's casual attitude. "Have you done this before?"

"Yes, and it's best to go just as it falls dark. The longer we wait the more likely men will be in the house."

Thankfully, he seemed to know what he was talking about. "Bigger chance of a fight."

"Exactly. Stay out of sight as best you can, but keep an eye on both ends of the mews, just in case. I'll spell you with one of the factory men as soon as they get here."

Ewan nodded, then smiled with total satisfaction. "Best news I've heard in days. Jacob is alive, Alexander."

The man nodded. "A great relief to his mother."

"And me. Now we can use that special license I have."

Alexander smiled. "Congratulations. We'll be in touch."

The sun was low in the sky when Barker, one of the men Ewan recognized from his day at the flour warehouse, appeared.

"Any changes in the front?"

"Haven't heard a thing, guv. Quiet day?"

"Very much so. Certainly no coaches coming through."

"They sure little Jacob is inside?"

Ewan nodded. "According to Daisy."

Barker grinned, exposing a cacophony of twisted teeth. "A looker, that. She have a lot of followers?"

"Not that I've heard," Ewan said. "Tell you what, we get the boy out safely and I'll stand you both a nice dinner."

Barker's grin widened alarmingly. "I won't so much as blink until the boy is safe in his mother's arms."

Ewan nodded. "Where am I to go?"

"You're staying here. Supposed to stand just in front of the back door, in case anyone comes out. I'm to stay in the mews."

Ewan heard carriage wheels on the cobbles.

"Probably the Redcakes, coming to block us in," Barker said.

Ewan nodded. "Very well. I'll go into the garden now." He vaulted the gate, not wanting to alert anyone by opening it, and walked cautiously toward the rear of the house. On the left side, he could smell sausages being cooked over a fire in the garden. On the other, voices rumbled in an argument. Above, a baby or three cried in hungry protest. Typical signs of habitation.

They were lucky today was a Wednesday. The house might have had company from Wyld and his friends if it had been his day away from the Murchie household. Once they had the child, they had to figure out who the lead kidnapper had been.

About ten minutes later, after hearing more carriage wheels on the other end of the mews, he felt the house shake as someone knocked determinedly on the front door.

He recognized Gawain's rasp and the slattern's rude tone. The argument continued for a couple of minutes before Alexander's Scottish burr joined the argument. Ewan pressed up against the back door, trying to hear better. Without thinking much about it, he tried the doorknob. It turned easily in his hand.

He pushed gently at the door. It moved inward. He crept in, careful to keep out of the thin trail of light from a lantern glowing on a table. Visibility was just good enough for him to see the room was indeed stone floored, as Matilda had said.

He leaned his ear against the only door. It must lead to the parlor. He could hear nothing. Had all the adults in the house moved to the front door?

As he stealthily turned the knob and pressed the door open, inch by inch, he heard more raised voices, including a male one joining the argument. But him? He was in. The parlor was empty, though a glass oil lamp glowed above the dark fireplace. Now what should he do? From the babies' cries, he assumed all the children were upstairs. The only staircase he knew about was in the front of the house, where all the commotion was.

The house was not that small, though. Could there be servants' stairs in the kitchen? He slid along the wall, searching for a door that didn't lead into the front hall. There.

He opened that door and found it led to a corridor. The front of it blazed with light, and he could see people, the open door. Directly ahead of him was another door. He needed to make his way across the three feet of empty space without any of them seeing him. Thankfully, Sir Gawain was arguing passionately, keeping everyone's attention.

Ewan all but jumped the hall and turned the knob. Locked! He flattened himself against the wall and moved toward the back of the house, searching for another door. His questing hands found a knob. This one turned. *Saints be praised*. He found himself on a back staircase. It smelled strongly of onions.

Creeping up the stairs as swiftly as he could manage without making noise, he made and discarded plans. Could he get Barker's support? What would happen if a man approached one of the Redcakes' carriages in the dark? Would they hurt Jacob before he was able to identify himself? But he was getting ahead of the game.

He reached the top of the staircase. The door was already open. If the layout matched below, there must be space for four rooms on this level. Jacob was unlikely to be in the top left room, where the woman had been with the babies. He'd be too visible.

He went left and opened the door of the rear left bedroom. Pitch black; he could see nothing. His ears strained for sounds of breathing. Leaving the door open, he crossed the hall to the room behind the staircase. Also pitch black, but when he stopped breathing in order to hear better, he did hear quick, childlike breaths.

Wishing he had a match, wishing for windows, he crept through the room, toward the source of the breathing. His legs met a wooden structure, a bed. He fumbled around until he felt a small warm body that felt too large to be an infant's. He tucked the sleeping child against himself and went into the hall. There; he had just enough light to see a thick dark thatch of hair, a hint of Matilda's stubborn chin. Surely this was Jacob. He'd only seen a portrait, but chances were excellent that this was him.

He went down the steps, hesitating on the bottom stair. The voices of arguing people seemed closer to him than before. Had Sir Gawain and Dougal Alexander entered the house? He had to pray no one was paying attention behind themselves. Quickly, his heart racing at double-speed, he crossed the hall and went through the parlor into the stone-floored room without stopping or glancing behind. He sped up in the garden.

"Open the gate!" he cried in a hoarse whisper.

A moment later, he heard the slats creaking as Barker opened it. He went through with the child as soon as there were a few inches.

"Close it again!" he ordered. "Give us time to get away."

"That him?"

"I hope so. I did the best I could. Which carriage?"

Barker held up a lit cigarette and peered down at the child, then shrugged. "The one to the left has Sir Bartley in it. Not sure about the other."

Ewan went left, followed by Barker. The door of the carriage opened. Sir Bartley held up a lantern. His mouth dropped open when he saw who Ewan held.

"How?" Sir Bartley asked.

"Sheer dumb luck, sir," Ewan said.

"You have my eternal gratitude, son," said his onetime employer, feathering his hand over the boy's hair as if not quite believing he was here. "Come in."

He slapped the outside of the carriage as soon as Ewan was inside and it started to move. Thanks to the lanterns, Ewan could see the boy more closely. His tension was relieved considerably when he saw the lad was undeniably brown-haired, with the ruddy complexion of his grandfather. He'd rescued Jacob; he was finally certain.

"My grandson," Lady Redcake said, wiping tears away. "How can we ever thank you?"

Ewan realized he was panting from the shock of the past few minutes. Holding the sleeping child as tenderly as he would hold the boy's mother, he was silent at first, but when they went in a direction he didn't expect, he finally spoke.

"Aren't we returning to Matilda's home?"

"No, we have a plan. Carriage to Swindon, then the train. We're taking Jacob straight to Redcake Manor in Sussex. Can't stay in London with Wyld on the loose. We'll leave you there, though, so you can get on with your business." Sir Bartley stared at the boy.

"I don't understand. What about Matilda?" He'd wanted to place Jacob in her arms.

"Securing Jacob is the first thing," Sir Bartley said. "We all agreed. Everyone will figure it out soon enough. But in London, please ring Bristol and let Mrs. Miller know for sure at the house. She can get word to everyone at the baby mill."

"It's two hours to Swindon," he protested.

"We have a hamper," Lady Redcake said. "Is Jacob drugged, do you think? Should we try to wake him?"

"It's a bit early for him to be asleep," Ewan agreed. "But he's breathing well enough." He didn't want the boy to wake until he was far away.

"May I hold him?" Lady Redcake asked.

Ewan's first instinct was to refuse, but he stood, crouching, and passed the heavy, limp boy over. "I wish I'd chosen the carriage with Matilda, to be honest."

"I understand," Sir Bartley said. "But she's in one of the carriages blocking the street. It never occurred to us to have you plot a rearguard action."

"Purely an accident," Ewan said. "I never thought the door would be unlocked. In the end, rescuing Jacob was almost easy." If you discounted what the past two weeks had been like for all of them. And until the boy was reunited with his mother, it didn't feel like their nightmare would be over.

Chapter Nineteen

Shadrach Norwich shook his head almost sadly on Friday morning. "My dear Mr. Hales, you knew this would find its way into the newspapers."

"Not so quickly." Ewan's mouth twisted as he reviewed the tabloid article about the kidnapping of the "Redcake heir." "Besides, Mr. Norwich, surely you can see that I have no regrets."

"Yet you attempted to go to the Douglas Industries office yesterday morning, as if Lord Fitzwalter was still willing to employ you."

"At the time, I assumed he was. I did not entirely shirk my duties to the business."

"No, you fired a respected manager and accused an entire warehouse of kidnapping a child." Norwich raised his bushy eyebrows.

"Albert Pigge is a fool, and I'm not wrong in saying there was a connection between the child and the warehouse in Bristol. We found the child in a house two blocks away. The tenant of the house is the estranged wife of one of the warehouse foremen."

"Mr. Hales, I really don't care. And certainly the earl does not."

Ewan's hands tightened on the wooden armrests of his chair. He'd received a note at his office that morning, requiring his hasty attendance on the solicitor. Anger had been simmering through him ever since Jacob had left his arms, gone into his grandmother's safekeeping. He'd watched the sleeping boy all through the long carriage ride, then on the train to London. There, he'd been left behind. It seemed Sir Bartley had no further use for him. So he'd gone to St. James's Square to request that Pounds, the family butler, telephone the Bristol house, then returned to his solitary room in London. Empty arms, angry heart. He'd had no word from Matilda. She'd likely been in transit from Bristol to Polegate in Sussex much of yesterday. Once she had Jacob in sight, would he even matter to her? Would she reject his love once and for all?

The door of Norwich's chamber opened with violence, the handle bouncing off the dented plaster wall behind it. The earl strode in, followed by a bearded man in a funeral suit and perfectly shined shoes.

Fitzwalter's color appeared off, his skin sagging on his jawline. Exhaustion? Fear?

Ewan soon realized it was outrage.

"You, sir, are a liar." The earl pointed a shaking finger at Ewan. "I will not have this. No, sir. You will be struck from the family."

"You cannot do that," Ewan said, reaching for calm. "I am your heir."

"That's what you think," the earl spat. "Not much evidence to show your legitimacy. I can tie this up in court for years and the title can go elsewhere."

"You wouldn't dare. The situation is too well-known."

"It is not. We have been in contact for less than a month. You can go back into the obscurity in which I found you and continue to play your little games with the Redcakes."

"They are talking about me in the clubs, sir. It is not for me to point out your unscrupulous dealings," Ewan said. "Though they must be evident in your businesses, my lord. But no one of high rank will accept your mistreatment of your heir."

The earl sneered. "Do not think to play games with me, Mr. Hales. I assure you, you are out of your league, and your mind, if you think to best me. Mr. Norwich, you have your orders."

Ewan watched in disbelief as the earl stood. A cough racked the bent frame, then he steadied himself, though his face had gone pale.

The earl, an expression of absolute disdain on his face, unsteadily stalked out of the office, followed by the other man, who slammed the door behind himself. A pile of books wavered at the top of one bookcase and fell. Dust rose when they landed.

Norwich was wiping his eyes with a handkerchief when Ewan swiveled back around. "Oh, dear." He pulled a sheaf of papers toward himself on the desk.

"Now what?"

"I can offer you three hundred a year," Norwich said, licking his finger and flipping through the papers. "You will have nothing to do with the family or the businesses."

"Can he really disinherit me?"

"What proof do you have? Parish registers can be lost. Documents can be burned. Memories can be bribed into forgetfulness."

"He'd really go that far?"

"You have led a powerful man on a merry chase these past weeks. And insulted him besides. An earl going to the extreme of kidnapping the bastard grandchild of Sir Bartley Redcake? Come, sir; it's laughable."

"I never said he knew about it," Ewan protested. "But I'm certain people in his organization are involved."

"Nonetheless, you've insulted his honor one too many times."

"Honor," Ewan muttered.

Norwich cleared his throat. "Well. If I were you, sir, I'd tour the Continent or the colonies or such for three or four years. Live simply and the money will hold out."

"I'm going to marry Matilda Redcake."

"I see no faster way to guarantee the disappearance of evidence of your lineage," Norwich said. "May I be frank?"

"Please." Ewan leaned forward.

"An earldom is worth a dozen Matilda Redcakes. You are a young man. Come back in four years. Get some polish in Italy. Learn to paint or something. You'll have your pick of the year's debutantes in, what, 1894, and the Redcake hoyden will be long forgotten."

"I can't forget her," Ewan said. Could she forget him?

"Then by all means marry quietly and live invisibly," Norwich said. "I am not without sympathy for the plight of a young man, and I do realize you have known the Redcakes for a very long time. I will not claim your affection is a passing thing."

"Thank you for that."

Norwich nodded. He cleared his throat, then opened his drawer and pulled out his brown bottle and a ledger. Taking a pen, he wrote out a draft and handed it to Ewan. "Your first quarter's income. I assume you didn't leave anything of value in your office?"

Spring had a more intense scent here in Sussex. Matilda sat in her parents' garden behind Redcake Manor, watching Jacob run across the sprightly green lawn, chasing Sir Barks. The boy laughed heartily, his short legs spinning, all troubles quite forgotten. He'd stayed close yesterday and slept in her bed the previous night, but now, in bright sunshine and soft breeze, all his cares seemed forgotten. Once again he was the cherished child of the house. She watched his brown ringlets bounce from a combination of breeze and movement. His hair had grown too long, but he hated to have it cut and she would do nothing to trouble him now.

Her sister Alys had telephoned, a couple of weeks out of childbed now, and suggested she bring Jacob to Hatbrook Farm. Equally free of London and Bristol kidnappers, she would have access to nursery maids and Jacob's beloved, slightly younger cousin, Lady Mary Ellen. Matilda wanted her father, though, more than she wanted nursemaids. How silly to be twenty-four, and a mother, and think her father was still her safe haven.

Yet he'd brought her son home to her.

Later that night, she lay in bed, Jacob beside her, breathing in little snorts. Afraid he was coming down with a cold, she'd refused to leave him in the nursery. Her mother had looked at her with sympathy and not argued. A strange expression had come over her father's face as he wished her good night and left the room. Even now, she could see him through her open curtains, a dim shape in the garden, a lantern at his feet. She wondered what thoughts had him in thrall.

Her mother had gone to bed. Gawain was still in Bristol, dealing with the police who were coordinating with London to search for Wyld and Augustus Hulk, though Ann had returned to her son in Battersea. Dougal Alexander had probably reached Edinburgh by now. Mrs. Miller had told her she and Daisy would be busy giving the house a thorough cleaning after so many houseguests, but she'd told her housekeeper to give Daisy a night off and money for a new dress, so she could have a nice evening with Mr. Barker, who'd been promised such. She'd told Mrs. Miller to take some time for herself, as much as she needed, after the cleaning was completed, and of course both women could attend Izabela's funeral, if her mother had one.

Her parents had separated from Ewan in London. She hadn't heard from him. Had he asked the earl's forgiveness and gone back to work? Surely he had access to a telephone. Or maybe he had written her a letter. She'd see it soon enough if he had.

The next morning, she sat in the breakfast room with Jacob and her mother. She had not been able to push her fiancé to the back of her thoughts. "When you left Ewan in London, was it his choice?"

"No, dear, but it seemed for the best. I'm hoping he could help the police there find those two horrible men who were involved," her mother said.

"So he's busy with the police, then?"

"I expect so, dear. Have you attempted to communicate with him?"

"I don't know how. I know where he lives, but all I could do is write him a letter."

"No telephone?"

"I don't really know where he is employed, and of course he could not have one at his room. He doesn't have much money, you know. He lives very neatly, but just in one room."

"You've been there?"

Matilda nodded sheepishly. "We were engaged, Mother."

"*Are* engaged," her mother corrected. "Nothing has changed, dear."

"But he's in London and I can't go there, not with Wyld and Hulk still on the loose. We still don't know the full story."

"Write him a letter. Ask him to telephone. He can use the telephone at Redcake's."

"I suppose you are right. I just thought he'd make an effort to contact me."

Her mother reached across the table and took her hand as Jacob snatched up a spoon from his porridge and spilled droplets of mush on Lady Redcake's sleeve. She chuckled affectionately and took the spoon away. "This is the man who risked his life to save your son, Matilda. He loves you. Don't risk his feelings now."

"I have felt myself so unequal to love," she admitted.

"Now Jacob is home and you are nothing but love. You are full to bursting with it," her mother said. "Save some of that overflow of emotion for your soon-to-be husband."

Did she love him? She needed to see him through eyes not glazed by terror, a heart not still confused by her agreement to marry Theodore Bliven. She had to go to London, but how could she leave Jacob?

Her father entered the room, his eyes looking red-rimmed and tired.

He stood upright, however. She thought he had lost a fair amount of his paunch these last couple of weeks. None of them had been eating much. Her stays had been much easier to tighten.

"Papa, I don't think I can go back to Bristol," she said.

"Not until we get to the bottom of our troubles," he said readily enough.

"You should give Ewan the position," she said.

"Pishposh, he'll be living wherever you are. Greggory can do it. He's been watching you, and he grew up around the factories. He'll be fine."

"But Ewan—"

"Needs to make his own way, Matilda," her father said. "Presumably under the iron fist of Lord Fitzwalter, but he does need to learn the family business."

"It's not a possibility. Not if he marries me. The earl made that clear."

"Everything can be mended in a family," her mother interjected as she dabbed at her flowing sleeves with a damp rag. "It just needs time."

"I don't think the earl sees Ewan as family, not precisely," Matilda said.

"He will come to love Ewan, just as we have," her mother said.

Her mother's placid tone held such assurance that Matilda was startled. "We have?"

"Of course. He's been in our employ for years. We've watched him become a man. I'm very happy he's to be my new son," her mother said. "London isn't far, and you owe him a duty, Matilda. Take the train up there for a day, as soon as you've made contact, and see him. Sort out your wedding date. Do you think you'll want to be married from here?"

I don't know what I want. I have to go to London. Matilda stared blankly at her mother.

"Don't panic," her father said. "Be grateful you have the opportunity to be a bride. And to an honest and intelligent man."

"A handsome man, too," her mother said with a twinkle.

"I'm not ungrateful," she protested, blushing. "Am I good enough for him, Papa? A future earl. So brave. He sacrificed so much for me." She put her head in her hands. He'd given her everything and what had she done? Made love with him a couple of times, and she hadn't even sacrificed her virginity for that. He was a better person than her. She didn't deserve him.

"He loves you," her father said. "That is good enough for him, and it ought to be good enough for you."

"Why?" she whispered.

"You have to ask him that."

She stood, tucking her hands under Jacob's legs as he wrapped his chubby arms around her neck and squeezed. "I'll telephone Lord Judah at Redcake's and ask him to send one of the deliverymen to Ewan's home with a note. Maybe he will come in tomorrow and telephone me so we can speak."

Her father nodded. "That would be an excellent idea. I know he needed to speak with the earl, but he's had yesterday and today to do that. Now he can turn his thoughts to matrimony."

While she continued to wait on Jacob, attending to all his needs, even his bath, which she had avoided in the past due to the damp mess of the procedure, her thoughts were consumed by Ewan. She reviewed their physical encounters, the pleasure of them. Without meaning to, she compared them to her experience with Theodore Bliven and found there was nothing to say. She and Ewan had been heat and light, passion and pleasure. Being with Theodore had been a terrible, unpleasant mistake with ruinous consequences. She hadn't even worried with Ewan. He made her feel safe. He attracted her physically. She respected him, appreciated his stubbornness. These were all good things, important things.

Did she like him? The thought struck her as she cut tiny bites of egg for her son on Friday evening. Had he ever made her laugh? Long for his company? She enjoyed sparring with him, but that involved a certain degree of lust. Those pomaded, glossy curls, so tightly contained for so long, now disturbed by this new habit of tunneling his hands through his hair, made her face hot when she saw them. That was still lust, not liking, but she thought her regard was more than just lust. Yes, she liked him, wanted to be in his presence.

Then there was love. She hoped for it. And she hoped he would love Jacob, too. He would be the only father her son ever knew.

* * *

On Saturday morning, she felt elated when Pounds, returned from London, came to her sitting room door to tell her she had a telephone call from London.

The crackling noise made him hard to hear, but she almost recognized Ewan's voice.

"Darling, hello?" he called.

"Yes, I'm here, Ewan." She smiled, feeling truly happy.

"How is Jacob?"

"He seems fine. He clings to me a fair amount, but he goes to my mother and father, too."

"Poor mite. Is he eating well?"

"Oh, yes. He'll have the weight put back on in no time." She hugged herself with her free arm.

"I spoke to Mrs. Miller briefly, when I called to speak to Gawain. She expressed her joy and hopes to see you soon."

"I can't go back to Bristol. Not now."

"I understand."

The line crackled badly, and she was afraid she'd lost him. "Hello?"

"I'm here. Do you want me to come to Polegate?"

"Aren't you busy with your work and the police?"

"I'm not working for the earl now, though he has given me an allowance. I'm walking the streets every day and stopping in with the police superintendent at teatime to spur them on. Wyld and Hulk have vanished, though."

"I am never going to feel safe until we've figured this out," she said.

"I know, and I'd like to offer you my protection. Can you marry me now, or do you want to plan a big wedding?"

His words made her smile with relief. "Heavens no; quietly, please. I'd like to see you. Shall I come up to London for the day, on Monday?"

"Yes, please do, if you can tear yourself away."

"It's important. I mean, you are. I owe you so very much; everything, really. What you did, going into the house. You could have been killed."

There was a long pause before he said, "I have no regrets. Listen, the line is getting worse. Come to Redcake's? I'll meet you in the tearoom, whenever you can arrive on Monday."

"I'll visit your room," Matilda said. She wanted to see him in private. "Wait for me there."

"Very well."

She thought she detected a note of humor in his voice.

"I shall have to do some tidying."

"You have two days in which to accomplish that."

"I shall spend them thinking of you. I've missed you."

She felt her eyes prick with tears. She had thought herself done with them, after all she'd shed over her son. "I've missed you, too." Thankfully, she knew it to be true. "I can't wait to see you, and make our plans for the future."

"Yes, I want that, too. Until Monday, then."

Chapter Twenty

"I had to confess to my mother that I'd been here before," Matilda said as Ewan drew her into his room. It fairly sparkled with cleanliness, and she was touched that he'd gone to such an effort for her. She also noticed that he hadn't done any packing. She could see no sign of a man about to take up a post in Bristol, or even with a thought of moving to the Redcake family home on St. James's Square. He'd even placed a small bouquet of violets in a chipped tea mug on his table.

"Your mother seems the sensible sort." He half-smiled and tucked his hands into his trouser pockets under his coat.

She realized he must have meant to embrace her and she'd missed a cue. How embarrassing. "It looks very nice here," she commented, craning her neck to make it clear that she really had missed his gesture.

"I thought we might spend our wedding night here," he admitted. "You must want to remain in hiding."

The muscles around her rib cage tightened painfully. "Are we marrying today?"

"We don't have to. I didn't make an appointment or anything like that."

"I'm not prepared." The words left her mouth before she'd thought them through. She put her hand to her lips. "Oh, Ewan, I'm doing this all wrong."

"I can completely understand you being unprepared." He put his arm around her shoulders, his expression softening. "It is such an important matter. Perhaps upon reflection, you don't even want to marry me."

"Why would you think that?" She let him take her to one of his two chairs and sat in front of the violets.

He took the other chair and leaned forward earnestly. She'd seen that look before, on the rare occasion when she'd been at Redcake's and he'd been expressing some important point to her father. His hair wasn't mussed today. She missed the curls that hid beneath his pomade.

"You haven't been yourself through our courtship. Extreme emotional distress. I know I wasn't good enough for Matilda Redcake in the past. You may continue to feel that way. I have little to offer financially right now."

"I don't care about money."

"Ha," he said. "Of course you do. You've always had it. You've no notion of how to live like most people."

"Should I be offended?" She stared at the violets.

"No, I'm just being honest." He sat back. "Regardless, you will never be poor, no matter who you marry. Your parents are very liberal. It's part of why I respect them so much."

"You must think I am not good enough for you," she said slowly. Was this his way of breaking the engagement?

"You know I don't feel that way at all," he countered.

"Do I?"

He touched her face. His elbow brushed the violets, but she closed her eyes to feel his touch more acutely instead of trying to rescue his teacup.

"I have missed your touch," she whispered. "In the south, it felt a little like nothing had ever changed, like it was two years ago, when I was still living there. But I was dissatisfied. I'd learned to want more than I deserved. I've learned to want you, Ewan."

"You have?"

"Yes." She opened her eyes. "I only had to hear your voice again to know that."

"What else?"

"You sound like the old Ewan, getting your business reports."

"I don't mean to." His fingers tucked around her jaw.

"It's who you are. You're a good businessman. I told my father to offer you Bristol, but he said you would not want to be apart from me."

"He is correct."

"I have so much respect for you." She swallowed. "Your work, of course, speaks for itself, but your kindness to me, the risks you took for Jacob, both physically and within your family. I can never repay you."

"You aren't meant to."

"I love everything about you," she said, feeling like crying. "I really, really do."

"Then why are you so sad?"

"I'm not worthy of you. I'm shallow and flawed, headstrong, not beautiful, not especially kind."

He ran his index finger along her chin, then cupped it. "You do not see yourself as others do. You are more than worthy of my love. So brave, my darling, so intelligent, so loyal."

Tears dripped from her eyes down her cheek. "Ewan."

"It is perfectly fine, my darling. Everything is. We'll go abroad after we marry, if we must."

"I can't take Jacob away from my family, not right now."

"Then I will figure out what happened, once and for all. We'll ask Dougal Alexander to return to the case if necessary. I hate to be apart from you for so much as a day, but whatever it takes. I will scour London; I will walk the streets of Bristol."

"Make love to me first, then find a vicar to marry us," she said. "Let us move forward together, as we're meant to."

He nodded. "You will not hear me disagreeing. Should we switch the order of those two events?"

She shook her head. "Definitely not. I need your hands on me."

"One of my more sterling qualities is my constant desire to please you," he said, pushing back his chair and standing.

She giggled and wiped away tears. They disrobed, watching each other. She drank in the sight of his strong body, slowly revealed. He could undress himself far better than she could. Soon, she needed his help. Every time his fingers brushed her flesh, she bit back a gasp. Every nerve ending was sensitized to his touch.

Finally, she was nude, her back to him. He cupped her breasts as his erection nudged her back. She leaned against his body, feeling herself soften, moisten, become ready. He played with her nipples and she ran her fingers lightly over his arms, making the hair there lift.

"We'll make love in far more luxurious surroundings than these over the years, my countess," he said into her ear.

"But it will never be so special. Equal, perhaps, but never better."

She felt his smile as he nipped her ear, and one of his hands dipped down her torso, then between her legs. Her head fell back on his chest as he stroked through her wet heat and began to circle her pearl with astonishing delicacy. How he treasured her body. How he loved her mind. She'd never thought she would have such grace in her life.

With a wrench, she pulled herself from him and turned around, grabbing his hand, pulling him to his narrow bed.

"How I love you, Ewan." With an animal cry of satisfaction, she pushed him down and mounted his thighs, fitting his erection to her. She plunged herself down, filling herself. He gripped her hips, moaning, his eyes open in pleasured shock.

She tossed her head back, laughed, and began to ride him in earnest.

Two hours later, Ewan slid from the bed. Matilda murmured and turned on her stomach, not waking. She'd worn herself out, his darling, both above and beneath him. He wanted her to rest, but he had his marching orders. A vicar to marry them tomorrow, and answers.

An hour later, he'd shown his special license and made arrangements at his parish church to be wed the next day. With resolve, he made his way back to Lord Murchie's home, hoping to find some clue to Richard Wyld's whereabouts.

Lord Murchie received him in his drawing room, though his face had lost the sunny air of their previous meeting.

"What has happened?" Ewan asked.

"Mr. Wyld is no longer in my employ," the lord said. "Dashed nuisance, having to find a governess for my sister."

"Perhaps it is worth the bother, given Wyld is a blackguard," Ewan commented.

"Yes, yes, of course." Lord Murchie lifted a hand and waved it about.

"Have you seen Wyld since we last met?" Ewan inquired after a moment's silence.

"No."

"Are his possessions still here? May I look through them for clues?"

"No, sir, you may not. They have been collected."

"By whom?" Ewan asked, his senses prickling.

"A solicitor." Lord Murchie sniffed.

Ewan smelled brandy on the man's breath. He'd been drinking away his irritation. "Can you give me his direction?"

"No, but I remember his name. Shadrach Norwich. What a mouthful."

Ewan swore.

"Sir?" Lord Murchie said, his mouth screwing up in distaste.

Ewan shook his head. "My apologies, my lord, but I know Mr. Norwich. I am afraid this whole mess has something to do with Lord Fitzwalter."

"You don't say?" Lord Murchie raised an eyebrow. "Well, I am sure you have some notion of the streak of madness running through that family. Mind you, I'd been told only the men named Walter were ever truly mad, so I saw nothing wrong with hiring a Richard."

"Are you saying Richard Wyld is related to the Douglas family?"

"Of course. He's an offshoot of the current earl's grandfather, I believe. Or was it father? He's so much older than I am, you understand. But certainly related somehow. Richard Wyld Douglas."

"His name is Douglas?" Ewan found himself standing without knowing how it had happened. "He doesn't use the name?"

"Hiding from creditors, I expect." Lord Murchie raised an indolent hand again. "Would try it myself, if I wasn't so well known."

Ewan bowed slightly. "Thank you for your time, my lord. I'd like to depart for Norwich's office before he leaves for the day."

"Yes, yes, of course. Do your worst." Lord Murchie forced a smile and rang for a servant to escort Ewan to his front door.

Ewan drew in a deep breath as he entered Norwich's office. The solicitor, who'd been warned of his arrival by a clerk, had his fingers steepled in front of his chin and his brown bottle at the ready.

"Asking for an increase in your allowance so soon?" he asked, an unusually acidic tone to his voice.

"I think you know why I'm here," Ewan said, keeping his own voice level with effort. "Richard Wyld."

"He is Richard Walter Wyld Douglas, in point of fact. I was hoping we could keep him out of it."

"Lord Fitzwalter was behind this mess all along, wasn't he?" Ewan said. "You've told me one lie after another. I can scarcely understand the timing, given that I had only just formed a connection with Miss Redcake when her son was taken. Which means these evil deeds must be about business."

"His intention was to weaken the family in order to draw you away," Norwich said. He lifted his bottle and drank deeply, his Adam's apple moving up and down his fleshy throat as he swallowed. "The adulterated flour was meant to destroy Redcake's high-end business. Kidnapping the boy was done to distract the family while the bad goods were whispered about among fashionable Society. Jacob Bliven was the easiest Redcake child to access. The earl didn't want you to risk continued ties. Business partners had told him you were doing well, but he wanted you dependent on him."

Poor Matilda. If he'd been a weaker man, he'd have wanted a soothing drink from the brown bottle himself. "So my relationship with her had nothing to do with this."

"It didn't help matters any," Norwich said, draining his bottle. He set it on the desk and glanced mournfully at it.

"What a foul man he must be," Ewan muttered. "What did he promise Wyld?"

"I imagine he wanted the earldom," Norwich said. "But he'd never have inherited. Money, though, well . . . A kidnapper can become a blackmailer easily enough once he's a taste for it, and he knew all about Lord Fitzwalter."

"I am marrying Miss Redcake tomorrow," Ewan said. "I expect Lord Fitzwalter to be in attendance, with a smile on his face no less. She and the boy are under my protection. I don't need his employment or his money."

"Understandably," interjected Norwich. "But the earl is confined to bed, Mr. Hales. Some sort of attack."

Ewan wondered if he'd suffered a true medical crisis or had merely gone into hiding. "Very well, but I will, in any case, expect him to protect my wife's name and welcome her into the family. By letter, if necessary."

"Yes," the solicitor said.

"I suggest Wyld be sent to manage that farm in Vermont," Ewan continued. "I don't imagine you will be able to make him confess his crimes to the police without implicating the earl."

"I would never do so," Norwich said stoutly.

Family. His urge was for vengeance, for trials and judges and prison, but he did not have the power to demand it. "I do not want Wyld in, or adjacent to, any country in which a Redcake resides. I assume he was Izabela Pickett's lover?"

Norwich nodded.

"Did he kill her?"

"No. He planned both kidnappings, but that poor girl took her own life. I don't imagine she knew what Mr. Wyld had been asked to do. He told me she became quite inconsolable when the boy was removed from her care."

"It can't have helped when she realized she was carrying the child of such a blackguard. Where is Hulk now?"

"I can ensure he goes to Vermont with Wyld."

"No, that isn't good enough. Australia for him, far away from his partner in crime, or prison here."

Norwich sighed.

"What about those miscreants at the house where Jacob was kept?"

"The Bristol police shut down the house," Norwich said. "They've lost their livelihoods."

"I want everyone from the Douglas warehouse who was involved in the scheme to lose their positions immediately. I will do what I can to make this family honorable again." He paused, then added, "If there is ever one unfavorable whisper about my wife in Society, I will come to Fitzwalter for reparation. He had best guard her as one of his own."

"Understood." The word was slurred. "But you will be earl soon enough."

Ewan knew he was done here. He stood, then bent and put his hands on the desk. "After you see the earl, I suggest you take a long voyage yourself, Norwich. You aren't looking well."

The solicitor nodded vigorously. "Haven't left London since my wife died seven years ago."

He wanted to tell the man he was out of a job but couldn't risk his files disappearing. Dismantling this mess would take time. "Anything else?"

"The best to you and your bride." The solicitor forced a wobbly smile.

"Go to some European spa, man, and get your health back," Ewan suggested, throwing the words over his shoulder as he walked out.

* * *

When he went into his room, he found his almost bride half-dressed again, sitting on the edge of the bed.

"I can't lace my own stays," she said, her cheeks pinking at his frank regard.

"I don't think you need them laced." He threw down a newspaper-wrapped package of fish and chips. "May not be what you're used to, but it will get us through the night. Then, tomorrow, you can dress at St. James's Square before our wedding."

"Oh?" Matilda pushed strands of fiery hair out of her eyes.

"It's done, my darling." Ewan sank onto the bed next to her and wrapped his arm around her shoulders. "I'm very afraid that it was all my fault. Fitzwalter wanted to make your family less influential. He wanted to hurt you to get to me."

"But Jacob?"

"A horrible coincidence," Ewan admitted. "They must have reached Izabela before they could act on the servants around Noel or Lady Mary Ellen."

"What happened to her?"

"Suicide, according to Fitzwalter's solicitor."

"So she felt so guilty in the end that she took her own life? And her baby's?"

"A sad ending," Ewan agreed. "But we have a new start for ourselves. I'm afraid Wyld is a blood relative of mine, however. Are you sure you want to marry into a mad family?"

Matilda leaned her head on his shoulder. "Given the adventures of my own siblings over the years, I can hardly declare us categorically sane, Ewan darling. At least Greggory and his family are a quieter lot. I think we should raise our children under Uncle Charles's influence instead of my own father's."

Ewan smiled. "I like your father."

"I know it."

He kissed her cheek. "But you are correct. We are bound for Bristol. I look forward to shaking the hand of every one of your men who helped us."

Matilda nodded. "I plan more than that. I want to throw a party, with gifts, a welcome home for Jacob that all the factory workers can join in on."

"It can be a wedding celebration, too. How about we stroll over to

Redcake's and make some telephone calls? Do you want your family at your wedding?"

"Will there be time?"

He nodded. "I suppose I will have to lace you back into your stays after all?"

"Just for today. Then you can spend the rest of your days removing me from them."

Her smile was so tender, so naughty and loving, that Ewan knew, if he had ever had any doubt, that he'd found his home within the Redcake clan forever. This redheaded hoyden would soon be his wife, and the mother of his children.

"If we can manage it soon enough, they may even be able to bring Jacob up to us tonight," he suggested. "Turn around, my love, and let's see you dressed."

Don't miss the rest of the Redcakes series, available where
eBooks are sold!

The Marquess of Cake
One Taste of Scandal
His Wicked Smile
The Kidnapped Bride (novella)
Christmas Delights

Some cravings
must be indulged…

The
Marquess
of Cake

THE REDCAKES

HEATHER
HIESTAND

His craving could be her undoing...

One Taste of Scandal

THE REDCAKES

HEATHER HIESTAND

First comes seduction...

His Wicked Smile

THE REDCAKES

HEATHER HIESTAND

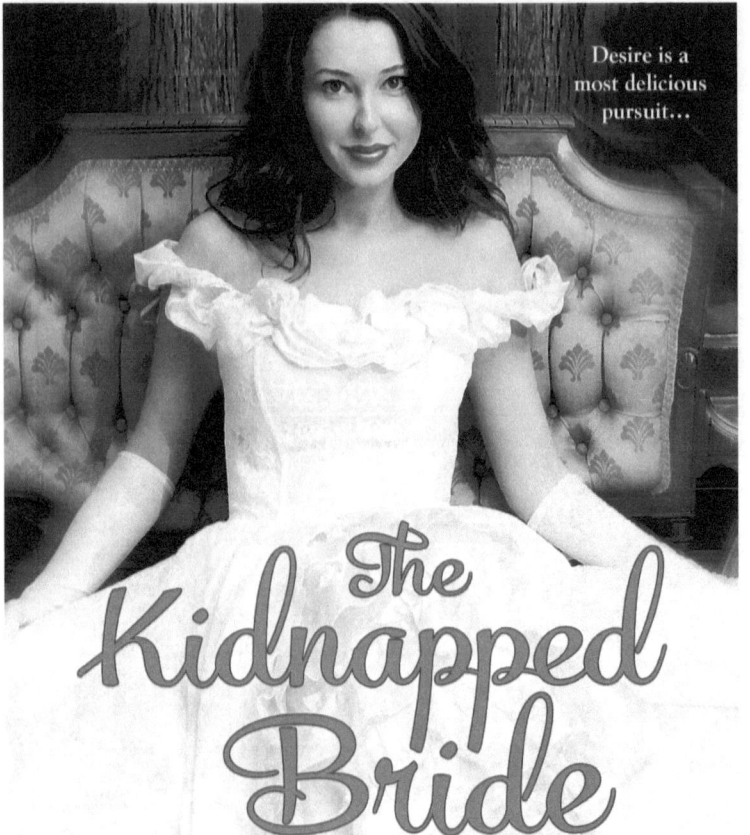

Desire is a
most delicious
pursuit…

The
Kidnapped
Bride

THE REDCAKES

HEATHER
HIESTAND

Nothing is
more delicious
than desire...
Christmas
Delights
THE REDCAKES
HEATHER
HIESTAND

About the Author

Heather Hiestand was born in Illinois, but her family migrated west before she started school. Since then she has claimed Washington State as home, except for a few years in California. She wrote her first story at age seven and went on to major in creative writing at the University of Washington. Her first published fiction was a mystery short story, but since then it has been all about the many flavors of romance. Heather's first published romance short story was set in the Victorian period and she continues to return to historical fiction, ever fascinated by the past. The author of many novels, novellas, and short stories, she has achieved best-seller status at both Amazon, and Barnes & Noble. With her husband and son, she makes her home in a small town and supposedly works out of her tiny office, though she mostly writes in her easy chair in the living room.

For more information, visit Heather's website at **www.heatherhiestand.com**. Heather loves to hear from readers! Her email is heather@heatherhiestand.com.

www.ingramcontent.com/pod-product-compliance
Lightning Source LLC
Chambersburg PA
CBHW020752250626
47155CB00003B/1043